MAKING

Promises

BOOK YOUR PLACE ON OUR WEBSITE AND MAKE THE ARABESQUE ROMANCE CONNECTION!

We've created a customized website just for our very special Arabesque readers, where you can get the inside scoop on everything that's going on with Arabesque romance novels.

When you come online, you'll have the exciting opportunity to:

- View covers of upcoming books

- Learn about our future publishing schedule (listed by publication month and author)

- Find out when your favorite authors will be visiting a city near you

- Search for and order backlist books

- Check out author bios and background information

- Send e-mail to your favorite authors

- Join us in weekly chats with authors, readers and other guests

- Get writing guidelines

- AND MUCH MORE!

Visit our website at
http://www.arabesquebooks.com

MAKING
Promises

MICHELLE MONKOU

BET Publications, LLC
http://www.bet.com
http://www.arabesquebooks.com

ARABESQUE BOOKS are published by

BET Publications, LLC
c/o BET BOOKS
One BET Plaza
1900 W Place NE
Washington, DC 20018-1211

All Kensington Titles, Imprints, and Distributed Lines are available at special quantity discounts for bulk purchases for sales promotions, premiums, fund-raising, and educational or institutional use. Special book excerpts or customized printings can also be created to fit specific needs. For details, write or phone the office of the Kensington special sales manager: Kensington Publishing Corp., 850 Third Avenue, New York, NY 10022, attn: Special Sales Department, Phone: 1-800-221-2647.

First Printing: October 2004
10 9 8 7 6 5 4 3 2 1

Printed in the United States of America

This book is dedicated to my father,
Charles Ivelaw Monkou
(May 12, 1932–March 15, 2004)
in loving memory.

Prologue

Zoe died lonely and rejected.

Amber Delaney sat still, mulling over that fact. Even she wasn't there to take the pills out of the hand of her childhood friend. Guilt weighed on her conscience. She wanted to fall to her knees and scream until her voice was mute. Instead, she folded her hands in her lap, trying not to think about it.

The unexpected tragedy had cast a pall over the events. But the imposing century-old church that held more than a hundred mourners was itself a monument of reverence. Back in the day, it was the focal point for the small town—religious and social. Now Libertytown had turned into a city with the usual suburban sprawl populated by families escaping the rat race of urban life.

A faint pine scent from the polish used on the pews lingered in the air, reminding Amber of the fun times she and her friends had spent at Sunday school. Nothing much had changed. Dark wood made up the framework, with thick exposed beams overhead supporting the raised roof. Only the altar area was carpeted in a deep purple shade. The lectern stood on one side, while the choir of at least seventy men and women sat in their exclusive box on the other side.

Zoe had been a member of the choir until she turned sixteen and claimed she was running away from home with a cute boy from high school. Amber smiled inwardly at the memory of Zoe's mother meeting her at the bus station, then dragging her home. Zoe's brother had been dispatched soon after to make sure the boy didn't think about sticking around for Zoe.

Amber remembered that the choir's robes were royal blue and gold. The new look of purple with gold trimming set a more regal tone. A large ornate cross in gold fabric was emblazoned on each member's back. Considering the grand sweeping motion of the robes whenever the choir clapped and bopped to their gospel melodies, Amber surmised that the robes had to be heavy and hot; although it was fall weather with a slight chill in the air and overhead fans were whirring, several choir members still fanned themselves. Yet Amber also suspected that a few only fanned so furiously because it was the church thing to do.

The funeral service had long gone over the one-hour mark. The unforgiving seats had no mercy on her behind—the downside of not being well padded. To take her mind off the torture, she focused on the stained-glass window above the pulpit. The crisscross beams of filtered light added splashes of violet, rose, and deep purple onto the floor.

Zoe would have loved the colors. She had wanted to be a painter, but never told her parents, knowing that they wanted her to be the first doctor in the family.

They all had dreams and sincere intentions. In Zoe's attic, the threesome had pledged to be friends for all eternity; nothing could divide them. Amber sucked in her breath, holding it for a few seconds before exhaling. She repeated the exercise a few more times, acknowledging the steady rise of bitterness winding its way around her thoughts. Heck, it had overtaken her heart.

People filed past her, heading to the podium to have their say. Some praised Zoe. Others spoke of wishing they had more time to tell her how they felt. By the time Amber had reconnected with Zoe, these friends had devoured Zoe as much as the public had. Listening to the tearful pleas set Amber's teeth on edge.

Her hand fisted around a balled-up wad of tissue. If she concentrated hard enough on the crack in the floor near her seat, she could block out the choir softly singing a mournful spiritual in the background. She gnawed at her lip to force back tears.

The conductor lowered her hands, signaling the song's end. Time for the minister's closing sermon.

"How are you holding up?"

Amber turned toward her best friend, Sylvia, sitting at her side. "I'm fine. I'm glad you came," she whispered.

Sylvia patted her hand and reached over to give her a reassuring hug. "She's my friend, too. I feel just as guilty. Through thick and thin, that was our motto, right?" Sylvia dabbed at her eyes, sniffing loudly. "Anyway, don't let this minister's fire-and-brimstone speech work your nerves."

Amber shook her head. "I'm just sitting here." Numb.

"You forgot who you're talking to. You keep biting your lip and it'll start bleeding. After today, you never have to see any of these people again. This place isn't home anymore. It hasn't been for a long time for any of us."

The plan had been to go to the same college, graduate and then get an apartment together. The plan, friendship, their lives went in different directions a couple months after getting on campus. Zoe, the beauty in the group, immediately soaked up the upperclassmen's attention. Several sororities vied for her membership. When she failed to show up at Amber's birthday because one of her many boyfriends had taken her away on his family's boat for the weekend, the group suffered its final blow up, ending with hurtful accusations flung among them. Amber didn't want to recall the nasty darts she'd shot at Zoe. Being friends for so long, they knew each other's insecurities and had each moved in for the kill.

The minister stood tall and erect from his pulpit. Glaring over his glasses, he pitched his words like an actor with his monologue. He shook his head, pounded his hand against the podium, raised onto his toes to drive home his message for salvation.

Words boomed down on the congregation about sanctity of the soul, sins of the flesh, greed of men. Sylvia placed a reassuring hand, or maybe it was a restraining hand, over Amber's. After listening longer than she liked to the condemnation in the minister's tone, Amber felt sure Sylvia's hand was to keep her from interrupting the proceedings and letting loose.

If Zoe's so-called friends and relatives turned their backs on her, those who didn't know her treated her with brutal personal attacks. Expert consultants, news reporters, and talk-show hosts rolled out Zoe's faults. How many high-profile women fell from grace with the IRS salivating at one end and the government waiting at the other end with an executioner's axe? It was news.

Headlines painted the picture of the executive who had a reputation for being hard-nosed but successful on her company's behalf. In vainglorious detail, they scrutinized the only female in the company's history who had spiraled from the top, with her designer suits and company car, to the bottom, where her reputation and accomplishments sat in an undignified heap. They'd fed on her like a pack of dogs.

Amber closed her eyes, desperately wishing she could close her ears, too. "Zoe Cantrell," she murmured. It had been a while since she had reason to say her name.

The white casket was now the final memory. Tears filled Amber's eyes. This time she couldn't stem their flow down her cheeks. She was dangerously close to breaking down.

"Here." Sylvia pushed a travel pack of tissues into her hand. "He's winding down, thank God."

Amber dabbed at her eyes. She had cried enough in the past week for all the mourners packed into the small town church. Zoe's parents wept in each other's arms. They had been angry and embarrassed by their daughter's fall from grace. Now it was too late for the words of love.

The minister ended his sermon with a powerful "Amen." The organist pounded the keys, playing a livelier piece for the congregation's departure.

Amber stood ready to negotiate her way out of the church into the fresh air. Suddenly the small building, the warm bodies, the heady scented air from the bouquets closed in on her. What had kept them apart?

"Hey, wait." Sylvia noisily caught up to her. "Don't march off without me."

Amber didn't respond. The clusters of people impeded access to her car. She wanted out. Lowering her shoulders, she drove through the crowd, marching to her own beat until she reached her compact car.

"Want me to drive?"

Amber nodded. The two-hour drive back to Maryland was long enough time for her to think and plan. She retrieved the note she kept on her person. Quite simply, she'd make sure that people remembered Zoe, learning from her mistakes, but also celebrating the positive things she'd done in her life.

Sylvia glanced over at her. "Want to share what's going through your mind?"

"I'm not sure, as yet. But from what I've learned so far, all the top dogs were dirty. All, except for one. I can't believe he didn't dip his manicured hands into the honey pot. I'm going to do what I can for Zoe. And I'm going to bury this guy if necessary."

Sylvia turned to look at her, a frown crinkling her forehead. "Since when did you become a superhero? What if he's not guilty?"

"Sylvia, all these guys are guilty. Whether it's embezzling or lying on their taxes. They can't get to where they are without a little help. Don't tell me Mr. Whistle-Blower didn't cop a deal with the prosecutor."

"Why so cynical?"

Amber refolded the note and tucked it into her pocket. "It's not being cynical. It's being practical, grounded. That way, you don't get hurt from trusting blindly. Look where it got Zoe."

"But she was guilty."

"Don't you start. Zoe was honest and hardworking."

"When you reached out to her in the end, there had been at least ten years where you or me were not a part of her life. You don't know her. All we have are memories of a pretty naive part of our lives."

"Now who's being the cynical one?" Amber rubbed her temples. The headache throbbed just under the surface, waiting for a moment like this to charge full throttle. "I don't want to fight, not today. You're right, I don't know the supercharged, workaholic Zoe. I don't know why she did the things she got indicted for. All I have is this note. She could have written that last note to so many others. She wrote it to me."

They rode in silence down the two-lane highway. Amber leaned her head back against the headrest and closed her eyes. Exhaustion had finally taken over.

"Do whatever you need to do, my friend."

Chapter One

All around Eddie Ashton, women moved like brightly colored fish in an aquarium, darting to their destinations, wiggling their behinds, flashing their evening get-up. He alternated between biting his nails and picking lint from his pants. Waiting for the event to begin had his nerves on edge.

The mirrored walls framing the lounge and dance floor allowed him to glance at himself, admiring his reflection. From his table, he'd be able to monitor his movements and gestures, fix his clothing, and admire himself. And why not? The amount of money that he'd spent on his designer suit made him feel rich.

The suit didn't come off the rack. Its dark gray jacket and pants accented with a white shirt and red tie spoke its own language—the language that spoke to the greedy eyes of women who openly flirted with him.

He sipped his ginger ale and tried to ignore the assault on his ears. The latest hip-hop noise blared with a chest-thumping bass. Meanwhile the trashiest women in their indecently short skirts and dresses paraded in front of him.

He fully expected that one in particular would catch his eye. It was what brought him to these loud, immoral dens every Friday night. There had to be at least one woman who hadn't fallen to her darker nature—flirtatious, deceitful, greedy. It would be like winning the lottery.

His mind spun with the dazzling possibilities. Tonight smelled of success. The adrenaline shot through his system. His senses sizzled. He wanted this so badly, he could taste, feel, touch what no other man could.

Under these mood lights, he transformed. Hell, he could be anyone he wanted to be, muscles to ripple off his frame, taller by a full foot, and equipped with the skilled art of conversation.

While tapping his feet to the club music, he created versions of how the courtship would unfold. No in-your-face declaration, which people seemed so fond of today. He'd be smooth like Sidney Poitier or Harry Belafonte.

Yeah, he'd be like those cats from yesteryear who made women of any race lose what little sense they had. He sipped his soda and continued to scrutinize each face.

All he had to do was remain calm. Impatience had gotten him into trouble on a few occasions. One doctor had suggested anger-management classes. After he'd broken the doctor's nose, he'd asked him what he'd recommend now.

Finally the emcee started the weekly speed-dating event with his usual corny announcements. The listing of rules no longer interested Eddie. He knew it by heart. The only sound he wanted to hear was the bell. Every seven minutes, a fresh face full of heavy makeup would sit at his table, spinning a yarn to make herself sound sexy and hip.

The bell sounded.

For the next hour, he listened and critiqued his dates. Eyes that had too much shimmer. Lips that had too much color. They were all like brown porcelain dolls that talked too much, dipped in heady, stifling perfume. Their dislike toward him was usually instantaneous. Some even curled their lips in disgust after he talked about himself. One had dared to call him chauvinistic. He should've selected her just to teach her a lesson.

The euphoria he'd only recently enjoyed now turned to panic. Where was the woman? His head pounded. Sweat beaded on his forehead. He needed a break—fresh air. Otherwise he'd have to leave early. The manager didn't like that. He'd already been warned about running out while a woman sat at his table.

"Well, hello." He smiled long after it was necessary at the woman seated across from him at another table. The oval-shaped face offering him a shy smile hit all his senses like a refreshing wave. He looked down at his tie, pleased to see that her red dress matched perfectly.

The bell rang, signaling a new date. She disappeared into the crowd. Maybe he'd get a sliver of a chance to talk to her, if she didn't come to his table.

It would be a successful night, after all.

Amber waited until her friend parked before bringing up the subject again. "For the last time, Sylvia, why are we doing this?" Amber surveyed the area, noting the crowd milling around near the doorway to the nightclub. "Plus, it's freezing out here. I'm going to get a cold showing all this skin."

Sylvia tossed her head and flashed Amber a mischievous smile over her shoulder. "Take a vitamin and stick with me, kid. I'll make sure you have a guy or two writing your name on their date cards by the end of the night."

"Great," Amber muttered. She followed her friend across the street, dreading the next two hours of her life.

The music pulsated out of the doors onto the street where women stood in line, waiting for the "cattle call," as she referred to it, to begin. According to her watch, the musical chairs of dating would begin in five minutes. She wished she could act as excited as the others, but so far her stomach had clenched into an even tighter knot. Food was so out of the question.

"Relax." Sylvia laughed. "You'd think someone dragged you here."

"Ah, hello, you did." Amber giggled. Good heavens, she was on the verge of hysteria. "I said I didn't mind meeting someone. I didn't know about this speed-dating crap. And what am I supposed to do once I'm in there?"

"Don't sweat it. They'll tell you what to do."

She and Sylvia made their way toward the door. IDs had to be shown before walking through the faux-leather padded doors. Small tables with a chair on either side lined the entire room. The bar stood in the center of the room, gleaming under the mood lights. A large shiny silver bell swung from the overhang.

A man standing behind the bar stepped up and rang it. "Ladies and gentlemen, welcome to Wednesday night at the Metrodome for our speed-dating event. Once you hear this bell, you may chat, ask questions, and check out your date for seven minutes. How many minutes?" He cupped his ear for the response.

"Seven minutes!" The women whooped and hollered.

Amber thought they all sounded and looked like noisy chickens waiting for the coop to be opened.

The man continued. "We have many sample questions, or you can use your own imagination. Don't be shy, ladies, just start talking! After the seven minutes, decide whether that person will make it onto your date card. You'll only receive their e-mail addresses, *if* you're also on their card. So, good luck and let the games begin!"

Amber watched Sylvia slide into the chair next to hers. Her friend had already launched into her pitch with the familiar toss of her head. Amber slowly turned to face the stranger in front of her. Her mouth opened and closed as her mind looked over the flood of questions. Doubts tumbled over each other.

"Hi, I'm Amber Delaney. Um. I'm here with my friend." A small smile trembled on her lips. "Um. I'm an only child. Oh, I work for a news magazine. You probably wouldn't have guessed that." She rubbed her hands together under the table, praying for the ringing bell.

"It's okay. This is my first time, too. I'm Jack Beard."

Amber slowly raised her gaze from the front of his shirt to his neck, then to his face. He wasn't bad-looking, kind of average. Nothing distinctive that made her heart go pitter-patter. So as not to appear rude, she chatted while mentally counting down the minutes.

An hour passed. In that time, Amber had met Tony—a part-time stripper and full-time law student; Sly—an uptight stockbroker; George—a shy flower-shop salesman; and several others who didn't make it to her memory bank.

"Can you believe that it's our last one?" Sylvia heaved a sigh. "I'm having a good time, but these shoes are killing my feet." Sylvia had the pair of offending red pumps in one hand and a cocktail drink in the other. "I know, I know. I make a classy picture. Bite me. My feet hurt. Maybe I can get lucky and get a guy who's willing to massage them."

Amber snorted. "He'd have to be pretty darn desperate for that humanitarian act." She playfully dodged Sylvia's shove.

The bell sounded for the final seven minutes. Amber slid into the chair like a pro. "Hi, I'm Amber Delaney. How are you?" She stretched out her hand and felt pleased at the returned firm handshake.

"Stu Jackson. Private detective, at your service."

"Wow. How cool. How long have you been doing that?"

"It's been five years with my own company. I mainly work for celebrities."

Cute face. Not mature features, but very boyishly handsome. "I work for—"

He blinked. "I've worked for several hip-hop artists, maybe you've heard of—"

"I don't listen to hip-hop." One check mark for rudeness.

"You don't? What are you into? Soft jazz?"

Contempt draped the simple question. The buzz from the evening fizzled. "I don't have time to be into anything. I'm mainly juggling deadlines."

"Deadlines? For what?"

Take a deep breath. "I'm in charge of the community connection for our newspaper. I do the research. Every now and again, I write an article."

"For the *Post?*"

"No." It killed her to admit that she wasn't writing for the top newspaper in the region. "I work for the *Nation's News Bulletin,* which is a—"

"A tabloid newspaper?"

When will the darn bell ring? "A national newsmagazine." *Nimrod.*

Stu smirked. Amber's irritation meter screamed to the peak. "Not all of us can be baby-sitters of the rich and famous." Catty, but it felt good. Not waiting for the bell, she stood. As far as she was concerned, it was over.

"Amber," Sylvia whispered from the table next to her. "What are you doing? You could get disqualified."

"Disqualified from what? I'm like a piece of meat on a conveyor belt being examined and reexamined." She raised her glass of Coke in Stu's direction and left.

The bell rang.

What a zoo. Amber couldn't say that she didn't enjoy herself, but some of her dates would never get another chance with her. Her last relationship, lukewarm and brief, had ended three years ago.

Sylvia caught up to her. She linked arms and they headed for the door. "I really want to chat with that Tyrese look-alike. I want to make sure he's got my name on the card." Sylvia craned her neck to look back into the throng.

"Why don't you get a man instead of those young boys? You're sounding desperate, girl. I'll buy you a vanilla latte if you leave now. No need to hang on to the bitter end. If they're interested, we'll get an e-mail. Let's go."

Sylvia tucked her date card into her purse. "I want a grande with two vanilla shots."

A club attendant ran up to them at the door. "Oh, ma'am, I have something for you." He handed Amber a single rose with a note.

Who did this? Amber looked at the rose, holding it a few inches away from her face. Some crazy guy could have put something toxic on the petals, expecting her to sniff.

Sylvia plucked the rose out of her hand and waved it under her nose. "Open the envelope."

"What if you were poisoned?"

"What if you were run over by a truck in the next five seconds?" Sylvia shrugged. "If stuff is going to happen, it's going to happen."

Amber wanted to argue the point. Instead, she opened the little white envelope, immediately noticing the neat, slightly slanted handwriting. *Seven minutes is not enough. How about dinner?*

No signature. Amber didn't care for juvenile high school notes when a grown man should know how to talk to a woman. She took the rose from Sylvia's hand and tossed it into a nearby trash can.

They stepped out the door. Outside, the cool night air brought a welcome change to the warm, sweaty, cologne-ridden room. The major road in front of the club in D.C.s' downtown had its unique hub of activity at night. Taxis and limos lined the streets. The noisy foot traffic made its way from one club to another. A few drunken souls in front of a neighboring bar simply collapsed on the curb, smoking and talking with each other.

The two women walked in the opposite direction to the end of the block. They waited for the light to signal them to cross.

"Yo."

Neither woman turned. They had discussed on several occasions the stupid ways for men to try to get a woman's attention. This was in the top three.

"Yo, Miss."

Amber turned because the young male voice was closer. "What do you want?" she asked in a crisp tone.

"My man, there, said you're makin' a big mistake."

Amber looked over in the direction the kid had pointed. Surprise, surprise, there was no sign of any man.

"I swear, he was just standing there."

She studied the kid. "It's okay. I believe you. What did he

look like?" If it happened to be someone from the club, she would make a formal complaint.

"He was a dude, like any other dude. His sh—I mean, his stuff was tight, though. He had on a bad designer suit, sportin' a mighty bling-bling earring stud. Dude had money." He looked her up and down. "You're not bad looking, either, in that hot red number. Explains why he was all over that."

Amber felt his adolescent leer over her body, lingering on her hips. Her hands curled at her sides. If he took one step toward her, she would kickbox his behind all over the sidewalk. She waited.

"Ah . . . Amber, I know you take those classes so you can fight the whole world. I, on the other hand, am a librarian. Paper cuts are about all I can handle. My chunky legs can't kick higher than my shins," Sylvia declared.

The young man threw up his hands. He addressed Sylvia. "What's wrong with your friend? Ain't nobody tryin' to mess with you. I'm just passin' on a message." He flicked his hand at Amber. The youth turned on his heels and stalked off down the street.

Amber took a deep breath, uncurled her hands, and headed for her car. Her heartbeat throbbed in her ears. The aftershock jitters had her entire body trembling.

Sylvia looked at her over the top of the car. "Boy, you sure know how to kill an evening."

Mondays sucked. Or maybe it was just the job. Amber stirred sugar into her coffee, making the small effort last as long as possible. In five minutes she had a meeting with her boss.

"What does old sourpuss want?" Gladys, another staff reporter, asked.

"The usual. He's going to chew my butt about something. There's no pleasing that man." Amber sipped her coffee noisily. She tried to mask her unease with bravado. Over the rim of the cup, she spied the top-gun reporter coming out of her boss's office. "Now, if I threw away my scruples, embellished a bit, and invaded someone's privacy, then I could share a chuckle with the boss man."

"This is true. But are you sure that you want to be like Marty?" Gladys threw a grimace over her shoulder toward the man heading their way.

"Break it up, ladies. Don't you need to be drumming up some stories? What about you, Amber? Come see me in my office. I've got a couple leads I won't have time to do because I've got the scoop of the year."

Amber hated the smugness that practically oozed all over Marty. She didn't have to doubt that he had the scoop of the year. Marty had lots of contacts and enough dirt on a few key local people that they did his bidding, willingly or not. "I'll take a rain check on that offer. Gotta run. I have an appointment with the boss man." She threw her empty cup in the trash and headed out. Just being in his company left a bad taste. What a jerk!

She approached her boss's office. He motioned for her to enter, where she had the pleasure of watching him clip his fingernails while he cradled the phone between his shoulder and ear. He nodded toward the chair opposite him. Amber slid in, sitting tentatively on the edge, somewhat like her nerves.

Her boss slammed down the phone and stared at her for a full two seconds. "Amber, it's time you stepped up to the plate. Marty is going to be busy for the next month or so working on a big story. My other top reporters are also under deadline. I can't have you covering the sappy stories you usually bring to me. We bring the news that people want to hear and know."

Amber opted for silence. Mr. Barkman had an agenda and nothing she said would detour him.

"You've nothing to say? You're too good for that, right? I had to take you in with no experience when you got tired of playing real-estate agent. You said you had a passion for writing, for reporting the news, for being responsible for sharing knowledge." He leaned forward. "I'm still waiting for the brilliance to hit me." He opened a file on his desk and scribbled notes on the top sheet.

Barkman's hostility didn't bother her. She needed this experience to move on to bigger things. Since her boss didn't save his piggish behavior for only her, she chalked up the experience to earning her dues. "There may be a story I can research." She hadn't thought any of this through. An ill-tempered boss provided the right amount of motivation, though. "Remember the pension fund scandal?"

"Ha. Which one? Every corporation these days has crooks running them."

"The Sandstone Corporation with its headquarters in Landover, Maryland. Software engineering. Had a lot of the local government contracts."

"Might be a bit heavy for you."

"Thought you wanted me to get started."

"Yeah. More in the vein of interviewing the mayor's wife and her favorite charity. Anyway, Marty covered the story a year ago and will be doing a follow-up once the trial is over."

It would be a fight to change Barkman's mind. She had to be careful how she manipulated the situation. "I have a couple weeks' vacation I want to take soon. It'll give me time to think about what you're saying."

Barkman squinted at her. His lip twitched. "Don't play

games with me, Delaney. I'll approve your vacation. The minute you get back, you'd better be ready."

Amber met the doubt in his eyes head on and didn't back down. "Yes, sir." She could now focus on Zoe's project.

"Where are you headed for vacation?"

"Not quite sure." Zoe's parents had turned over boxes of their daughter's possessions. They had even given Amber her front-door key while they made arrangements to clean up the condo before selling it. It would take a few days to sift through all the papers and personal effects. Adding the emotional ride it would be, it would probably take even longer.

"Maybe you'll discover something worth printing." He closed the file on his desk and slapped his hand on top of the file. "Or else re-up your real-estate license. And no one will be able to save you." His phone rang and he waved her away before picking up the receiver.

Amber walked through the rows of cubicles to her area in the back. Her mind ticked off the list of tasks she had to complete. First item was to organize a game plan. She couldn't do that until she had finished reading all the available materials about the entire story.

Out of the articles, one central figure intrigued her. The man who had been labeled the whistle-blower proved to be mysterious and reclusive. There had to be a way to get to him.

By the end of the day, she knew more details about this do-gooder, including the court transcripts about the infamous Bodine Pemberton. He was a senior vice president of benefits who didn't believe in the company's philosophy of using pension funds to bankroll the dubious expenses of the executives. The only personal tidbit she'd managed to glean was that his family was based in Breezewood, Texas. One reporter had managed to take a photo of him unaware in front of the family home.

With dirt heaped on all the executives, she wondered how Bodine would fare under her scrutiny. No one was squeaky clean—at least that's what Marty always crowed right before he slammed someone.

Photos and articles covered her desk. If she could learn enough about Zoe to honor her wishes with a more human-interest approach to her life, maybe the gnawing guilt could dissipate.

Deep in her gut, she sensed that there was more to be told about this pension scandal. No one had really focused on the only remaining figure that survived the handing-down of the indictments. But she didn't want any discovery to over-shadow Zoe's story.

The next week Amber continued gathering the back-ground materials. She avoided the boss by spending her days out in the field trying to get firsthand reports about Bodine Pemberton.

Barkman still pushed her about when she would take va-cation. His concern puzzled her, until he reminded her that she said she'd think about the new game plan. As long as he didn't put any unreasonable pressure on her with his impa-tience, she'd take her time researching and organizing her notes.

So far, she determined that the whistle-blower was a short beat away from sainthood. No one disliked him. If they couldn't like him, it was only because they didn't know him. When she drew the circle around the top executives, he stood out against the rest. If she made up her mind to write the story, she'd need to discover the real Bodine. How did one man not fall under the spell of greed and power?

She parked her car and headed into the salon for her reg-

ular eyebrow waxing. As usual, the small beauty shop bustled with the regulars and several eager new faces. Hair dri-
ers hummed. Patrons, sitting side by side, gossiped and
shared a joke or two. Even the stylists joined in the frenetic
noisy surroundings with animated conversations over their
clients' heads.

Amber walked through the shop quickly to avoid the
piercing scent of hair relaxer and acetone from the manicur-
ing area. She'd be a dizzy mess if she had to work there all
day. With her constant nagging for three months, she had
managed to convince Sonny to have additional fans in the
facial spa area.

Stepping between the psychedelic curtains, she entered
another world. Music played from a mini stereo system. She
recognized the rhythmic chants from the South African
group, Ladysmith Black Mombazo. She smiled, appreciat-
ing Sonny's eclectic taste. The loud conversations didn't
occur behind the curtains. It was all hushed whispers and
hand signals.

Every week Amber visited the shop. One week she got
her eyebrows waxed and reshaped, the other week she got a
facial and shoulder massage.

"Hey, Sonny. I'm not late, am I?" She brushed her cheek
against Sonny's in greetings.

"No, honey. Right on time. We're ready for you in Salon
Deux. Sidekick Sylvie is in the Paradise Lost Salon." He
made a face and waved his hand.

"I hope both of you behave."

"If she'd stop popping her gum like a teenager, stop wearing all that darn pink, I wouldn't have a problem. She looks
like a pink hippo."

"Look, don't pull me into your fashion wars." Amber
laughed and made her way to the back. "Sonny, can I have a

Coke?" He shook his head. "I know. I should be drinking one of your herbal concoctions, but not today. Okay?" She waved to Sylvia. "Hey, girl, any good news for me?"

"I'm fine. Thank you for asking. Ouch." Sylvia flinched as her brow was tweezed. "You owe me big. I'm putting my career, my reputation in jeopardy—"

"Cut the drama. I'm sure your lawyer boyfriend didn't even notice he was spilling his guts when you were blowing in his ear."

Sylvia giggled. "How'd you guess? Anyway, I got some great news. Your man is in Texas hiding out at the family homestead."

"I know about the home in Breezewood. How the heck am I going to get him to talk to me?"

"Don't even look at me when you say that. You're the one playing detective. Take your butt to Texas and go detect."

Amber waited for the strip to be pulled off her brow before speaking. She blinked away the natural tearing. "Sure you don't want to take a vacation with me?"

"I'm sure."

Sonny arrived with her Coke and a gift-wrapped little box. "Someone dropped this off for you. Didn't tell me you had a new man in your life." Sonny put his hand on his hip. "Hell, I can't recall when was the last time you did have a man in your life."

"Why don't you go make yourself useful and get me an iced tea?" Sylvia ordered.

"Why don't you get a colonic?" Sonny quipped.

Amber stared at the little box wrapped in blue and silver paper. She turned it over. There wasn't a note attached. "Who dropped it off?"

"Donna, at the front, said it was a regular guy with a

baseball hat. He didn't smile much, but he wasn't rude either."

"I don't want to open it. Sylvia, do you think this is the same creepy guy who gave me flowers from the club?"

"How would he know you're here?"

"I'll open it." Sonny took the box and retreated to an available chair.

All eyes focused on him as he pulled the paper off the box. He held it to his ear and shook it. Without ceremony, he pulled open the top. A folded piece of paper fell to the floor. Inside was a pendant that had two pieces for His and Her. The Her piece was in the box lying on the cotton square.

Sonny held up the note. "Today we are two separate pieces in the world of confusion. Soon we will be together to build our world of love. Happy birthday."

Sylvia pushed away the stylist's hand and propped herself onto her elbows. "I don't like this. I think we should call the police."

Amber was glad she had a firm table under her body. The message in the note scared her, making her limbs shaky to match the nervous quiver in her stomach. "I'm not afraid to call the police. But what are we going to tell them? We don't have any idea who is doing this. Obviously he knows I'm here. It must be someone I know." She mentally went down her very short list of the men that recently had been in her life. There were two candidates, both highly unlikely. One guy, after a few dates, confessed that he was on the rebound and married the woman he'd dated before her. The other guy announced on the first date that he would be entering the seminary and wanted to go out with a bang.

Sylvia walked over and retrieved the note. "I don't like the fact that he says you'll be together with him on your birthday. Your birthday is three weeks away. Makes it seem as if he's planning on some type of reunion."

Sonny waved the wrapping paper. "I think you should listen to Sylvie."

"I'll go to the police tomorrow. So far, it's been harmless." Amber poked at the pendant, having no desire to wear it anywhere close to her body. "Throw it away, Sonny."

Later that night, Amber settled on the couch with a cup of hot chocolate and a book. The television played the latest music videos in the background. Her nerves had settled down somewhat, but she took precautions. The doors were locked, curtains drawn, and her softball bat on the floor next to the couch, just in case.

The phone rang. She jumped, spilling the drink onto the page. She uttered a curse. "Yes. Hello." She was in no mood to be civil.

"Hi, sweetheart. It's Mom."

"Mom? Where are you?" Amber set aside the book. Her mother hadn't called in weeks, since Zoe's funeral.

"Still here in California. I'm having such a wonderful time. The weather is absolutely fantastic."

Amber heard the contentment in her mother's voice. "Good. Have you seen her as yet?"

"No, not yet. But I'm participating in several readers' groups who love her work. We've been writing letters to her in hopes that she'll come and talk with us."

"That's good. How long do you think you'll be there?"

"I'm not sure. But I'm so close, I can't possibly entertain not staying here for a little while longer."

Amber smiled to keep her voice light. She stared up at the

ceiling, hating the direction the conversation took. "But you can't afford it, Mom."

"I know, which is why I'm calling you."

There. Her mother had said what she'd tell herself after each call. The calls weren't out of loving concern or a desire to catch up with her daughter's activities. Necessity dictated the occasional communication. "Do you really think it's a good idea to be hobnobbing in California? You don't have much income beyond your social security and small retirement."

"I didn't call to fight with you, Amber. I'm really close to meeting Alice Walker. I feel that meeting her will inspire me and motivate me to finish my memoir. I can't walk away from it. Can't be distracted."

"Distracted? How about just being responsible? Alice Walker doesn't know who you are and, if she did, she probably wouldn't care that you're there in California. And I've got my own bills to pay." Amber's chest heaved from anger. Why did she feel like the bad guy whenever she spoke to her mother?

"Fine. Fine. I didn't mean to be a burden." Her mother sniffled softly at the other end of the phone. "It's just that I put aside what I wanted to do all my life. I gave up my dreams, my goals without complaint. I asked for nothing through the years."

Amber squeezed her eyes shut to block out the accusation. How long would her mother punish her? For years their relationship had drifted apart to a careful, cordial acquaintance. She wanted the warm, loving person who was her constant cheerleader from her childhood. She wanted the mother who hugged her and shared her views of cheating boyfriends after her first heartbreak. Obviously that was too tall of an order. "Where do you want the money sent?"

"Are you sure you can manage? You can send it to Williams Liquor Store."

A liquor store? She wrote down the information. Not long afterward, the conversation died and Amber hung up, tired of asking questions to keep her mother engaged. The book and hot chocolate, now cold, sat on the side table forgotten. Amber leaned back into the couch and fought against the urge to scream angrily or to cry in desperation. Is this how Zoe felt when her parents, especially her mother, turned away from her?

The phone rang again. She answered.

"Did you like my gift?" the male voice asked soft and low.

"Who is this?"

"Someone you'll meet soon."

Amber looked around the room, turning in her seat, half expecting to see a stranger staring back at her. Her grip on the phone tightened. "I got the gift," she gasped. Think. Keep him on the phone. Get clues. Her breathing grew ragged. If she noticed, he would, too. But her fear soared to panic at the realization that he knew her phone number.

"I can tell that you didn't like it. You don't wear it. I promise that you'll like your birthday gift. I'm planning for a very special celebration."

"Who are you? Are you one of those men I met at the club? How did you get my telephone number?" She found a pencil and began writing on the pages of the novel. *Slow. Deliberate. Light voice. No special accent.*

"All will be revealed when the time is ready. I think you'll be pleasantly surprised. I can't wait." He sighed deeply. "You'd be surprised what I know about you—Amber Lee Delaney of Pineywood Lane."

Amber clutched the arm of the couch. Her nails dug into

the soft fabric. "Don't call me again," she squeaked and slammed down the phone. She covered her mouth with a shaky hand to keep her terror quiet. The fear that overtook her body had now rendered her mute. She sat and stared at the wall until her heart returned to a calmer state.

The next morning Amber groggily turned over and blinked at the clock. "Damn, I'm going to be late again." She jumped out of bed and headed for the shower. It'd taken several hours before she could fall asleep after the terrifying call.

Thirty minutes later, she ran through her home, grabbing paperwork. She had two items on her priority list: send money to her mother and visit the police. Now that it was daylight and a sunny day, the mind-numbing fear she'd experienced last night had almost disappeared.

She came out of her town home with her face upturned, soaking up the sun rays. As she approached her car, she noticed something odd. On the driver's-side window, a word had been sprayed in white frost. *Apologize!*

The parking lot was busy for a workday morning. Adults went off to work or jogged, while the kids waited for the school bus. How could a man spraying her car not raise any alarms? So much for neighborhood watch.

She wasn't going to wait another minute, though. She pulled out her cell phone and called the police. If this nut thought he could continue with this mad behavior, then she'd show him that he picked the wrong girl for his victim. Today was a brand-new day and she was in the mood for a fight.

The police arrived promptly. Amber knew from their questions that she couldn't provide them with enough information. She disclosed everything she'd thought of, while they told her how to change her routine and to travel with at least one other person. Their last piece of advice sounded like the best thing for her. Could she take a vacation for a little while to see if that would head him off?

Since she had planned to take a few weeks to work on Zoe's project, she could take this opportunity to get started in earnest.

That night she lay in bed with all the lights on in the other parts of the house. Exhaustion pulled at every muscle, draining her energy. This was no way to live. She called her best friend. "Sylvia, I'm following the police's advice, sooner than later. I'm heading out of town for a couple weeks."

"You know you could stay with me."

"I know, but it gives me the perfect opportunity."

"For what?"

"To head to Breezewood, Texas."

Chapter Two

Thirty years old and sweating like a pig in this stupid car. Of all times for Texas to have an unseasonably warm winter. *Happy birthday to me. Big whoop.* Amber wiped the sweat puckered on the tip of her nose. It wouldn't matter, though. In a few seconds, her nose would be moist again, just like Old Faithful.

Dry heat, everyone said of the southwest. It wouldn't feel as bad as the humidity in Washington, D.C. What a bunch of crock. Heat was heat. Her body reacted regardless of the type of heat by sweating from every pore.

She adjusted the ineffective vents to aim down on her bare legs and up at her face. Air flowed, barely. It wasn't really cold, but it beat facing the heat. Thank goodness she'd ditched the wrinkled blue linen suit for a pair of denim shorts, a bit shorter than she'd wear, and a crop top. If she hadn't seen other adult women wearing the midriff-bared tops in town, she'd swear she had shopped in teenage heaven.

The sun hadn't reached its peak for the day, but its brightness made her squint. She drove west on Interstate 35, glancing at the signs dotting the roadside, marking the miles of upcoming, major cities. Breezewood, sandwiched between Dallas and Fort Grant, was only fifteen miles away.

Traveling on a cheap flight with two connections to an out-of-the-way airport and a drive that took an additional three hours, Amber wanted to feel the firm ground under her feet. Never mind the nervous jitters that had her stomach in knots. The cockiness she'd started with had taken a detour at the last pit stop. What made her think she could pull off her master plan? Better yet, who made her think she could?

On the passenger side sat a yellow folder filled with papers, photos, and newspaper clippings—bits and pieces of Zoe's life. She knew the contents by heart, but brought it on the trip as a constant reminder of her mission.

Among Zoe's personal effects, she'd found an official memo from Bodine Pemberton addressed to her friend. The one-page letter alerted Zoe about discrepancies in the pension fund. He'd notified her of a meeting with all the senior officers a few days later.

There were no follow-up memos on the situation. It did confirm that they had some level of interaction. While she took on the formidable task of uncovering Pemberton, she could also learn about her friend's business behavior that had put her on the road to self-destruction.

Zoe had started off her career on a high and soared even higher. Meanwhile, Amber had fallen into the real-estate business and caught the bug for selling high-end houses. After ten years of earnings, awards, and various titles announcing her massive success, she walked away. Maybe approaching thirty started her thinking about her contribution to mankind, her reason for living, and a host of other highbrow topics she'd gotten off the latest TV talk show. Gathering her courage, she'd marched headlong into a new career, staring at the bottom of the ladder at a newsmagazine.

Now her money appeared to be going in one direction: out of her hands. She'd been hired on a trial basis, and if she didn't land something big, she'd be looking for a new third career. From Washington, D.C., to Texas with one suitcase, she focused on her target—Bodine Pemberton.

She wanted to dissect this man into little pieces. Who was this man who had fallen from grace? It was clear she wasn't the only one who thought he received a deal from the government. He'd lost his sizable pension fund and perks, had been offered a hefty sum to pose for the infamous *Every Woman's Fantasy* magazine, and now had turned urban cowboy on his family's cattle ranch. Bodine Pemberton could be the ticket to getting Zoe's life story in print.

WELCOME TO BREEZEWOOD. The billboard greeted the town's new arrivals in bold black letters, announcing its population at the 20,000 mark. She was a long way from the nation's capital's dense urban scene.

Small Town, U.S.A.; the semirural scene was not really her thing since childhood. At least on a more positive note, she'd made it. Thank heavens. Her legs cried out to be stretched. Amber followed the directions she retrieved off the Internet and turned off the two-lane highway to aim for the center of town.

Side streets intersected Main Street. Signs for a library and elementary and middle schools intermittently dotted the road. She guessed the law-abiding citizens must still be home at this early hour because the street only had a few cars, mainly in front of the local meat market. Time had certainly taken its time with this place. Maybe Clint Eastwood would want to direct his next Western here.

She slowed the car as she approached a jean-clad young man and pushed the button to lower her window. Immediately the heat rushed into the cool interior and her face and scalp prickled. On cue, the floodgates in her pores opened. "Could you tell me how to get to the Pemberton Ranch?"

"Yes, ma'am. Go on about a mile and then after you pass the Smithers House—big and yellowlike—you'll see a dirt road on your left. Turn there and it'll take you to the main house."

Amber thanked the young man, hoping she understood everything he'd said in his thick Texan accent.

Once she had driven out of the city limits, the road curved, and there loomed the Smithers House. The large three-story farmhouse stood back off the road with a wooden perimeter fence around the property. She'd never seen a yellow house, at least not this particular buttery shade. It reminded her of a great ball of sunshine—a good target for a flock of birds with a vendetta. Staring at the eye-catching structure, she rolled on past a dirt road.

"Darn it!" She slammed on the brakes and yanked the steering wheel toward the dirt road.

No street sign marked the road, or, rather, trail. The dry dirt and small craters qualified the need to call it a trail. The small car squeaked and grunted. Amber, with head bobbing, wasn't going to be deterred. Nothing about this assignment had come easily, so why should she expect the final leg to be any different.

Already her nerves tingled, the adrenaline pumping. She pressed down on the gas pedal, ignoring a new sound emitting from the car. It was a rental. Whatever that *grrrr* sound was, it wasn't her problem.

"Who the heck would live this far off the main road?" she

muttered. She wanted nothing more than to soak her body in a tub and scrub herself clean of all the grime. Her foot sunk the gas pedal a few more inches.

The *grrrr* sound graduated to a hiccup and the steering wheel shook with a frightening vibration. Amber stamped onto the brake and the car skidded to a stop, but only after she had hit a fence post. In her opinion, it was too darn close to the roadway. "Great, Amber. You really know how to do it."

She popped the hood and stepped out of the car, propped the hood open and stared down into the engine. Hoses, cables, a big square thing in the middle—what to do now? Her ever-present nerves reminded her that she had a predicament. Not a soul happened to be in sight.

The cell phone wouldn't help. It hadn't gotten any signal once she'd turned off the main road. She looked up and down the road, trying to decide which direction to take. If she headed back into town, at least she knew what to expect. On the other hand, the person she'd come to meet lived somewhere in the vicinity from where she stood.

Maybe she could drive at a crawl pace. She leaned against the side of the car and tucked her head again under the hood. Why did an engine have to be so complicated? She shook her head at the grimy . . . stuff. What could she check?

The oil.

Bo sat atop his Tennessee walking horse Onyx, admiring his family's property. A painter's brush couldn't add another detail to the verdant landscape. Two hundred acres of lush prairie grass rustled in rhythmic swirls under a gentle breeze. Wild flowers dotted the field with rich splashes of yellow, blue, and pink. Faint, familiar sounds of mooing from the cattle punctuated the air.

This was home. He'd jumped on every opportunity to separate himself from Pemberton Ranch, where his great-grandfather and his great uncles settled more than a century ago. Over the years, the families combined property and finances and created the ranch. The name came with its privileges, but it also hung around his neck like an annoying weight during high school and university in his bid to be independent.

Bittersweet emotions swirled through his heart, making him feel guilty for not stepping up to be the head of the ranch as he knew his father expected of him. Yet he couldn't deny the pride that nestled in his heart for his family's ancestral home and for all they had done for Breezewood and their place in Texas history.

His head, though, was not raised too high. No youthful arrogance present. The circumstances of his return clung to him like a dark unrelenting shadow.

Onyx snorted and nodded his head. "There, boy. I know, we're suppose to be taking you on a run." Bo patted the steely neck of his horse, who promptly flicked his sleek head. With a click of his tongue, he led Onyx in a canter along their usual path within the perimeter of the field in front of the house.

A soft roar pierced the quiet surroundings. Bo looked around. What on earth was that? It grew increasingly louder as the roar turned into a choking gurgle. A red bullet of a car shot down the road heading toward the house.

He frowned. He didn't expect a visitor, at least none in a sports car. With a quick nudge in Onyx's flank, he guided the horse along the low fence separating the field from the road. What idiot would drive down the dirt road at that speed? Well, whatever they were selling, he wasn't interested.

Tires squealed. The car fishtailed and then straightened out before plowing into a fence post. He squinted into the sun, trying to make out who had trespassed and destroyed his property. Hopefully, the person wasn't hurt. It would hinder him from telling them about their reckless behavior.

Bo rode up behind the car and dismounted. "What the heck?" he muttered. His mood went south. A long pair of legs in denim shorts was visible from under the raised hood. Not only was she reckless, but she wore those silly platform shoes that belonged to the seventies. He pushed his Stetson back, scratched his forehead, and gritted his teeth. A woman, for pete's sake.

Either she was ignoring him or she was consumed with whatever was going on under her car hood. Still draped over the side of the car, one leg rose as she reached farther under the hood. If they were in a horror movie, the car would gobble her up and he could return to tending his cattle.

Instead he found himself staring because he refused to admit that he actually admired those legs—smooth, shapely, and the color of caramel, his favorite candy. Never mind that his eyes traveled up to the hem of the shorts and farther up to her curved—

"Darn it!"

The trespasser held up the dipstick, flicking oil off the edge. Keeping a wary eye on her and the airborne oil spills, he cleared his throat. "Ma'am, may I help you?" He rounded the car in time to see her miserably failing to get the dipstick back into place.

"Here, you take it." The woman stuck the offending object at him. An oil smudge marked her cheek. Seeing her lips pursed and light brown eyes mirroring her frustration, he opted to keep his observation about her new face paint to himself, especially since her hairdo had obviously wilted along the sides of her face.

Bo retrieved the stick and replaced it. "What happened here, other than you knocking down the post?"

She placed her hands on her hips. "The post is too close to the side of the road. There's no shoulder. Where are people supposed to walk?"

Maybe she was crazy. "No one walks up here."

"Look, I'm hot and will need a tow. Something is wrong with the car. Think you can go ask the folks at the house to send a car?" She gave a dismissive wave and walked over to the car.

Leaving her stranded entered his mind. "How about riding with me back to the house?" The panic that shot through those eyes made him want to chuckle.

How ridiculous. Amber took a deep breath. No need to run screaming down the road just because the thought of getting on that huge horse scared her. Even though it nibbled a grassy patch, she knew that, if given the chance, the horse would take a chunk out of her legs. She'd rather walk.

The cowboy stood in her path. She strode past him, raising her chin in defiance. He and his horse could take a flying leap. She hadn't gotten this far for nothing. Her ankle twisted and she stumbled forward. Strong, tanned arms supported her before she fell into an unsightly heap.

Embarrassment warmed her face, which was pressed against his chest. His forearms supported her under her chest. "Thank you," she mumbled. Her lofty attitude fizzled.

His hands dropped from around her. Not only did she have to worry about the horse, but also its owner. Sitting on the horse next to this man would reduce her to schoolgirl antics of blushing and giggling. Amber couldn't see herself physically touching this tall hunk of man. "Um . . . I think

you'll have to go get help. I don't do horses." *Or cowboys.*
She ignored the disgust on his face—square-jawed with
sculpted nose and full lips.

"Take my word for it, this is your best choice."

She bit her lip, contemplating. Stay in this heat until her
cowboy rode on his massive black snorting beast to get help
or pretend she was some prairie princess and sidesaddle her
way to Pemberton Ranch.

"Times a-wasting." The cell phone rang at Bo's side. He
looked at the number, but didn't answer. "Ready?"

"I thought cell phones didn't work?"

"Only cheap ones."

Amber noticed the smirk. She'd wait to pick her battles,
until she was in safe surroundings. "I'm Amber, by the way."

"Nice to meet you. I'm Bo."

"Bodine Pemberton?"

Bo froze. Iced water could have been poured through his
veins. She looked at him with a gleam that had him take a retreating step. Her interest went beyond casual recognition. It
showed in the excitement barely hidden. Curiosity burned in
her eyes, fastening on him as if he were a prize. He didn't
care if she had a small, pert chin, delicate features, and soft
brown, albeit wilted hair. It didn't matter. This woman had
better be leaving when the tow truck arrived. "Yes, I'm Bo
Pemberton."

"Nice to meet you. Amber Delaney." She offered her
hand in greeting. He shook it, a bit self-conscious that his
callused hands may offend. He rubbed his hand against his
jeans to erase her softness.

Bo untied Onyx and led the horse back to where Amber
stood.

"How am I getting up there?" She shrank against the car.

"Like this." His eyes drank her in like a fine wine, admiring not only her good looks, but the edgy toughness that seemed second nature. He walked purposefully toward her and, in one swift motion, scooped her into his arms and set her on the horse before she had a chance to object.

"Ooh."

He bit back a smile, sensing her ready response to flee. Just as quickly, he pulled himself behind her. "Comfortable?"

"No, but I'll manage." She stiffened when his chest brushed her arm.

The slight adjustment of her body didn't go unnoticed. At least he was not the only person to suffer from the closeness. It would really help if she didn't have that light, floral fragrance that drifted past his nose and scrambled his thinking. Amber Delaney had invaded his domain. Completely unacceptable.

He pushed Onyx in a trot back to the house. The ride proved difficult with another body on the horse, especially when they both remained rigid for the duration. But the faster he could get her taken care of, the quicker she'd be gone. He needed his space, with its daily routine of managing cattle, paying bills, and recuperating from his broken heart. No second opinion needed to tell him that Miss Delaney had an intensity that set him on edge.

They rode up to the front of the house. He dismounted and reached for her. She threw a leg over the horse and slid down before he could hoist her off. "Come on in." He ushered her into the cool interior. "Have a seat. Would you like something to drink?"

"Sure. Water is fine." Like a first-time visitor, she openly gazed around, taking in the cathedral ceilings, polished pine hardwood floors and matching trimmings. Over the years, the house had been renovated to mix a bit of old with new.

Her real-estate expertise recognized the quality in mixing the ranch style with a contemporary flair.

Bo went in search of the housekeeper. "Tessa?" There was no sign of her. He let out an exasperated sigh and headed for the refrigerator to get the water. On the door, posted with a magnet, a light blue paper had a note scrawled on it. He pulled it off and read the loopy handwriting that belonged to his housekeeper. "Tessa!" he roared. How could she do this?

"Bo, why are you yelling?"

"Oh, hi, Mom. Didn't know you came over."

His mother pointed at the note in his hand. "I knew Tessa was leaving. Figured you'd need help."

He read the note again. "How could she leave without giving me notice?" Tessa had been with the family most of his life. He depended on her. She kept his world calm and normal, like a second mother.

"She gave you notice three weeks ago. You ignored it." His mother retrieved a parcel of meat from the freezer and set it on the counter. She shook her head at him.

"I told her not to marry that moron." Tessa was too good for Ben. He had nothing to offer her. Now she'd taken off like a young teenager and headed for El Paso.

"Who died and made you king? She works . . . worked for you. You don't own her. She loves Ben and she left to get married."

"That's stupid." Love didn't last. It was like a shoe that got worn out sooner or later. In his case, it came sooner. In Tessa's case, it might be later. She had a boatload of patience to put up with overbearing men, like Ben.

"Um . . . excuse me. May I have that drink of water, please? I'm a little parched." Amber stood in the entryway between the open kitchen and hallway looking disheveled in a cute, sexy way.

Still scowling over the news of his housekeeper, Bo opened the cupboard, snatched a glass, and slammed it down on the counter.

"Here, let me get that before you break it." His mother retrieved the glass from him and filled it from the refrigerator door. "Hello, dear, I'm Martha Pemberton."

"I'm Amber. Thank you." Amber drank the cold liquid, savoring the wetness as it soothed her dried throat. Her mind had been working overtime with a plan on how to get close to Bo. Now that she was in his home, there had to be a way she could stay. She sipped the water, peeping over the rim at her target as he explained to his mother why she was in their home. Amber cleared her throat. "I apologize for this intrusion." She ignored Bo's grunt.

"Not at all, dear. Have a seat? Were you coming to see Bo?"

"Is there anything to eat? Did Tessa at least cook before she abandoned me?"

"Actually, I'm here to see Bo." Amber didn't lie.

Martha's eyes lit up and she turned a bright, welcoming smile toward Amber.

"Why?" Bo backed away from her. His eyes narrowed to slits, confusion written all over his face.

Amber had to think fast. "I need a job." Not a lie, but could be true back home if she couldn't nab Bo for her article. Plus she'd overheard most of the conversation.

"We don't have any openings." A smirk crossed his face when her eyebrow shot up.

"Not so fast, Bo. You need a housekeeper. You know I would help around the house if I could." His mother kept her friendly smile on Amber.

"Yes, but I need someone experienced. Mature," he warned.

So he wanted to be difficult. Let the games begin. "I heard

in town that you would be needing someone. Something about a housekeeper. I'm looking for work until I can get enough money to get me to D.C."

"What's in Washington, D.C.?"

"Nothing. A new life. New start."

"Look, I'm not interested in hiring short term nor in anyone running away from something or someone."

"Now, Bo. You're being rude. We'll take what we can get. I'm sure Amber has references?"

"As a matter of fact, I was a researcher for Sylvia Monroe, legal librarian in Virginia for several years. I have her contact information in my car."

And there was that other reason for running after an assignment so far away from her home. Her creepy admirer had promised to make her birthday an event to remember. She suspected that the speed dating was at the root of her problem.

Being talked into looking for Mr. Right had landed her in this predicament. The police couldn't help her and she didn't have any big brothers to protect her. So she did what any sensible woman in her position would do, she ran like hell and went into hiding.

Bo folded his arms and planted a wide, disapproving stance. "Can you cook?"

Amber caught the challenge and held her tongue for the moment. His dear sweet mother took her glass and refilled it.

"Most times it's just my husband and Bo. My other boys only come over on Sundays for dinner or when they want to butter me up for something." She chuckled.

Bo glared at his mother, who didn't retreat from her son's dark looks. "I don't understand why you came to me for a job when you passed an entire town where you could've looked for work," he said.

"It doesn't matter, does it?" Martha waved aside Bo's protest. "Where are your people from, young lady?"

"Um . . . District of Columbia. Well, actually, Maryland. Did you mean where they were born?" Half the time, she couldn't keep up with her artsy parents. Her mother and father had lived very separate lives since she was a teen. Her mother wrote poetry and wanted to write a story about the women in their family. Meanwhile her father, long since divorced from her mother, played the cello in a jazz band and toured constantly.

"The question wasn't supposed to be so difficult," Bo pushed.

Martha playfully smacked Bo's shoulder. "Take her references, if it pleases you. But I like her. I can't bear to be the only female on the premises." Martha approached and wrapped her arms around her in a welcoming hug. His mother smelled of talcum powder and baby oil, comforting nurturing scents that drew her in. "I don't actually live in the main house. We built a small guest house next to the house, hoping that when Bo took over that his father and I could retire. Say you'll stay."

Amber couldn't help but respond to Martha's hospitable nature. She only came to Amber's shoulders, with a full head of shockingly white hair. She was probably gray by her forties. Bo didn't really resemble her, except for the contours around the mouth and chin.

"Yes. I'll stay." Amber shot a quick glance at Bo. One thing was for sure, he had no telepathic powers or she'd be six feet under from his icy stare. Instead she hugged the older woman, who provided a wonderful thaw.

Martha clapped her hands. "Great news. Bo, isn't this great? Well, I'm heading out to run errands. Bo will show you around the house. I know you'll love it here." Martha, in her busy print dress, bustled out, taking all the liveliness out of the room.

Please say something, Amber silently begged. The new job didn't intimidate her, but her new boss certainly did. Not exactly the way she'd pictured her assignment unfolding.

In her plan of action, she'd arrive at the house and state her case that the American people wanted his side of the story. How did it feel to know that his company had swindled its employees' pension funds? Judging from the size of his family's property, he had most certainly landed on his feet. How could he sleep at night, knowing that his staff who may have looked forward to retirement had to work, harder and longer, while he enjoyed the privileges of his class?

"Don't bother getting comfortable. You may stay until I find a better fit."

"Suits me." She met his stare. Let him go find his perfect mature housekeeper. In the meantime, she had two weeks to do her thing. This handsome, ornery giant with healthy bronzed skin wouldn't know what hit him by the time she was through with him.

"Follow me." Bo led the way through the house. "There's not much more to see on this floor. We've got a full bathroom on the first floor, with the standard family room and living room."

Southwestern hues decorated the house in a warm sea of coral, soft greens, and hints of purple. Light, sheer curtains muted the harsh light coming through the large windows. Placed around the hallway were potted plants, bringing a little outdoors into the home.

"What's this door?" Amber laid her hand on the knob.

"My office." His voice left no doubt that it was off-limits.

"You don't want it dusted?" Getting in there would be like

earning thousands of bonus points. Since she expected Bo to guard the inner sanctum of his life, she'd zero in on papers, books, and other personal items to probe these dark corners.

"This house is too big for one person to keep straight. A cleaning service comes in twice a month." His eyes flicked over her, dismissive.

The familiar anger percolated. "I understand your hesitation; after all, it's not every day that someone drops in on your doorstep. I do appreciate you helping me out in this way."

Another grunt was the reply.

She followed him up the stairs, declining his prompting to lead the way. Instead of him having full view of her rear as she climbed the stairs, she had the pleasure to enjoy his jean-clad rear end. She needed Sylvia to share this moment, and giggled at the thought.

He turned and frowned at her. Shaking his head, he continued up the stairs. She rolled her eyes at his back, knowing that he again had dismissed her as if she were an annoying child.

High cathedral ceilings accented with skylights allowed the natural light to fill the great hall and stairway. Large, gold-plated frames of family portraits lined the wall leading up the stairs. Bo's quick march didn't afford Amber time to stop and study the various generations of Pembertons.

Suddenly Bo stopped in the hallway, causing Amber to bump into his back. "I don't get you," he said. "You seem to be a together person, clean—well, reasonably so—articulate, kind of good looking. Why would you need a hand out?"

If I hadn't met your mother, I would think you were raised in a barn. She'd almost said that and more. He sure could get her dander up. "I'm taking an impromptu vacation and I'm short of cash."

Bo didn't reply, instead he continued down the hallway.

Amber marveled that there were five large bedrooms and three luxurious bathrooms. "Should I turn down your covers each night? And place a mint on your pillow, perhaps?"

He smiled. She couldn't believe it. She'd actually made him smile. The simple action of his full wide lips did wonders to transform his face into an approachable, friendly person. She answered with her own smile, breathing a sigh of relief that maybe it wouldn't be bad after all.

"Where are you staying?"

She had stayed in a motel in Dallas, but checked out earlier that morning. With her credit cards charged to the max, a one hundred dollar–bill in her pocketbook, her choice for sleeping arrangements were limited. She shrugged.

"Look, I don't need a housekeeper on the premises. I probably only need a part-time cook to help my mother."

"I can cook." Sylvia would have fallen over with laughter at that lie. "If you tell me of a cheap place, I'll stay there." She tried to mask her desperation. He could hear it, though.

"I'll make a deal with you. You can stay here, play housekeeper until I find a real one."

That could be a day later or three weeks later. To come so far and let the fear inhibit her was unthinkable. "Deal, Mr. Pemberton." She stuck out her hand and shook his, letting him know that she was no wilting flower to be bowled over by his presence.

"I'm going to call for the tow truck. Was there anything you needed from the car?"

"My suitcase."

"No problem. I'll bring it." Bo picked up a phone sitting

on a hall table. He dialed the operator and requested the number of a local tow-truck company. "And call me Bo."

She grinned; a noisy sigh of relief escaped.

"I've one request," he added. "Don't make me regret my decision."

Chapter Three

Snooping didn't rank as one of her strengths. The lengths she seemed willing to go for a story wrestled with her conscience. Marty, the head jerk reporter at her company, couldn't be her source of inspiration. That would leave her at the level of a slug.

But she had to tap into something motivational. Why not think about some of the TV talk-show hosts she admired? They managed to get interesting people in front of America and specialized in extracting information that could make you hate or love these people.

Amber wanted that power, that ability.

Her hand paused over the doorknob to the master bedroom. It wasn't as if she'd dig through his drawers to see if he wore boxers or briefs. After all, she had a job to do as the housekeeper. On that premise, she'd knock three times and then, if no answer, go in. The loud tick of the hall clock matched her heart's pounding.

The sound of the garage door opening drew her attention.

From the window, she saw Bo's silver-gray Mercedes drive out and head down the road. His daily routine remained unknown to her, so she'd better act quickly.

The bedroom door opened easily. A part of her expected it to be locked, given its occupant's personality. She slipped in and closed the door quickly behind her. All her favorite spy movies inspired her to be in character as she swiveled around to keep a roving eye on her surroundings. All clear.

The other rooms in the house exhibited soft, warm hues steeped in the region's culture. In contrast, this room didn't identify with any abstract decorative themes. Dark burgundy boldly dominated the room, linens, and borders around the walls. The masculine theme continued with hunter-green accents in the scatter rugs and pillows, with a worn armchair in a small sitting area.

Amber ran her hand over the dark wood furniture, heavy with bold, defining lines. A neatly made four-poster bed took center stage, sitting high on its frame. No wonder the man acted as if he had direct lineage to royalty. His day consisted of sitting on his monster of a horse and sleeping on a bed so close to the ceiling that his nose could touch it.

Wonder how many women shared his pillow? She pursed her lips, tossing out the question before her mind sprung an answer.

She walked over to the tall chest of drawers, resisting the urge to start opening drawers, but failing miserably. After closing the first drawer, she made a decision.

He was a boxers man.

She trailed a finger along the curlicues on the edge of the piece of furniture. No dust. Either Tessa was a whiz of a housekeeper or Bo had the dubious distinction of being a neat freak. A small bottle of cologne sat among his other personal effects: small change in a ceramic cup, cuff links that winked with their diamond studs, a comb, and brush. She popped open the cologne and her memory of riding with him came back in a rush. His light woodsy scent acted as an indelible signature she secretly savored and filed away under miscellaneous tidbits.

She'd stepped into the lair and liked it.

Continuing on her tour, she headed into the bathroom, which was equally tidy. Shaving cream, razor, aftershave lotion were all out of sight. The bathroom didn't have the modern touches with the standard his-and-her sinks, a minor detail that didn't detract from its purpose. Her eyes lit on the medicine cabinet set over the sink.

Amber stared at her reflection in its mirrored door, her hand already on the bottom edge. She wasn't looking for anything in particular, but she still wanted to know what was on the little shelves behind the door. Was he the kind of man who preferred liquid cold medicines or the small caplets? Did he have bottles of expired prescription pills marking the history of each illness?

She popped open the door and stared—bandages of all sizes, rubbing alcohol, tweezers, a comb, packaged soap from a hotel. Nothing earth-shattering, just functional. Oh, well, she didn't know what she'd expected to see. She swung the door closed.

"Aah!"

Bo's scowling face glared at her in the mirror. "What are you doing in here? In there?"

So this was how a mouse felt cornered by a cat. She spun around. The bathroom suddenly shrunk, with her behind pressed against the sink while her tall, displeased boss towered over her. "I—I needed—" If only her brain would cooperate and understand the gravity of the situation. "My finger. I needed a bandage." She nodded for emphasis and quickly held up her pinkie finger. "See." She promptly pulled her hand behind her back in case he wanted a closer inspection.

With his familiar grunt, he stepped aside. She needed no further prompting and sidled past him. The entire length of her body brushed against his.

Time slowed.

Her senses flickered to life and revved in a matter of seconds to full speed. The entire length of her body tingled with a delicious jolt. Given the differences in their height, they didn't exactly line up together in the doorway. That made it even more disturbing as each heady breath she inhaled caused her breasts to rise against the base of his chest. If she didn't move soon, she'd be breathing into a paper bag to stop hyperventilating.

But she didn't want it to stop.

Maybe Bo didn't feel the same way. She slowly took her eyes off his Adam's apple and met his eyes, smoky gray and filled with desire. Oh, my! If she tiptoed, their lips could meet.

"Bo! Bo, I'm back with your car."

Thank heavens for Martha. Amber squeezed past Bo and ran from the room. She didn't want to face Martha right at this minute, knowing that the older lady's shrewd gaze would sense something odd had occurred. In the haven of her bedroom, she sat on the bed and lowered her face into her hands in an attempt to control her ragged breathing.

Teenagers had more sense than she did. It was bad enough that hers had taken that moment to disappear into oblivion. But she didn't expect to see that hunger in Bo's eyes. It didn't repulse her. It didn't make her feel uncomfortable. It didn't incite any warnings that she cared to heed.

The best thing she could do was focus on her house-keeping duties, find a way to get Bo to talk to her, and leave

Pemberton Ranch. Now that her pulse had returned to normal, she straightened her clothes, smoothed back her hair into its ponytail, and took a deep breath to face her duties with firmer resolve.

Bo still had his head against the door frame when he heard Amber's door close and her light footsteps walk downstairs. When he saw her in his bathroom, surveying his cabinet, the emotions she stirred confused him. Only his halfhearted attempt to act angry could keep it all straight. Even then, he couldn't stand up to Amber's charm, especially when she stood less than six inches away from him.

He'd smelled the fresh scent of her shampooed hair, felt her soft curves, and had easily surrendered to the sexy pull of her whiskey-colored eyes.

The only cure to get Amber's soft lips out of his mind was work. He needed to use his muscles until they ached. Time to go look at his cows. Shoving his hat low on his brow, he walked down the stairs and out the door before he ran into his bewitching housekeeper. He must make a note to start the interview process.

Tomorrow. He'd start tomorrow.

Amber washed the few dishes in the sink. Not too much needed to be done. She expected Bo to pop his head in for lunch. Sometimes he'd call and cancel at the last minute. The sandwich or whatever she'd made would remain uneaten until she threw it in the trash. If he canceled on her one more time, though, she would have to sit him down and tell him about his lack of consideration, even if he was the boss.

Martha waved from the freshly dug flower bed. Her short white hair was perfectly styled around her animated face with its ever-present smile. She waved a gloved hand covered with dirt, motioning to Amber to join her.

Amber poured two glasses of lemonade and headed outdoors. "Here you go." She handed a glass to Martha, who'd taken off her gloves, then placed the glass against her forehead. An appreciative sigh escaped.

"I was calling for Bo. Where did he head off to?"

Amber shrugged.

"Oh, well, we'll have fun just the two of us." Martha hooked her hand through Amber's elbow. "You know I made Bo hire you because I selfishly wanted someone to spend time with me."

They strolled arm in arm toward Martha's house. Martha's handiwork around the surrounding area showed in the assortment of low shrubbery lining the graveled stone path leading to the back door.

"I always wanted a girl."

Amber could identify with that wish. As a young girl and an only child living in a broken home, she had dreams of the perfect family. Maybe that's what brought her and Zoe together. Zoe had been an only child and her parents were going through a rough patch. She envied Zoe's life, with their big house and family vacations. Sylvia came into the picture a little later; she lived in the same block of apartments as Amber. The threesome became fast friends and a force to be reckoned with against the female bullies in their school.

Martha placed her freshly cut herbs in the sink. "Three boys, each two years apart. Boy, were they a handful." She washed her hands and dried them on a hand towel draped through the refrigerator handle.

Amber helped herself to a cookie from a nearby cookie jar. Martha had been insistent that she was a friend, not her son's employee, when she was in her house. Nibbling on her snicker doodle, Amber followed Martha into the small living area. In no time, she had bonded with Bo's mother without ulterior motives.

"Honey, I'm here with Amber." Martha nodded toward a closed door off to her right. "Are you going to join us?"

"In a bit." Bo's father sounded weak.

"Will is having trouble with his back. I'll let him rest. Maybe he'll join us for dinner tonight." Amber nodded her understanding. She looked forward to meeting the patriarch of this family.

Small, silver-framed photographs decorated a few end tables. A larger portrait sat on the wall showing Martha and Will in their younger days. They made a handsome couple, with strength and a certain tenderness in the way Martha rested her hand on her husband's hand.

"Before the kids?" Amber examined each face in an effort to determine whom Bo resembled.

"Bo was born by then, suffered a bit of jaundice, but since then he's been strong as an ox. Out of all my boys, he's the most stubborn."

"Was he always groomed to take over the ranch?"

"Not really. After college he went to New York on a brief stint. Then he landed a high position at Sandstone in Atlanta." Martha sighed. "He worked so hard. We were so proud of him. After a big promotion he relocated to Maryland. We expected great things for him." Martha grew silent. A faraway expression touched her face. "Terrible what happened to all those people."

"Was he ever under investigation for it?"

Martha's eyes turned hard. "What are you getting at?"

Amber knew she had stepped over the line. She wished she could retract the insult. "I'm sorry. I didn't mean to be so tactless."

Martha covered her face with her hands, peeping over the tips of her fingers. "My, my, I'm like a mother hen ready to peck at you." Martha laughed. "I'm sorry, honey. Bo doesn't talk about it. I figure they may have investigated him because of his position. If they did, nothing came of it. All I'm thankful for is that he's back home where he belongs." She took a seat and rested her hands in her lap. "I'm glad we still have the ranch in the family. Because of Will's condition, we've thought about selling it, especially since none of our boys seem to care. But in the last six months, this home has served as a place of refuge for family and friends, alike."

Amber picked up a framed photograph of three boys in their Sunday best. "Bo and his brothers?"

"Yes, his other brothers, Josh and Zack. They all live here in this part of Texas. Josh is a doctor and has an apartment in Dallas. Zack travels a lot on his job and lives on the property whenever he's in town. Then there are a few cousins and a couple grandnieces. You see, one uncle didn't have children, but the other had four. Do you come from a big family?"

Amber shook her head. "My parents are artists, so they tended to move as their spirits dictated. They're divorced." Her early childhood was spent living in various states. Each move tore her heart because it meant she was always the outsider. She learned to turn inward with no friends, no attachment.

A clock chimed. Eleven o'clock.

"Oh, dear. I've got to get lunch prepared." Amber scrambled up to leave.

"I'll help you."

"No need. I'm okay. I'll give you a buzz when it's ready."

"You know I'm stubborn. Besides, I want to find out what you're hiding," Martha said, with no trace of malice.

"What?"

Martha tapped her temple. "I had three mischievous boys who were always playing sneaky games or feuding about something. You have a quiet nature, but sometimes you seem to be conflicted. I can't guess because I don't know you well enough. But you look like you need someone to unburden some of those issues. I've got ears and pretty strong shoulders."

Amber squirmed under Martha's scrutiny. So much for sneaking up on the family. There was no way she would tell Martha everything. She couldn't bear the disapproval, her look of betrayal, or, worse, the end to their budding friendship.

Martha relented. "It's okay. I don't mean to make you uncomfortable, sweetheart. I'm here whenever you need me."

Bo sighed.

"What's eating at your gut?"

Would he ever gain as much knowledge as Joe, the best foreman in the state, as far as he was concerned? "Ah, nothing. Just thinking about stuff."

"Don't worry yourself into the ground. It takes time to learn everything."

What if he didn't want to learn any of it? He'd run away right after high school and entered college on the East Coast. His parents had tried to hide their disappointment, but he knew he had to find his own place in the world. Or at least that's what his mother whispered in his ear at the airport before he left.

Four years later he graduated with a business degree and pursued an accelerated program for his MBA. Armed with his master's, he breathed a sigh of relief that he had what it would take to ensure he never had to be a cattle rancher. The lifestyle had no place in the 21st century when the big meat-packing corporations could churn out plastic-wrapped meat in supermarkets at lower costs and in high numbers without the hassle of his average-sized business.

A brown, furry calf ambled over to the fence. Bo leaned against the fence, observing the animal's curiosity. Its big round eyes fastened on Bo. The broad pink nose twitched to pick up his scent. Seconds later a thick, rough tongue flicked over Bo's fingers. "Hey, girl, you're a cutie." He scratched the space between her eyes. The calf mooed, nodded its head, and returned to the herd.

The moment sparked a childhood memory. Bo and his brothers loved playing with the calves. They'd hold mooing competitions. Each boy had to moo and coax the calf into coming to him. Any brother who couldn't do this feat had to do the other brother's chores for a week. Many times he held the honor as sole winner, enjoying his brothers' stint of working his chores.

Time sure flew. So many years had passed, faster than he cared. He'd left a boy and returned a man, but what did it all mean when he had nothing to his name? Because what had he proven when he came back to the life from which he'd tried to escape?

Joe cleared his throat. "Since you're fading on me as I go over my exciting report about the shorthorns' dietary needs, I'm going to change the subject. How's it going with the new housekeeper?"

"Why are you asking?" Bo fanned himself with his hat to give himself something to do. He sensed that Joe had more on his mind than a casual question.

"No reason. Just some of the guys said she was cute as all get out." Joe's amusement blazed in his vivid blue eyes that stood out in stark contrast against his sunburned face.

"You're almost married," Bo stated.

Joe raised his hand in mock surrender. "I haven't seen the woman. I'm only going by what I've heard."

Bo grunted. Amber's bewitching skill had far reaching power. First his mother, now Joe had fallen under her spell. He counted himself lucky that he had sense enough to block her wily ways.

He kicked the hard dirt, loosening a few pebbles. Her lost-girl charm had sucker-punched him. He picked up a handful of stones and flicked them across the land.

Darn. There he went again. He couldn't go for more than an hour without thinking about her. As a matter of fact, what was the wretched woman up to at this time?

He checked his watch. Almost eleven-thirty. She was probably preparing lunch with her froufrou sandwiches for him. Some of the meals had to have come from a magazine. The parsley trimmings and baby carrots arched around his dinner plate raised his suspicion.

"Plus I heard that Tessa left to get married."

"Why did everyone know except me?" Bo asked testily.

"Your mother told us. Hey, don't get mad." Joe edged away from Bo. "She had to tell us. We all love Tessa. By the way, where did you find the new lady?"

Bo threw the last stone, watching it arc through the air. He concentrated on keeping his voice light. "Actually she found me. Can't figure out why she expected me to give her a job."

Joe laughed. "I bet she's one of the town girls who has her eyes set on you. And you fell for it."

Bo wondered if he really was being played for a fool. Although she came from Washington, D.C., she seemed to know who he was.

Fine. No problem. He'd raise his defenses in preparation for an eventual invasion, possibly a war.

He dragged his heel, drawing the symbolic line in the dirt. A chuckle escaped.

"What's up?"

Bo slapped his thigh. A wide grin pasted on his face. "Round up all the guys. Today, lunch is on me at the house. I want everyone to meet the new housekeeper."

"Everyone? Even the kids on winter break?" Joe frowned, shaking his head. "You know Tessa didn't like us surprising her and all."

"But this isn't Tessa. I'm sure Amber won't mind. She's got lots of experience." Bo walked off, whistling. After he mounted Onyx, he looked down at Joe. "Lunch is usually at twelve-thirty, right? Come at noon." He resumed whistling, happy with himself. He'd prove that Amber Delaney was no housekeeper and was out of her league.

Amber finished making a thick submarine sandwich and placed it on a plate with a side of potato chips and a pickle wedge. She poured a glass of lemonade, set it down, and waited for the phone to ring. It was close to twelve and she knew Bo was going to call and cancel coming in for lunch.

That man! Her fingers drummed an insignificant beat while she waited.

A knock on the back door startled her. "Who is it?" Bo didn't usually knock and Martha had said she was going to rest a bit. Boisterous laughter and loud chatter came from the other side of the door. "Who is it?" she repeated, slightly alarmed.

"It's us, guys."

She looked out the small kitchen window, shocked to see several faces smiling back at her. A few even waved. "Yes?"

They looked friendly, but she didn't know a single person out there.

"Miss Amber, I'm Joe, the foreman." A tall blond man stepped forward, grinning from ear to ear. "Bo sent us over for lunch. I only brought the guys who work in the stable. I don't think you'd want the guys from the sorting pen and loading dock walking all over your clean floors, not to mention the smell."

"Pemberton, you're a dead man," she hissed. Pasting on a welcoming smile, she opened the door and watched at least twelve to fourteen men jostle their way into the kitchen. The one lonely sandwich on the table made a bad prop for the ugly scene about to play out when she told these men she didn't have lunch.

What was she going to do? *Calm down, Amber. Think.* She walked over to the refrigerator and pulled out a large pitcher of freshly made lemonade. They had to be thirsty. "Anyone for a tall, refreshing drink? However, I'm not serving anyone until you wash up. You boys smell like those cows." She wrinkled her nose. The men roared, pleased at her bluntness. Obviously they liked a woman with attitude. A few of the younger men stared dreamily at her, following her around the kitchen. Oh, boy!

In a matter of minutes, the men formed a queue with disposable cups in hand. Serving the guys provided a few more minutes to highlight her predicament. Bo thought he had her figured out. He thought she didn't have the backbone to stick it past his clumsy sabotage attempts.

"Amber?" Martha popped her head in the house. "Heard all the commotion and had to be nosey." Martha waved to the men, giving hugs here and there. "What's the celebration?"

"Amber!" Joe shouted over the din. "Bo said Amber had

lunch for all the guys as a welcome and introduction." He touched his forehead in a salute. "I say that's pretty nice of her."

Martha surveyed the group and faced Amber, turning her back to the men. "Need help?" she mouthed.

Amber gave a small nod. Martha didn't make her feel threatened. Accepting her assistance was the smart thing to do. As for Bo, she wanted to give him a good punch to the gut.

The men had to wait despite her attempts to get lunch prepared quickly. They didn't seem to mind with Martha fussing among them, asking about their lives, family, and work. Amber had nothing to say, but listened closely to the various conversations. Apparently the Pemberton ranch had the world's happiest employees. Amber refused to give Bo the credit.

Martha and Amber made several sandwiches in record time. Side by side, they had a perfect assembly line adding turkey slices, cheese, lettuce, and tomatoes. The mayonnaise and honey mustard she'd leave up to their individual tastes. Since the potato chips were long gone by the time the sandwiches appeared, Martha brought over her homemade potato salad.

"Hey, is there a party without me?"

Amber looked up to see an older version of Bo standing with the aid of a cane.

"Will, you came over. How nice." Martha hurried over to her husband and supported his free arm as he maneuvered over to the table. The other men stepped aside, leaving a path down the middle for his progress. A respectful silence bathed the small area.

Even Amber had to admit to sensing the quiet dignity of Bo's father. Although slightly hunched over, he had to be at least six and a half feet. His hair matched his wife's crisp white hair, which he wore low.

"And are you Amber, who I hear about all day long?" He took his seat and offered his hand to Amber. From the bottom half of his bifocals, he peered down at her.

"Yes, I am. I hope you only hear good things. Your wife is such a sweetheart."

"That, she is. I'm Will, pleasure meeting you."

After introductions were over, Amber took a deep breath. The men chatted among themselves, now that most of the food was finished. Martha, the life of any party, enjoyed their attention, as she told adventure stories about Will and his brothers.

Bo hesitated at the front door, deciding that he'd let Amber stew long enough. Despite his initial enthusiasm for a good prank, he felt sorry for her. He shifted the six large pizzas with the works in his left hand as he put the key into the lock with his right.

"Hey, everybody." He walked down the hall with his prize. "Figured you would be starving, so I brought some pizzas to save the day. . . ." His words trailed into the air.

"We've eaten, boss." A teenage boy grinned and patted his stomach. "Miss Amber and Miss Martha fed us with the best sandwiches I've ever had. Then we had strawberry shortcake Miss Martha said she'd made for you, but you wouldn't mind because you're on a diet."

Bo stared at the boy until he got the message to stop talking. The other men went back to their conversations, except for Joe whose bright grin could be a beacon in a lighthouse. He deliberately didn't look over to Amber where she stood quietly at the sink; her rigid shoulders provided enough of a warning to him.

Bo's eyes must have been deceiving him because if he wasn't mistaken, his father sat at the table with his mother. "Hey, Pop, I'm glad to see you."

His mother turned her head. He swore he felt the lightning bolts of anger in her eyes. Once again, the minx had wrapped his mother around her fingers.

"What do you plan to do with those pizzas?" Martha asked, her arms folded across her chest.

"I don't know." She still had the knack of making him feel like a bad little boy.

"We'll take it." Joe walked over and relieved him of the pizzas, handing it off to the other men. "Well, everyone, this was a lot of fun. Miss Amber, you're the best. Welcome to Pemberton Ranch; I hope you'll be here for a long time."

"Nice meeting you, Joe. All you guys were really great. I couldn't have done it without Martha, though."

Bo watched the drama playing out, feeling like an outsider. He didn't like it one bit. Fine. When his kitchen was back to being quiet and Amber had time to cool off, he'd venture back in to talk, maybe to apologize. Maybe.

Chapter Four

Bo waited until the house had quieted before peeking out of the study. The silence reminded him of the surreal calmness before a summer thunderstorm struck with a ferocity that shook windows. Not only did he have to keep a sharp eye out for Amber, but his mother was not one to let the matter drop. Sooner or later, she'd corner him and give him an earful about his bad behavior. Maybe his father would come to his rescue.

He headed out of the house, realizing after the fact that he'd tiptoed. His conscience continued to betray him, prodding him with guilt. Spying his mother relaxing on the screened-in porch, he skirted the area and softly opened the door. He eased it closed. "Dad," he called softly.

"In here. I'm watching a movie."

Bo followed his father's voice into the bedroom. Propped against several pillows and equipped with the remote in one hand, his father looked contented, pain-free. His father's expressions would tell him what kind of day he was having.

Will pointed to a chair. "We haven't talked in a while. Have a seat."

Bo obeyed. New, deeper lines etched his father's face, adding character. His father carried the air of an elder doling out wisdom. It was a relationship he treasured and respected. "How's your back? You've been up and about the last few weeks."

"I'm hanging on, but some days I feel like someone is pulling out my spine." He grimaced as he pulled out one of the many pillows behind him and tossed it to a vacant chair. "How's the business? Joe tries to keep me updated, but I know he's busy and is indulging me with his visits."

"Joe's doing a great job. Makes me wonder why I'm here. I feel useless next to him."

His father waved aside his comment. "You know just because you're the boss doesn't mean you have to know everything."

"But that's the problem. I don't feel like the boss. Frankly, if I were Joe, I'd be offended about having to deal with the boss's son who doesn't know squat about anything."

His father clicked off the television and turned his full attention on him. "All of you boys learned the fundamentals for life on a ranch. Don't sell yourself short. You can earn his respect, although I doubt that Joe hasn't given or shown you respect." His voice held no accusation, only concern.

Bo allowed the advice to sink in past his doubts.

"You have to decide whether this is what you want do. I asked you once and I promised I would never ask you to head the ranch again." Will raised his hand to halt Bo's retort. "Not that I don't believe you can do it, but I'm putting unfair pressure on you. While you're here, for however long, I won't stand in your way or hover around you." Will slapped his knee and chuckled. "Not that I could even if I wanted."

Bo frowned, puzzled with the admission. "Excuse me? How are you in the way when you're . . . here?"

His father grew agitated. His hands plucked at the comforter covering his legs. "I mean that I'm still too involved. I never showed you that I trusted you or your judgment," he stated in a choked voice. "It's only natural that you grew up thinking that this was *my* business, instead of *our* business."

This sounded good. It would be easy to let his father carry that unfair burden. But Bo remembered his father taking him aside after he came home from school to explain the grazing habits of the shorthorns. Or when his father told him stories about his grandfather and how the family banded together to hold on to the land.

His father sighed. "I must tell you about the fun I had today. Eating lunch with the guys made me feel young again. It wiped me out, but it was worth it." A wide grin spread across his face. He retold the many conversations he'd shared with the younger men.

Bo listened patiently, chuckling at some of the exaggerations that his father boasted. It never occurred to him that his father suffered so deeply. His life with limited mobility must be frustrating.

"I'll invite the guys more often to the house," Bo said.

"Next time clear it with Amber, though. The poor girl worked her fingers to the bone, but she did it. That's a tough girl."

Bo nodded. Playing the bad guy didn't sit well with him. "Well, I just stopped in to see how you're doing. I'll be heading back now."

"Okay. Bye, son."

Bo walked over and hugged his father. Once upon a time, his father's shoulders seemed wide and strong with the naturally built muscles bulging through his shirt. Now, hugging him, he felt the frailty of his shrunken frame beneath his clothes. Only his eyes held the fire that had the charm to win his mother's heart and his workers' loyalty.

He closed the bedroom door behind him, smiling to himself when he heard the television click on.

"You sorry good-for-nothing."

He froze. Not only did the words zap him like an electric shot to the shoulder blades, but the coldness in the familiar voice slapped him with contempt. "Hello, Amber, nice to see you." Apparently she'd been on the porch with his mother. She probably heard him with his father and lay in wait, like a spider with a fly. Maybe he should roll over and play dead.

Her eyes continued to blaze at him. Heaven help him if she didn't look sexy in a light sleeveless dress that fell softly along her slender frame. While she bit at her lip, he admired the material seductively clinging to her full breasts, small waist, and slim hips.

"You may be the boss and I may be fired in the next few minutes, but I'm going to have my say. Let's go over to your place." She stormed past him, not waiting to see if he would follow. A tropical dress became a swirl of color as she marched into battle.

If he thought hesitating was an option, his mother stood with both hands on her hips, lips pursed, waiting for him to object. He threw up his hands in surrender. "Don't worry, I'm going. It's clear that my mother has abandoned me."

He followed on Amber's trail, albeit a little slower.

She waited for him in the kitchen, leaning against the counter. "Why?"

"You'll need to give me more," he stated calmly.

"Don't play games with me. You invited those men to make me look bad." She started pacing. "But it didn't work, did it?" She offered a smug grin. "Instead, you looked really stupid with all those pizzas."

That stung. "Any real housekeeper would have been able to handle it." Small lie. Tessa would have strangled him if he'd done that to her. "And those job references you gave me . . ." He snorted. "Try getting current telephone numbers. The Sylvia woman couldn't provide any details beyond yes and no. I'll need another reference." Bo heard the sharp intake and paused. He'd hit a nerve, but didn't know what had swiftly taken the anger out of her.

"Look, I'm not a—"

The phone rang. Bo raised a hand, halting her. Then he walked away with the cordless phone cradled between his ear and shoulder.

Amber threw up her hands and went upstairs to her room.

"Good morning." Bo spoke first.

Amber mumbled a greeting as she aimed for the freshly brewed coffee. Her head pounded. She didn't sleep well again.

"Already poured you a cup."

She took the proffered cup, enhanced it with cream and sugar, and took a satisfying sip.

"I'm sorry." He didn't look at her, but stared into his coffee.

"No problem." She glanced warily at him. "Don't know what got into me."

He grinned. "No one probably bullied you on the playground."

"Got that right." Her mood improved one hundred percent with his smile. "By the way, what are you doing today? The rental car company called. They have a new car for me."

"Isn't that a waste of money? I have a car you can use."

Great. She only needed it for another week. "Thanks. I also have to go to the post office. I'm expecting a forwarded package of my mail."

"Well, let's go. You can decide about that car on the way to town."

The ride to downtown Breezewood only lasted a few minutes. The small city sported its share of outlet malls and super-warehouse stores. An old-world charm existed, despite the occasional fast-food restaurants. Most of the city had retained the Western charm through its architecture.

Neither she nor Bo spoke, but it was an easy silence. Comfortable. He parked in front of the post office.

Amber walked into the building that had a sizable bustle of people being serviced. In a matter of minutes she retrieved the large envelope of mail that Sylvia forwarded. The bills couldn't wait while she was on assignment. Maybe her mother had written news about the latest Alice Walker sighting.

"Thanks for bringing me," Amber said after climbing back into the car.

They pulled away from the post office and headed for Dallas to the rental-car company. She ripped open the envelope and leafed through the various envelopes, which were mostly junk mail. A bright red envelope caught her attention. From its size, she suspected that it was a card, probably a belated birthday card. She pulled it out, noticing no return address.

"Good news from home?" Bo asked.

"I think it's a belated birthday card."

"Your birthday? Did I miss it?"

"It was the day I first met you."

"You'd think I'd noticed when I had your license."

"You were preoccupied with trying to throw me out," she teased, enjoying his rueful grin. Sitting side by side, she acknowledged the physical magnetism. There was more, though—an underlying theme of courage and inner strength.

She flipped over the envelope and read the writing on the outside. The card slid out of her fingers to the floor of the car. The familiar panic surged through her limbs and every fiber.

Bo glanced over. "What's the matter?" He pulled over to the shoulder of the road amidst angry car horns blaring. "Talk to me." He reached down for the card when she didn't respond. "What is this? A secret admirer?"

"No," she hissed. "I want it to stop." She wrapped her arms around herself. The shock that it was not over sent icy shivers through her body. "He knows I'm not there."

"Who? Amber, talk to me. Look, we're going back home. Then we can talk about this."

Home. She wished it was really her home. She closed her eyes. The fear ebbed a little, but her legs felt like jelly. She looked out the window on the ride back to the ranch. How to explain what had occurred, without revealing too many other details?

Bo led her into the study. He wanted her comfortable and to feel protected in his presence. She declined his offer for a drink. "Talk to me," he coaxed. He resisted the urge to place a protective arm around her. It unnerved him to see this sassy young woman taken under by an immobilizing fear.

She rubbed her brow and exhaled. "About two months ago I attended these things called speed dating at clubs in D.C. and Maryland."

"I've heard of that. It's when the man or woman meets

several people in one night. Their meeting is timed and at the end of the meeting you decide if you want to meet again or move on."

She nodded. "Some friends had suggested it. I think this creep is someone I met at one of these places. And the problem is that I don't have any proof. Meanwhile, it started out fairly innocent, although a little creepy. And now look at this." She held up the crushed envelope. "I've told the police, and they are investigating. Those clues are few. I've no witnesses. Nothing."

His anger sprouted like wild ivy climbing rapidly to its peak. Observing Amber and listening to her story kicked his protective nature into full gear.

"When I left home to come out here and see . . . and see Texas, I really wanted to get away." She grabbed his hand and looked him squarely in the eyes. "I know I'm far away, but I wonder if he'll find me."

"Well, let him come," Bo challenged.

Bo looked down at the handwritten message: *See you on the fifteenth.* "Seems unfair that you have to uproot your life. Now I understand why you're sticking around. Whoever this nut is must be sorely disappointed that he couldn't find you on your birthday." Because he couldn't resist not touching, he smoothed the hair out of her face. His hand lingered against her soft cheek and trailed a finger down to the corner of her lips. The seductive outline of her small mouth, with its full lips, tempted him.

"May I?" he whispered, his throat tightly laced with desire. She nodded and leaned forward with barely a movement. Ever so lightly, he kissed her. A soft sigh escaped from her lips, and her warm breath brushed his face. "You're so beautiful," he praised. Then he reclosed the gap between them, kissing her with a passion that was stoked by her answering response. His tongue explored and conquered, drawing on her sweetness that drove his senses wild.

The doorbell rang.

Bo jumped out of Amber's arms. What had he done? His chest rose and fell as if he'd run a marathon. This couldn't happen again. Number one, losing control wasn't his style. Number two, although kissing Amber could be a new strong addiction, what he'd done wasn't cool. He backed away from her, putting more than an arm's length distance between them.

"I'll get the door." Amber didn't want to believe that she'd made such a stupid mistake by kissing her target. After the hot and heavy episode in his study, he probably thought even less of her.

She opened the door. In front of her was a tall, slim woman in expensive finery.

"And who might you be?" The woman removed her shades, sizing her up.

"I'm Amber. How may I help you?" It killed her to remain pleasant in the face of outright snobbery.

The perfectly coifed woman turned and waved away the taxi that waited. "Tell Bodine I'm here to see him."

Oh, it was one of Bo's women. From the looks of things, he opted for the gold-hued-foundation types with cold gray eyes—a complete opposite to her, she noted. Amber stepped aside, irritated with herself for noticing. As the visitor grandly swept past, she noticed the matching suitcase and makeup case left at her feet. It crossed her mind to leave them outside. She wasn't a bellhop.

Martha came from the front door with her usual gardening clothes and gloves. "We've a guest, Amber?" She pulled off a glove and offered her hand with her trademark welcoming smile. "I'm Mrs. Pemberton. How may we help you?"

"Mrs. Pemberton, I'm Cassidy. We've never met. I'm Bo's fiancée."

"Oh, my." Martha looked at Amber as if for further explanation.

Amber had to focus on the process of breathing, otherwise the knot in her stomach would have her doubled over. At this rate, she'd need an antacid to get her through her assignment.

"Please come in and have a seat." She tried to keep her voice leveled. To her ears, it came out forced and flat.

Thank goodness Martha had taken over being the solicitous hostess. "Would you like anything to drink or eat?"

"No. I just want to see Bo. I've missed him so much. Don't know if he'd mentioned that we'd a little lovers' spat." She flung out her arms like a diva onstage. "But I'm back."

Her smile was a little too bright. Her hair was a little too auburn. Her clothes were too tailored. So he liked his women tall and elegant, reeking of money. As for the hired help, a tumble on the office sofa would suffice. Her anger cooked on a slow simmer heading for scorching level.

The trio sat at the small breakfast table, each person quietly contemplating.

"Here's a fresh cup of coffee." Amber slid the mug over to the manicured nails. She curled hers under her lap out of sight.

"Where's Bo?" Cassidy flashed Amber a toothy smile.

"He's around." Amber crossed her arms. "I take it he wasn't expecting you."

"Nope."

"He's been home for about six months and he's never mentioned that he was engaged," Martha said. A frown played on her forehead.

There was that false smile again. "Here's the ring."

A beautiful, heart-shaped diamond that could weigh a finger down blinked at Amber from Cassidy's finger.

"It's gorgeous." Martha smiled, but Amber recognized her hesitation. Martha looked expectantly at her future daughter-in-law.

Cassidy ignored their avid curiosity. "I'm a bit tired. If I could go settle down, let me know when he comes in."

She'd expected the flamboyant arrival would've drawn Bo out of his study. Since Martha didn't know he was home, she'd keep the revelation a little while longer. Amber knew she was being unprofessional, but didn't care. Her feelings stung knowing that he'd been kissing her only a few minutes ago. What made it worse was that she'd enjoyed it. "I'll show you to the guest room."

"I was expecting to stay in Bo's room."

"A girl in my day didn't do such things," Martha said sharply.

Amber bit back her smile.

Cassidy turned stony stares at the offending pair. With a huff, she picked up her makeup case and headed for the stairs. "Would you bring up my suitcase?"

Martha stepped forward. It was her turn to paste on a fake smile. "Amber can't go up the stairs with that load."

"Okay, fine." Cassidy stomped out of the kitchen and thumped her way up the stairs with both suitcases.

Martha and Amber waited until they heard the door close before collapsing with laughter against each other.

"I'm so wicked, but I can't help it. I don't care for her. What on earth is Bo thinking?"

"I guess we'll find out soon enough." Amber wanted to know what could possibly draw him to such a callous creature. Maybe he was a man who didn't go beyond the exterior.

"Well, I'll see you, honey. Can't wait to tell the news to his father." Martha bustled out of the house.

Amber stared up the staircase, working up the effort to go and play nice with snooty girl. Being nice could garner her more information.

"Who came?" Bo walked into the hallway.

Amber turned to face him. Should she drop the news like a ton of bricks or make him feel like a heel, then drop the news like a ton of bricks? "I'll get back to that in a second. Answer me this. What happened with us, just now? Did it mean anything to you?" She'd kept her voice leveled, like a casual discussion about the weather. Her heart pounded in her ears.

"Yes."

Ha, so he could lie like a cheap rug. She wasn't going to be sucked in by the fake sincerity. He must think her a fool. "Good to hear. Come over here, please." She stood aside at the bottom of the stairs. "Cassidy," she called. "Come on down." In her best game-show-host imitation, she flashed a wide smile and pointed up the stairs for the surprise behind door number one.

The bedroom door opened and an irritated Cassidy looked over the railing. "What?" Then she spied Bo. "Oh, darling." A happy face slipped into place.

"Cassidy?"

Amber turned on her heel. In the softest whisper, she leaned in. "Did I really mean anything to you?" This time she didn't wait for an answer. She walked out of the house not sure where to go, but refusing to witness the touching reunion between beauty and the beast.

Eddie stood in front of the town home, the only one completely dark. For two weeks he'd driven through the neighborhood, ending up at Amber's place. At first he thought she may've gone on a quick vacation, but now he was confused. He'd never actually seen her in the home, but it was the only information he had.

It was no use standing there any longer. He flicked up the collar of his coat and blew into his hands. Obviously she had pulled a disappearing act on him. No need to get bothered by the inconvenience. His plan had a purpose and was destined to be. In time, another path would unfold to him.

He turned to head back to his car. His body shivered from the frigid temperatures. As soon as he turned on the engine, he blasted the heat. Slowly he thawed while he tried to figure out his next move.

A car pulled up next to his and a young woman hopped out. She caught his interest, mainly because she was wearing an obnoxious shade of green. The sweat suit made her look like a curvaceous frog. He watched her run up the few stairs to Amber's house. Dare he hope? She reached into her pocketbook and retrieved a key.

His hand was on the door handle before he clearly thought about his next move. Outside, he walked up the stairs, the shiver he felt no longer due to the temperature. Excitement heated his body. The door had been left open. A few more inches and he'd be in. It'd be great if he could stay there to surprise her when she returned.

His luck had turned quickly. He couldn't believe that he stood in the foyer. "Hello!" he called. Taking his time, he surveyed the living room, noting that it wasn't cluttered. There was a practical side to the small amount of furniture and decorations in the room.

"Can I help you?" the curvaceous frog croaked.

"Oh . . . I saw the door was open, a crack, really. And I wondered if Amber was back." He backed up toward the door. Women liked their space. He didn't want her to feel threatened.

"No, she isn't here. I'm here to pick up the mail so I can forward it to her. Are you a friend of hers?"

Should he lie? "No, not really. I'm just one of her neighbors and I tend to keep an eye on everything around here." He shuffled for a show of embarrassment. "Like Neighborhood Watch."

"I understand. I'm Sylvia."

"People call me Eddie."

Sylvia offered her hand. "Nice meeting you. Amber won't be back for about a month or so. You'll have to get used to seeing me around here."

"I think that's not so bad." Smile. Woo her. See, she's already grinning like an idiot.

"Well, I've got to be going. I'll be back in a couple days."

"I'm looking forward to it." He turned to open the door. Over his shoulder, he proffered, "Or it doesn't have to be in a couple days. How about a coffee at the local coffee shop down the street in five minutes?"

"I'd like that. I'll meet you there."

He drove behind Sylvia in the best mood he'd had for a while. Sylvia looked like the social butterfly who could chat about any subject, inane or otherwise. His plan didn't include anyone else. But he had to be flexible for his ultimate goal. At least Sylvia was a close friend of Amber's.

They shared their thoughts over coffee. Sylvia did have a colorful life, but it all meant nothing to him. With Amber almost within his reach, he could relax. Sylvia would be useful until she bored him.

He purposefully ended their coffee session in the middle of their getting-to-know-you phase. Better to keep her wanting to be in his company. It could come in handy for later when he wanted her to not only tell him where Amber was, but actually facilitate the meeting.

"Well, Eddie, it was nice chatting with you. Think we could do this again. I'd love to introduce you to this great Italian restaurant."

He nodded. He could almost hear the wheels grinding in her head, speculating about how much he was attracted to her. He hoped he wouldn't have to go out on too many dates before he got his information. Otherwise he may have to deviate from his plan and that would be a waste of energy.

"Well, I'll be seeing you. Here's my phone number."

He took it from her, careful to keep his fingers from touching hers. "How about tomorrow evening?"

"Perfect."

At last the curvaceous green frog left his company. From the coffee shop to her car, she turned several times to grin at him. He mustered the effort to return the acknowledgement. How could a well-bred young woman like Amber have such shallow friends?

With nothing left to do for the remainder of the day, he returned home. At least that's what he called the tiny apartment near the university that he subleased from a graduate student on a research assignment. It was a bit noisy sometimes, but it afforded him some level of anonymity. Moving from one town to the next didn't build much of a reference list or credit history for renting an apartment.

A file stuffed with papers and pictures lay across his bed. He pulled out a small ceramic piece from his pocket. The sculpture of a dolphin arcing in the air caught his eye when he was in Amber's home. Lying on his back, he stroked the piece to get closer to Amber's spirit in some way. Since he'd taken something from her, he'd be sure to put something there from him in return.

Amber had drawn his focus from the first time he'd seen her. He had observed her more than once on the dating scene, coming from her job, attending church, and jogging around the neighborhood park. But it wasn't until he talked to her, felt her breath on his face, brushed against her that his attraction transformed into a deeper, purer emotion. It was difficult for him to put the experience into words, except that finding such a perfect mate gave him strength.

Chapter Five

The weekend approached. Amber looked forward to having the days off. She hadn't really thought about what she'd do on the weekends, considering there were no friends or family to visit. The alternative to sticking around and seeing Cassidy and Bo act as lovebirds didn't appeal to her.

Before the household rose, Amber left the house, taking a change of clothes. An informal agenda unfolded as she drove into the downtown area. She'd spend the night in an area hotel. During the day, she'd tour the country stores and chat with the local vendors. They had to have an opinion about Bo and his family.

Amber parked near City Hall and opted to do a foot tour. According to the historical notes she'd researched, the town had been built around gold mines. The mines dried up and so did the population until a few powerful ranchers found the land suitable for their cattle. Beef became the town's primary commodity before a few oil wells popped up in the late seventies. The influx of such wealth changed the landscape.

The town had a precarious balancing act between the old and new. Land developers were razing the land for massive housing communities with self-contained shopping and recreational centers. The old frontier was changing into a series of small forts with high-income occupants.

The buildings all gaily painted provided a warm burst of color. A prominently placed barbershop on a corner featured a white storefront with bright blue shutters. A steady flow of business streamed in and out of the little shop. As she walked past the large window, she looked in on the lively conversation among the patrons, many of whom were gray-haired. It reminded her of Sonny's shop. This was her week for a massage. She sighed, already missing her weekly rituals.

Farther down the block, she strolled past a restaurant and watched a group of girlfriends meet another group before going inside. Their lively chatter and obvious bonds of friendship pushed her homesickness button further.

She wanted to be able to tell Sylvia about the homemade ice cream that was to die for, served at the restaurant. She wanted to tell her about the gorgeous sandals she'd bought at the outlet mall. But most of all, she wanted to tell her how wretched she felt when Bo didn't deny Cassidy's declaration.

Food always worked as a good comforter. She spotted a breakfast diner on a corner and followed the appetizing smell of bacon and eggs. Already her mouth watered and stomach rumbled. She'd fill up and then continue her tour.

She entered the busy diner, noting a mixture of singles, couples, and families with small children. Obviously the buffet seemed to be the hit; there was a tight crowd around the steaming serving trays.

With the nip in the air, a hot bowl of oatmeal sounded fabulous. She selected her seat in the corner, situating her back to the door. No need for distractions or any unwanted conversations. While she ate her oatmeal and sipped on coffee, she'd draft the outline of Zoe's story.

The story's angle still created a measure of difficulty. Her research didn't highlight any new friends or introductions of any oddities in Zoe's life. It merely highlighted a driven woman. Her parents had remarked that she slowly drifted away, only returning to their hometown for the major holidays.

As she gathered the information on Bo, his story didn't appear complicated. Another driven individual, but very different outcomes. Amber hadn't decided if she wanted to show Bo Pemberton as the cowboy, wildly independent, rebelling against the establishment at any cost, or Bo Pemberton, the man uncomfortable with the title of hero to some, traitor to others.

Her small breakfast fare arrived with a complimentary plate of warm corn muffins. For the next hour, she scribbled her thoughts and perceptions of her current adventure into her journal.

Bo stood outside the diner, waiting for his brother to show up. Zack was never punctual and today would be no exception. He'd give him five more minutes and then he was heading back home. This was their monthly ritual, since they both led busy lives. Although Thanksgiving was around the corner, they liked having their one-on-one time. Plus he liked listening to Zack's exploits as he embraced his eligible-bachelor title with sadistic glee.

Glancing at his watch one more time, he wasn't aware of Zack's presence until he felt a stinging slap on the back of his neck. "I see you haven't matured one bit."

"Hey, big brother, I'm famished." Zack grinned, blowing into his cupped hands. "Don't just stand there, let's get a move on. I want biscuits, eggs, hashbrowns, and Canadian bacon."

Bo rubbed the back of his head, tuning out Zack's list since it was the exact list of breakfast foods he always ordered. Besides, he was already planning retribution for his stinging neck.

They sat in their usual spot near the window that faced the entrance. The menus remained unopened, stuck between the ketchup and mustard bottles.

"Big brother, what's up with you? You know Mom told me about your so-called fiancée." He chuckled before downing a glass of orange juice.

Bo groaned. "Cassidy came unexpectedly."

"Were you hiding her? No one, not even your baby brother, knew about this."

"It was spur of the moment. Actually she proposed to me. We're no longer engaged, no longer an item. I have no idea why she showed up."

"You're so naive. You were a powerful mover and shaker getting to the top of that corporate ladder. What's not there to latch on to?"

"You don't know Cassidy. She's filthy rich. She could buy and sell me."

"Is that why you felt it necessary to hook up with her? Did you think she was giving you respect?"

Bo glared at his youngest brother. His bluntness was trademark and the root of many arguments. "Stop being an idiot."

"Don't get mad at me. According to Mom, you've got a new housekeeper who could give Cassidy a run for her money."

"Sounds like you and Mom have been doing some major talking about me." Bo rubbed his face in an effort to erase the stress of his impending decision to tell Cassidy to leave. Behind her back, her girlfriends called her "Queen of Drama" and he expected her to live up to the title.

Zack finished off his biscuit in one last bite. "Yep, you have given us lots to talk about. It used to be me who'd get all the attention and lectures. Looks like you're the bad boy of the family now. Congrats!"

Bo debated flicking a pat of butter onto his brother's forehead. Fighting back the adolescent urge for now, he leaned back in his seat, satisfied with the alternative to pop his brother's neck as they walked out of the diner. It would serve two purposes. Retribution was the top reason, but also he didn't care for the mirror his brother had held up to his face.

He glanced over at the other patrons, wondering what drama had wormed its way into their lives. Hearing the amount of laughter present within the numerous conversations, he surmised that these were a lucky bunch.

Although, coming to a diner by yourself had to be a lonely affair. He wondered what kind of lives they led when eating alone was by their choice.

"What are you looking at?"

"Nothing, really. People who eat by themselves make me wonder." He glanced over to the back of the diner. The fork slipped from his fingers. A deep crease furrowed his brow.

Zack turned his head in the direction Bo had turned. "What's up?"

Bo didn't respond.

"Do you know her? Never seen her in here." Zack drained his cup of coffee in a noisy slurp. "Probably a tourist driving through on her way to Los Angeles."

"Nope. She's the housekeeper."

"Get outta here." Zack pushed back his chair and stood. "Can't see much of her with her back to me. I'd better go introduce myself, maybe check her out a bit. I can tell she's not like our old housekeeper."

Bo's hand shot out and grabbed his wrist. "Don't. She wants to be alone."

"Because she doesn't know anyone." Zack had wrenched his hand away and was already halfway across the room.

"Well, I want to be alone," Bo almost shouted. He knew his brother would not be deterred.

"Hi. I'm Zack, the youngest member of the Pemberton family."

Bo could hear Zack's booming greeting, but strained to hear Amber's response. She offered Zack a shy smile. He walked toward the couple engaged in a conversation dotted with laughter and forced himself to relax. His legs moved like a robot and the seconds to her table felt like minutes.

"Hello." His voice sounded like a frog with a cold. He coughed to clear his throat. "We were just eating."

"We already covered that part. We're now at the part with how she ended up at the ranch."

"It's just for a little while."

"Really? You didn't say that." Zack pouted at Amber.

"I—I don't really know how long it will be." She stared at Bo. "Unless there are other plans." The question hung in the air.

"If I have anything to do with it, I'd say you can stay forever." Zack grinned and Bo hated the classic boy-next-door smile.

Bo looked at his watch and glared at Zack. "It's time for me to get going."

Zack waved him away. "Go on. Cassidy is waiting for you, isn't she? I'll keep Amber company."

Just because it was a fact didn't make it sit easily with him. He didn't feel any spark of excitement about heading back home where his ex-fiancée was. Instead he wanted to sit down and order another cup of coffee and chat with Amber. He liked her quirky ideas and passion for the underdog. Plain and simple, he wanted his brother to take a hike.

"Well, I'll go settle the bill." Bo walked away and then paused. "Bye."

Zack waved him away. Amber didn't even turn to acknowledge his exit. He didn't think she was the type to fall for someone like Zack, all surface and no depth. He shoved his hands into his pockets and walked away.

Bo drove past the diner, witnessing Zack's animated chatter and Amber freely laughing in a manner that never happened in his presence.

Amber walked out of the diner with Zack; her sides still ached from his hilarious stories about his brothers' wayward activities that inevitably got them in trouble. From Zack's description, she got a clear picture of each brother. Zack was the spoiled brat and she was willing to bet he still held on to that role with uninhibited pride. Jake suffered the middle-child syndrome, which had the local law at their parents' door many nights with a rebellious teenager in hand. Bo didn't match the funny, spirited big brother that Zack laid out. What she saw was a man who had a short tolerance for spontaneity. The world couldn't get past his wall, guarded with a fierceness that could intimidate.

She was glad she'd decided to take this time off to get away from the ranch. Being outdoors with no schedule stirred her creative spirit. She walked briskly away from the diner, not sure of what she'd do next.

The scent of freshly baked goodies drew her down a quiet side street. She opened the door, startled by the little bell announcing her arrival. Her taste buds perked up at the delectable feast of desserts displayed behind the glass enclosure. Never mind that she'd had a bowl of stick-to-your-ribs oatmeal.

That didn't stop her. She walked up to the counter where a fresh-faced teenager showed a bright smile, braces in place.

"Everything smells so delicious," Amber praised. "Oh, my gosh, you've got breads, too." She walked over to the small variety of loaves. "I'll have to come back for that cranberry walnut."

"It's our best-seller," the teenager offered.

Other drooling customers made their purchases and departed the little shop. Amber wasn't quite finished because she'd discovered lemon squares at the other end of the store.

Another woman behind the counter who'd finished helping a customer walked up. "Are you new in town?"

Amber looked down at her clothes. "Is it that obvious?"

She nodded and smiled. "Don't think it's something like your hair or the way you're dressed. I've been around this little town—I guess now we've graduated to being a city—for most of my life. Sooner or later, everyone comes to my little bakery and I get to meet them."

"Well, I'm brand-new. Right now I work at the Pemberton Ranch."

"Oh, wow! How is it at the Big House?" The teenager paused in her task of dropping a brownie into a pastry bag.

"The Big House?" Amber giggled at the teen's exuberant description. "I guess you could call it that. I'm the new housekeeper. Amber Delaney."

"I'm Patty and this is my boss and the owner, Miss Barb."

"Now, I've told you not to call me that. Makes me feel

old. I'm fighting it all the way to the top of that hill. So if you want to keep your job, you'd better call me Barb." The woman appeared to be a couple years older than Amber. She'd be called solid, big-boned, but her size supported her tall frame. Amber immediately took a liking to her warm personality.

"Yes, ma'am."

Barb shook her head and winked at Amber. She rang up the few items. "Have you met any of the guys on the ranch?"

"Yep. But I can't guarantee that I can remember their names."

"My boyfriend is the foreman, Joe."

"Really? He's a nice guy."

"Look, what are you doing later? I'm closing up around five."

"Well, I didn't really have any plans. I'm giving myself a tour. I'm planning to go to the library next. After that, I guess head back to my room at the Breezewood Inn."

"No way. You don't have any family or friends in the area?" Amber shook her head. "Bummer. I've got room. You can spend the night."

"I couldn't."

"It's no big deal. Plus I want to hear about the new Mrs. Pemberton-to-be."

Amber rolled her eyes before she thought better of it.

Barb smacked her hands together. "See, I know there's lots to tell."

Amber nodded. But she was no fool. Spreading the family business through town would be a career-shortening move. Playing the game right could also get more intimate details.

"Good. Come on over at dinnertime."

"That sounds lovely." Amber got the directions and then said her good-byes. As she headed back for her car, she marveled at how her day was turning out so far. Everyone was so friendly that the homesickness that hung around before had lifted.

She drove the short distance to the library that lay nestled in a residential neighborhood with small box-shaped houses with storybook white picket fences. Cars, mainly SUVs, and pickup trucks filled the library parking lot.

Amber strolled into the medium-sized building. She always loved the smell of books and loved visiting her area library to complete her research for her stories.

There was an area with the title LOCAL HISTORY that caught her eye. She thumbed through several books, quickly absorbing the colorful details about the dynastic families that were the founding fathers. There was little information about the Pemberton family, but that did not surprise her since there was little documentation about the African-American experience in the small town. Nevertheless, the background provided her with enough information to gain an understanding of the city's social and cultural structure.

She spent an hour browsing, making pages of notes she may never directly use, but would add flavor to uncovering Bo Pemberton. He definitely deserved his own story. She'd expected this coldhearted, money-loving shark. From the first time she'd met him to now, he had not revealed that side. Instead he almost seemed to want to retreat.

She stretched her arms and rolled her head to ease the bunching muscles at the base of her neck. Time got away from her. It was already five o'clock and she had promised to have dinner with Barb.

Amber followed Barb's directions over the cell phone and only realized when she was a minute away that Barb lived in the bright yellow house that had caught her eye when she first drove through town.

Her new friend stood at the door already welcoming her in with a warm smile. Amber ran up the steps, easily falling in love with the charming farmhouse. She entered the living room, inhaling the rich smells of dinner. Her stomach growled in appreciation.

Barb laughed. "Let's not delay. Help me in the kitchen, hon."

Amber nodded and dropped her pocketbook on the side table. She walked down the long hallway decorated with a vast array of framed photographs featuring family members.

"Those are my sisters and brothers with their significant others and kids. I used to be good and remembered names and birthdays. But it's getting to be too much for me. I think I have about twenty nieces and nephews and I'm about to be a great aunt." Barb pulled out a roasted chicken from the oven and carried it to the table.

The table was already set for two on a brightly colored plaid tablecloth. Amber opened the bottle of wine and poured. "You have a beautiful house."

"Thank you. It's one of the few remaining farmhouses that is still with the original family."

The two women passed each other from the dining room to the kitchen as they brought out the side dishes and dessert fare.

"Do you cook like this every day?"

"Only on the weekends. I'm too busy during the week with the shop and the farm."

Their conversation wended its way at a meandering pace about who they were, what they liked or disliked.

Several glasses of wine later, Amber and Barb sat in the living room with the fireplace going.

"What do you know about Bo Pemberton?" Amber asked.

"Bo? I went to school with him and his brothers. They

were a handful for the teachers. They're all cute, you know. I used to feel sorry for Bo. He had so much pressure to take over the farm and you could see that he was screaming to get out of this small town."

"Would you say he is a kindhearted person?"

"That's a strange question. You're the housekeeper working for him; do you think otherwise?"

Amber thought about her answer, knowing that her honest opinion could drive a wedge to the new burgeoning friendship with Barb. "He seems fine. But there is that mess with the company he worked for. I mean, it made national news."

"I don't know about that stuff. I only know that he's a fair employer. We went to the same school and his family is pretty honorable. Bo left with the best of intentions and I can only imagine that it must be hard for him to return and play the rancher."

Amber studied Barb's face. "Did you ever have something with him?" She'd really rather not have a big-girl's slumber party with one of Bo's former girlfriends. She didn't want to examine why this would be an issue, other than that the thought didn't sit comfortably with her.

Barb laughed. "Naw, honey. Bo was never in my sights. I had eyes only for Joe."

"Getting married soon?"

"I'm hoping he'll propose by New Year's."

Amber raised her wineglass. "Here's hoping, then."

"How about you? Anybody ready to sweep you off your feet?"

"No. I had some creep following me around. But other than that, there's no one else waiting in the wings."

"That's because you're too quiet. I've been watching you and you have a shy nature. Ain't too much to pick from in this town. But I know a few fellas who wouldn't mind taking you out to dinner."

Amber shook her head. "Thanks, but no, thanks. I'm not one for blind dates."

"Well, how about your boss?" Barb poured another glass. "Don't look at me like that. Why not? You're his type."

"Oh, and what would that be?" If her memory served her correctly, she looked nothing like the leggy bombshell that popped up at his doorstep. "And he's engaged."

"Hmmm. But she's a high-fallutin' type, or so I've heard. Naw, she's not going to make it up against Martha."

Amber shrugged.

"Hey, don't look disheartened. How did it go with Martha? Bet she didn't like her."

"That's an understatement," Amber replied.

"Martha is very protective of her boys. The father is the brains behind the ranch's success, but Martha is running things. When Martha first came to Breezewood, she hated it. My mother used to tell me funny stories about how Martha would come to cookouts in dresses and heels. When the economy went south and folks started to lose their farms, she decided Breezewood was her home and she was here to stay. I'm sure when she looks at that citified girl she can recognize someone who may not have the heart to be her son's partner in good and bad times." Barb yawned. "I'm beat, but if you'd like to stay up and watch TV, feel free. Let me show you your room before I head to mine."

Before parting ways in the hallway, Barb touched her arm. "Hey, don't count yourself out of the game. I can see you've fallen for him."

Amber offered a small smile, hoping that Barb wouldn't spread the latest about the new housekeeper and her crush. Barb's hospitality and trusting nature appealed to her.

She loved the bedroom. The walls had a country-style wallpaper in powdery-blue shades. The heavy wood furniture gave the room a frontier style. Amber especially adored the four-poster bed with goose-down comforter and lots of plump pillows.

She changed into her nightdress and climbed into bed. Sleep eluded her. Maybe Sylvia was still up and hopefully home. She dialed Sylvia's number. "Hey, what's happening?"

"Nothing much. Do you have your story yet?"

"Nope. I'm doing a lot of research." She filled her in on the latest, including her budding friendship with Barb.

"Not a bad thing, right?"

"I don't know. Zoe's part still bothers me."

"Why is it tearing you up so badly? We were adults gone our separate ways."

"I feel as if I let her down. I never told you. After our big blowup, she wanted to make amends."

"Oh, man. So?"

"I told her to stuff it. Said a few other things I'd rather forget."

Sylvia didn't speak immediately. "Did you ever try to reconnect after you cooled down?"

"Yes, but my calls weren't returned. I even went to her parents' home when I knew she was there. She saw me, but it was very cold. Tight." Amber recalled that Zoe's appearance had drastically changed. "She had lost weight. She didn't look sickly, but chiseled. Remember what a health nut she was in college? I think she took it to an extreme. That's what scared me about her in the ten minutes we chatted. The Zoe that I had come to see had taken a sabbatical. It was all about work and how far she had gotten and how quickly she got there."

"That's heavy," Sylvia said. "How does Bo tie into it?"

"I've pretty much figured that there wasn't much of a tie-in. It's looking like two separate stories. His story is equally intriguing."

"The main thing is did he cut a deal before they hauled him to jail?" Sylvia asked.

"Sylvia! You don't know anything about him. He cares about what he does. He's conscientious. His employees are loyal to him. I can't believe the mess this is turning out to be."

"Calm down. You can't hop the fence on this one, Amber. Take a stance and hold it. Maybe I need to come and see this great and wonderful Bo."

"Would you? Gosh, I miss your company. How about after Christmas?"

"Christmas? Hell, we haven't even gone past Thanksgiving."

"I know your family travels during that time. Plus I want you to come for more than a quick weekend."

"Guess you're not planning to come back anytime soon. Must be going deep, deep undercover." Sylvia howled with laughter.

Amber rolled her eyes. "That's the other thing. I have that stalker guy on my case. I'm actually enjoying my detective role. I'm going to ask Barkman for an extension, but this time on the company's time." She said it with as much bravado as she could muster. Deep down, though, the reality was that Barkman would have her head on a platter with such a request. So what.

"Okay, you win, Amber, I'll be there. By the way, I met this guy. I think I may be falling in love. No sex, as yet, but it makes it all the more appealing."

"What's his name?"

"Eddie. He's not cute or attractive. More like a geeky guy

with some cash. Very introspective, so not like me. I must be growing up."

"Sounds good. I'm looking forward to seeing this guy who makes you all ga-ga. Tell him your best friend can't wait to meet him."

Shortly thereafter, she hung up with Sylvia. She couldn't wait to see her best friend and new boy toy.

After a long day of playing housekeeper, Amber normally did not have trouble falling asleep. It had been three days and counting since Cassidy's arrival. The woman had made Amber her target. She criticized the food, the way she cleaned her room, and even rebuked her for the way she answered Bo. Only Bo's attempt at diplomacy saved his precious fiancée from a strangling. This situation had to come to some type of resolution, fast. Amber especially didn't like not being able to talk to Bo without Cassidy suddenly appearing and placing herself between the two. One more sleepless night and she'd scream.

She got out of bed and paced around the room, fidgeting with her toiletries on the vanity, then glanced up at her reflection, standing in her pajamas. What a stupid ninny! Only one thing at Pemberton ranch should have her interest: writing an exposé on Bo Pemberton. Instead she had taken on the role as housekeeper so completely that she forgot she had a life back in Washington, D.C., and a job she could barely hang on to.

Maybe a warm glass of milk would soothe her unrest. She slipped on her dressing gown and opened her door slowly to make sure she was the only one on a midnight raid of the kitchen. The hallway was dark except for a narrow strip of light coming from Bo's bedroom. Instinctively, she looked over to Cassidy's room and saw that her door was ajar.

Nix the warm glass of milk. She just wanted some fresh air. Thoughts of Cassidy and Bo getting their groove on in the home tortured her. It wasn't that someone like Bo wouldn't be pursued. But personally she couldn't see why he would want the likes of Cassidy. She was too high-society and clearly was not impressed enough with Bo's home or mother to be respectful. All she had going for her was her looks. Amber snorted at the thought.

The floorboards creaked as she made her way to the top of the stairs. She didn't want to interrupt the two lovebirds, although she doubted that they were paying attention to anything or anyone beyond each other. She tried to think of something else; the visuals of them together sickened her.

Bo's door opened with a thud as it hit the wall. Cassidy came storming out of the room, her dressing gown gathered in a bunch in one hand. Amber quickly ran down the stairs, pausing halfway to witness the events at a safe distance.

"I said it was over." Bo's voice boomed from the room.

"I'm not going to beg for you, Bodine Pemberton. We had something good between us, something special and—"

"Yeah, but you didn't think so when you told me it was over. That marrying me would create a scandal. That your father suddenly didn't think I was good enough for his little girl."

Amber went down a few more steps as Bo's voice grew closer. He must have stepped out of his room. Cassidy had moved into view at the top of the stairs. She still held her gown tightly, facing Bo's room.

"That's why it's such a big risk that I came to see you. My father threatened me with disinheritance."

"Don't let me keep you from your money."

Cassidy began to cry. "You ought to be glad that I still want you, now that you've lost your big job. What did turning in your co-workers do for you? Nothing. Who knows, you probably pocketed your share of the pot before pointing your self-righteous finger. Yeah, I bet that's what you did. All that time you kept telling me about how you didn't want to be a farmer. You were busy trying to wash off the stink of all these cows while you tried to convince them in the boardroom. Then I came along to give you credibility. I gave you contacts. I introduced you to a set of people that your low-class family ties couldn't do for you."

Amber put her hand over her mouth to keep from screaming. The hatred that oozed from Cassidy sickened her. How could Bo stand there and take her abuse? She wanted to go into battle on his behalf.

"I'll call a taxi for you."

Even when Amber and Bo had their occasional battles of words and wills, she had never heard his voice resonate with such anger. It had lowered to a deep rumble. It seemed that common sense had sunk into Cassidy as she turned and ran to her room.

Amber took a deep steadying breath, wishing she was in the sweet haven of her room. Instead she had no other choice but to continue downstairs and hide out until Cassidy's departure. When she looked up, Bo stood at the top of the stairs, looking down on her. With the light from his room outlining his body, she couldn't make out his features. She gulped, her ears burning as embarrassment washed over her.

"Had your fill?"

The words sliced through her. "I was going down for some milk." She dropped her gaze from the dark profile. Without another word, she turned and headed for the kitchen, staying there sipping the milk, listening to Bo announce that the taxi had arrived. Cassidy never spoke another word, but Amber could tell when she had walked to the front door as her heels clicked along the floor. She also noted that Bo had closed the door before the taxi drove off.

He walked into the kitchen and stopped short of her. "Sorry for what I said back there."

Amber waved his apology aside, keeping her eyes averted. "No problem. Would you like coffee?"

He opened the refrigerator and pulled out a beer. Holding it up, he said, "Somehow I think this calls for something a bit harder." He twisted off the top. "Cheers." He took a long draw. "I'll be in the study."

Bo finished the beer by the time he reclined on his couch in the study. He wasn't in the mood to get drunk, just wanted something to squelch the bitter taste harbored in his mouth. There was no need to ponder where it had gone wrong with Cassidy. When he was at the height of his career, he thought he needed someone like Cassidy. From the first day, he suffered under her snobbery. If he'd been honest with himself, he wouldn't have continued with the charade to the point of asking her to marry him. What would his life have become?

A soft knock on the door brought him out of his reverie. "Come in." He watched Amber enter, a bit hesitant.

"I know I'm interrupting, but I didn't want to leave you alone."

Her concern touched him and he found that he did want her to stay. "Worried that I may throw myself off the roof?"

"That or fall into a depressive funk and never eat again."

"Was that a hint about my weight?"

She shook her head.

"What are you thinking?" He raised his hand and offered

a weak smile. "Don't tell me: I'm a low-class opportunistic bastard." He scrutinized her face to see if there was any glimmer of agreement.

"I'm not joining you in your self-abuse. Seems to me you'll be thanking your lucky stars years from now when you think of what could have been."

"Actually I am wishing that time could race forward." He dragged a weary hand over his head. For the first time he acknowledged that he was tired. Tired and exhausted from the repercussions of his actions.

"You still have the trial to deal with."

He frowned at her. "You know about it?"

"You're in a small town, Bo. Everyone knows, and what they don't know, they make up."

"Well, you've got lots to tell them now."

"You think I'd gossip?"

"Why wouldn't I think so?"

"Then you don't know me."

"No, I don't, do I, Amber Delaney?" He swung his legs off the couch and patted the empty seat next to him. "Let's start right now. Tell me who you really are. I can't believe you go around working in homes to fund whatever it is that you do."

"I do what I have to. I wasn't as fortunate as you to have a two hundred–acre home."

"I didn't mean to belittle what you do. Looks like you have your private side, just as much as I try to protect mine. As for this place, my father and his brothers each had a plot of land. Some of my cousins still own it, although they don't live on the property. My father bought one of his brother's pieces because my uncle never married or had children. Everyone invested in the farm as a way to ensure that we have the capital to keep hold of the land. It was a family decision among my uncles and grandparents to put my father in charge of everything. Now it's time for the next generation to take over." His voice died away as his thoughts raced ahead. Everyone had looked his way to take the reins. To him it was like or equivalent to walking into a windowless room with no idea of when the door would open.

"You know, just now, at the moment when you talked about your family owning the land, you had an expression full of pride."

He drew himself up on the couch. His face flushed with embarrassment from the frank revelation. "My father would be ecstatic to hear that. He wants me to run the farm permanently."

"Why don't you? You've got to keep it in the family."

"I'm not farmer material. I went to grad school for my MBA. What a waste if I didn't use it."

"I have a real-estate license I don't use. I don't consider it a waste because I'm pursuing something I want to do."

"What's that?"

"Um . . . I'd rather not say. But working here is helping me."

"How mysterious." He picked up her empty glass. "Would you like a refill?"

Amber tried to shield a yawn behind her hand. "Sorry." They both laughed over the moment. "Yes, please. I'd love another glass of milk."

Bo walked out of the room to fulfill his errand. In a short space of time, he had two distinctly different women in his life. One from his former days when he was ambitiously making his move in corporate America. The other had managed to work her way into his life with her strong opinion and liveliness that he appreciated. Amber had earned his respect where Cassidy could never hold his.

He poured the milk and grabbed another beer. Although it was two o'clock in the morning, he looked forward to continuing their talk. Dare he say that their relationship was starting on a new page?

He paused before entering the study. This new feeling about Amber may be the aftereffects of Cassidy's departure. He wanted to retreat and think about what this all meant. Time to end this shoulder-to-shoulder chitchat. He opened the door. "It's getting late. I think . . ."

On the couch Amber had fallen asleep with her knees drawn up. There was even a gentle snore. Bo set down the drinks and pulled out a blanket from the closet. Gently he pulled off her slippers and set them down. Then he draped the blanket over her, tucking it around her shoulders. She mumbled and turned her head, causing her hair to fall across her face. With a gentle brush of his finger, he pushed the stray tendrils off her skin. The softness of her cheek electrified his fingertips. He couldn't pull his hand away. Amber shifted her head again, softly muttering until her lips rested against his palm.

A peaceful, beautiful picture lay before him. Openly, he admired the graceful line of her forehead sloping to the tip of her softly rounded nose. He couldn't help lingering at her lips with their whimsical lift at each corner.

"Sweet dreams," he whispered, before reaching over to turn off the light.

Chapter Six

Amber heard the door slide shut, but didn't turn around. Martha had given her the day off with no place to go; she chose to sit on the deck and catch up on the latest buzz in the newspaper.

"Isn't it too chilly?" Martha approached with her ready smile.

"A little, but the view is so breathtaking, I convinced myself I could last an hour out here. Plus, I have a cup of hot chocolate right here." Amber raised the oversize mug as evidence.

"Ever since Will brought me to Pemberton Ranch and I saw this land, I knew I would always love this place. Have you been on a tour of the property?"

Amber shook her head.

"Well, if you'd like, I can take you. We can take the golf cart so we can go off the road. And make sure to put on something heavier. I think that hot spell is over. Meet you outside in, let's say, ten minutes?"

"Sure." Amber looked forward to seeing the rest of the ranch. Maybe she'd even get a chance to see Bo at work. Not that it mattered. She only wanted to see firsthand what a cowboy's life was all about. Bo on his horse, Onyx, was a perfect picture.

They drove over the terrain that spanned various landscapes, from the rocky terrain to lush pasture. The red soil provided stark contrast to the prairie's grassy carpet. Amber could finally understand why Texans were so proud of their state. The land mirrored the history and lives of its dwellers in a rich tapestry of untamed beauty that mixed the Wild West with the modern urban sprawl. Although she was riding in a golf cart, she could easily imagine the pioneers on their wagons making this home.

"I can see in your face that you have that same appreciation, that sense of awe. I came from New York and I never looked back."

Amber turned in surprise to the petite woman driving the cart. "New York? What did your family say?"

"Honey, I didn't have much of a family life. My parents married young and my mother became a baby machine. There were seven of us running around. I was the third youngest and probably the most rebellious. I met Will in New York when he did a brief stint in the Army. God, but he was beautiful in that uniform." She laughed, her eyes twinkling merrily with thoughts of her younger days. "He was tall and striking and I was this pint-size thing, but we used to go out and jitterbug all night long. Then when his time was up in New York and he got sent to California, I wanted to go with him. I knew that I wanted out of New York. My parents were in the middle of their breakup. My older brothers and sisters had long since flown the coop. I fantasized about getting free of it all. So, yes, I saw Will as my ticket to freedom, but I truly loved that man."

"Is your mother still alive?"

"No, she died. It was all very neat and quiet. She died in her sleep. She was always the lady, never given to displays of affection. I made a promise that when I had my own children, I would hug them and kiss them until they had to beat me off." Martha pulled to the side of the trail. "I hope I don't sound bitter. I'm not."

Amber sifted through the turmoil of her emotions with regard to her mother. "No, you don't sound bitter. If anything, you sound like you enjoy your motherhood experience."

"Yep. I do. Don't get me wrong, there were some bumpy moments, and Lord knows, Will wasn't always a saint, but I valued what we had. I had three little boys who looked up to their father, as they should. When he wasn't here, I raised them the best way I could with lots of love and a few swats every now and again."

"Was Bo the troublemaker?"

"No. Actually he was the peacemaker. He was so protective of me. It's because of him that Will retired from the Army and decided to settle down. Bo was only ten years old, but he felt his father should be home with me, with all of us."

"Sounds very admirable."

"Over there is Zack's house. He's my youngest. It's more like a bachelor pad, if you ask me. Anyway, he's rarely home. Works for Delta airlines up in Dallas. I'm expecting him home for Thanksgiving. You'll get to meet all of them then. Quite a rowdy bunch."

Amber tried to hide the panic. Martha reached over and patted her hand.

"Oh, honey, I'm so sorry. Gosh, what am I thinking? Your family is expecting you for Thanksgiving. Here I am assuming you'll be with us."

"I'm an only child. My parents aren't together. I don't really deal with my father and his new family." She squirmed, not really enjoying having to share. Thanksgiving was her least favorite holiday with all this emphasis on family. "My mother is in California." She definitely wasn't going into her mother's obsession with Alice Walker and her pilgrimage to meet the author.

"Then would you please accept my invitation to our Thanksgiving dinner?"

"Oh, no, thank you. I don't mind working. And it's your family."

"Family is more than blood. When you've lived as long as I have, you'll realize that and come to appreciate it. I'm not taking no for an answer."

Amber nodded. "I'll still help with the meal. Sounds like you've got boys with appetites."

"I'll take you up on that."

The two women rode to the south side of the ranch where the cattle were penned. The area proved to be livelier, with field hands busy at work. Amber surveyed the scene, looking for one familiar figure.

"There's Bo. Why don't you go over there and talk to him while I talk to Joe?"

Amber got off the cart and walked toward Bo, all the while pretending to examine the large holding pens. Just beyond the structures, the men bustled along with their various jobs, shouting their coded lingo to each other. She couldn't help but crinkle her nose at the distinctive scent from the cattle.

"Takes a little getting used to."

She grunted, a little afraid to open her mouth in case the pungent smell could have an aftertaste.

"My mother brought you out, I see."

"She wanted to show me the place."

"She's my resident tour guide. And she's probably checking up on me." He laughed. "While she does her spot inspection, I want to show you my favorite spot."

"I can't. Your mother is waiting for me." She couldn't help the whispery rush of her words. Standing so close to him sent her nerves into overdrive.

"Believe me, my mother is too busy with my foreman to notice your absence. She's always got a million ideas and he's kind enough to listen to all of them."

Amber still hesitated. "Are we taking the golf cart?"

"No, where we're going can only be reached by horse or an SUV."

"I don't know how to ride."

Bo walked ahead of her and turned to wait. "I promise that the horse I'll pick will be on his best behavior."

His charming declaration didn't change her mind—it was the secret longing that she could spend some private time with him. "Okay, let's go."

Bo led a large gray horse in her direction that offered a hearty snort. The thick muscles rippled under its skin as it pawed the ground, waiting for her to mount. Amber took a deep breath and pulled herself onto its back.

They trotted past the stable and headed toward a clearing where Amber expected Bo to show her his favorite picnic area. Instead the horses slowed down as they peaked a small hill and then went down toward a pristine lake. The cool air stung her cheeks, but it refreshed her.

Without waiting for him, she dismounted and secured the reins. She looked at the water, barely a ripple marred its surface. The magnitude of the landscape that made up his family's property had her awestruck.

"It's all so beautiful."

"When I was younger I hid out here because I was tired of cleaning the stables. Gosh, I was a pain in the butt for my father. But then I got all turned around and ended up lost farther along the property. My father almost had the lake dragged because they couldn't find me by the end of the day."

"Why did you resist so much? It sounds like you really hated life here. All this land, openness, natural beauty feels like what paradise would be like."

Bo gazed into the distance. After taking a deep breath, he nodded. "It took a particularly bad experience to make me appreciate what I have, what my parents worked hard to make successful, what my uncles had the foresight to do to keep all this property in the family."

"With that impressive legacy, how does the entire mutual-fund scandal make you feel?"

He fixed her with a steely glint in his eyes.

Amber kept talking, hoping he would relax. Trust. "I always come back to that because I'm truly curious. People want to know how it's affected you in the short term. Others may not have had a family business to fall back on and have to make major important choices. The housing community near the company has a record number of foreclosures because the company laid off so many. This may sound strange, but do you ever wonder what would have happened if you hadn't said anything? I'm not accusing you," she ended softly.

"Could have fooled me."

"Listen, Bo. Think about the people you worked with, the people who worked under you. They may not have a family ranch the size of a small neighborhood to escape to for family love and support." She grabbed his arm as he turned away. "The woman, Mildred what's-her-name, she was an administrative assistant with the company for twenty-five years. She diligently put aside her money for retirement. No husband. No children. Her job was her life. Her life was her job. And now she's without a job, without a pension." The passion for the underdog and hatred for the injustice exploded. "Do you know what happened to her? Do you?" Amber circled around him until she faced him. Stared him down. "Heart failure brought on by stress." The tears welled in anger, in sympathy, in frustration that all this corporate greed impacted people's lives in irreversible ways.

"Don't you think I wake up at night thinking about the devastation? Not only did I work in the den of lions, but then I made it all explode by going to the SEC. Even though I came forward, don't think that the Securities and Exchange Commission bigwigs didn't put me through the wringer. Everything I worked for went up in smoke, along with my reputation." He wrenched his arm away and put some distance between them. "Since you want to get on your soapbox and make me out to be the lowest thing on earth."

"I didn't say that."

"You didn't have to. Your eyes speak volumes. In your mind, I killed Mildred."

They stared at each other. Both recovering from the impact of their admissions. Bo moved first, breaking eye contact.

"Let's go to my brothers' clubhouse."

They walked a few more yards where a small one-room house stood. The white paint had now faded to a filthy gray, but Amber could make out the faded black letters that read CLUB HOUSE.

"My brothers would have their meeting here. I only came here a couple of times, mainly to get them so they could do their chores. I was too old to appreciate it."

"Jealous?"

"Nope. But here is where they decided what they wanted to do with their lives. They had dreams and they went after them. Zack became a publicist. Josh became a pediatrician. But I was expected to go to college and after graduation come back here. Well, I rebelled and went on to work with a few companies before landing a low-level management position at Sandstone. I threw myself into the job. I worked as if I owned the company and moved up the ladder. I trusted the leadership. I believed in all the directives, carrying out the home-office message with a soldier's precision. With each promotion I'd call home with the news to my parents, my father especially. Even though he'd congratulate me, I knew he wouldn't settle for anything less than me saying I was coming home."

Amber kept her head down. She looked at the walls, trying to imagine the sibling rivalry and love. Being an only child limited her perspective, but she could still believe it was a wonderful, full experience.

"What did Cassidy say when you told her you would blow the whistle?"

"I never told her."

Amber looked at him with surprise.

"I didn't want to be influenced by anyone's opinion."

"But I'm sure your decision, or at least the aftereffects, affected her, too." Despite how it sounded, she refused to think she could possibly be defending Cassidy.

"Well, the other reason is that we'd already broken up by then."

"Sounds like you all have spent more time broken up than together. Couldn't make up your mind?"

"I have made up my mind. Some people can't take no for an answer. I did what I did with the company because of values my parents taught me. I broke it off with Cassidy because of the values my mother taught me. Have you come to make me pay for my sins, Amber Delaney? If so, get in line." He walked past her and exited the small structure.

Amber knew she had overstepped the line on several levels. She didn't know why she was so angry or what it meant. From a human-interest perspective, she wanted to raise everyone's awareness. Right now her easiest target was Bo. What if he hadn't said anything? The folks would still be out of their pension money.

A headache formed in the middle of her forehead. She headed out of the clubhouse before Bo left her in the middle of nowhere. There would be no easy chatter as they returned to the hub of the ranch. Her amateurish attempts at discovery had frozen any connection that might have been occurring.

"My mother is over there. I have to get back to work."

"Thanks, Bo. I'm sorry." She turned to offer a smile, a sign of truce, but his back was already turned—stiff, proud.

Amber stood in the kitchen, shaking her head at the amount of the food covering the counter. Thanksgiving was only a few hours away and an army-sized meal was in the works. Maybe she should have gone back to D.C. and spent the holiday in her usual way, quiet and alone.

Instead, the house buzzed with a level of heightened activity. It made her more acutely aware that she didn't belong. She couldn't share in the childhood stories or participate in reminiscing about one of the unfortunate ex-girlfriends who had been brought to the ranch.

She had to admit that the feeling of isolation stemmed from Bo's cold distance. They had never quite gotten back to their playful bantering. Her employee status was made clear in the way he talked to her or dismissed her with an averted gaze or slight turn of his shoulder.

Now, in three hours, she'd be sitting at the dinner table with him. She'd already crafted a plan to be the last one seated so she could hopefully not have to sit close to him. She didn't want him to feel any more uncomfortable around her than he already appeared.

"Amber, can you pull out the turkey and baste one more time? Bo, call your brothers so they can get the drinks out of the garage. Will, don't you think you're getting out of anything—here, cut up these maraschino cherries so I can decorate the ham."

"Cherries and ham. What the heck are you giving me to eat, woman?" Will popped a cherry into his mouth.

"The cherries sit in the middle of the pineapple circles. I don't even know why I'm explaining anything to you. One slurp and you'll eat it all up, anyway."

Amber bit back a giggle and basted the turkey. Martha had learned a few military command talents from her husband.

The Pemberton brothers walked into the kitchen in a noisy cluster. Bo stood off to the side, listening to his other brothers finish an argument about who would go to the Super Bowl that year.

"Ma, I've got a friend joining us for dinner. She should be here at any moment," Zack announced.

The doorbell chimed.

"I love a girl that's prompt." He headed for the door to let her in.

Everyone waited for the mystery guest to make her grand entrance. Amber also found herself waiting.

"Everyone, this is Sasha."

Martha came forward with an outstretched hand. "Hello, dear. I'm Zack's mother, Martha. Welcome to our home." As if an afterthought, she asked, "What's your title?"

"Excuse me?" Sasha looked around the room in confusion.

Zack stepped to her side. "Mom." He said the word through a gritted grin.

"I only wanted to know her title. You know Zack always dates a beauty contestant."

Sasha turned an obviously fake smile on the youngest Pemberton. "Oh, really. I'm Miss Black USA."

"Let's go in the living room and you can tell me about your trip." Zack ushered his guest out of harm's way.

Bo and Josh dutifully fetched the drinks from the garage.

"Bo, help Amber. Jake, make the punch while you tell me how the business is going."

Bo didn't know how to approach Amber. Avoiding her couldn't be an option, at least not with his mother directing everyone like it was a school play.

She'd cut him to the core with her direct questions. Her accusation had slammed into him like a punch to the gut. Later he'd realized that it wasn't merely the underlying blame in her voice, but his own guilt that overwhelmed him. Amber stirred all his feelings into a chaotic mess, leaving him feeling out of control. But he also didn't want this schism between them. He walked up slowly behind her as she washed vegetables in the sink. "May I help?"

Her shoulders jerked, but she remained focused on her task. "I can handle this. No need to stand over me."

He fought the urge to retreat. "I'll cut up the vegetables you've washed." He stood at her side and reached into the sink in front of her for the vegetables that had been cleaned. He cut the carrots into thin slices, thinking through various versions of his apology. "I'm glad you're spending Thanksgiving with us."

She shrugged and took the bowl of vegetables and placed them into the steamer.

"I'll go ahead and mash these potatoes."

Amber did her familiar shrug and pulled the pies out from the pantry. She left the kitchen and headed toward the dining room with an apple pie and sweet-potato pie in each hand.

Bo didn't waste any time. He dropped the knife and potato and went after her. "Amber," he called from the doorway of the dining room. He could hear Zack still trying to make nice with his girlfriend. He lowered his voice. "Amber," he repeated.

"Yes?" She laid the pies on the side table and headed for the other entryway to the room.

"Don't avoid me. I want to apologize."

"No need to apologize. I was out of line. My emotions get the better of me and then no one can shut me up."

"You'd make a good prosecutor."

"You mean persecutor, don't you?"

Bo laughed not because she was witty, but because he sensed a thaw in her attitude. He jumped on the opportunity. "Move over, city girl, let me help you set the table."

"Don't you have a cow to harass?"

"Yeah, but I'd rather be here with you."

"Swell."

They finished up their tasks in easy silence until Martha declared that dinner was served.

*   *   *

Bo couldn't believe that the bowl of mashed potatoes, platter of honey-baked ham slices, and dish of macaroni and cheese lay empty with only a few crumbs as evidence. Personally, he wanted to open the button to his pants. He just had to have that second helping.

The family's tradition was to play a couple rounds of cards until they could squeeze in the dessert.

"Amber, do you know how to play Hearts?"

She shook her head.

The table erupted with disbelief. Only Sasha and Amber remained silent throughout the barrage of questions.

"Okay, ease up on her. I'll entertain Amber and Dad while you guys play," Bo said.

"No funny games with my Sasha," Zack teased.

Bo already knew Sasha wasn't his type from the moment she came through the door. She was as opposite from Amber as could be.

Sasha stood tall and erect like a ballerina. Her skin was so fair and thin, he could see thin blue veins snaking from her temples into her hairline. She reminded him of a porcelain doll with a shy, tentative nature.

Amber, on the other hand, had an earthy quality that made him appreciate her natural beauty. She may not have been the perfect model height, but she walked with a purpose that brooked no nonsense. The only time he picked up any hesitation on her part was around his family. Listening to the roar of the winning team, he could empathize with both women, being the outsiders.

"This is how you entertain our guests?" His mother interrupted his thoughts. "Each of you sitting here looking like statues. Bo, take over my hand. I'll keep the party rolling along."

Bo didn't mind his mother's interruption if she only

planned to take Sasha off his hands. He wanted more one-on-one time with Amber, and with his entire family present, that wasn't going to happen.

He cleared his throat, swallowing some of his nervousness. "Amber, would you like your dessert now?"

"Oh, no, thank you. I'm going to head over to Barb's, Joe's girlfriend. I met her in town the other day and she invited me to Thanksgiving dinner."

Disappointment washed over him. "Do you need me to drive you over there?"

"No. She should be here shortly. I'll be back tomorrow afternoon."

He wanted to say, "Don't go," but the thought seemed so ludicrous, he forced himself to remain quiet. All he could do was sit in the living room as she waited for Barb to call her and say she was on her way.

"You don't have to sit with me," Amber said.

"It would be rude of me otherwise."

"I'm not used to you being . . . nice to me."

"I just want to get to know you."

She turned and raised inquiring brows at him. "Are you looking for something other than what you need to know?"

"I want to know why you're so wrapped up in what I did with the company. I want to know why you aren't with your family this holiday weekend. I want to know why there's no special man in your life." His questions faded away. Even to his own ears, he sounded obsessed.

"Well, Bo, looks like we are both dying for information about each other. I want to know how long it took for you to make a decision to tell about your company. I want to know if you have kept in touch with any of your staff. I want to know if Cassidy is gone for good or if this is Part Two in an elaborate play."

"She's gone," he said softly. "No regrets. No second chances."

From the kitchen, Martha bellowed the message that Barb was on her way.

He pulled her to him, embracing her in a long sweet hug. "Happy Thanksgiving, Amber." Her breath tickled his neck as she responded in like manner. He wanted to kiss her so badly, but held back, not sure that a second kiss wouldn't land him in hot water.

Chapter Seven

Bo hung up from talking with the special prosecutor. He had answered more questions than he'd ever thought he would have to. Questions came at him about his work, his family life, about him personally. His bank accounts had been examined, paperwork submitted, and he was sure they had a file on him a mile thick. He must have passed their test because the prosecutor was moving forward with the fury of an avenging agent.

Meanwhile his former bosses and others in the top ranks had proven to be formidable enemies. Copies of internal memos revealing his role in the scandal, written on his letterhead, lay on top of an overnight envelope. The prosecutor had also received a copy, and had only called to tell Bo that they had received the package, and, after a preliminary examination, deemed it a fraud. Bo was relieved to hear that someone believed in his integrity, but knew this would not be the end.

He sat behind his desk in the study, rubbing his temples.

The case wouldn't begin in earnest for another six months. In the meantime, he knew better than to send out his résumé. Not only did he work for a company that had committed illegal acts known by the compliance department, but he was a whistle-blower, the man solely responsible for massive layoffs as the company lost its major clients and faced imminent bankruptcy.

"Can I talk to you for a minute, son?"

"Sure." Bo tried to put on a brave face.

"How is it going?"

Bo hadn't shared the sordid details of the latest turn of events with his family. They had enough to deal with and he'd do everything he could to protect them and their privacy. "We may lose the sale to La Salle, but I met with the principals and I think we're back on track. The Whitetail ranch is our competition, basically undercutting us."

"Sounds like you've got it under control."

"Yep. It's not all clear, but I'll keep meeting with them."

His father stretched, then fidgeted with his clothes. Bo knew that smile meant his father was about to touch on the sensitive subject between them. "Bo, I know we said we would talk about this in the next few months . . ."

"Dad, please, I don't want to talk about this."

"You mean you're not ready to talk yet?"

"You want me to make a life-altering decision."

"Nothing so dramatic. I just want you to accept what you keep running from."

"Dad, I watched you be the responsible one. The one who skipped starting your career and watched the ranch while your brothers got to fly the coop. Now history will repeat itself."

"It was the one way we could keep all this land. It was worth the sacrifice."

"You always take the high road."

"The Carlyle Development Company came knocking again."

"They can't take no for answer?" He didn't like their persistence.

"I told them I'd meet with them."

"What?"

"I told them they'd have to meet with the entire family."

"Mom knows about this? I can't believe she agreed to that. What about Zack and Josh?"

"Your mother knows. I told Zack and Josh earlier today."

"You're seriously thinking about doing this? What about the cousins?"

"They said I should at least talk to them. I haven't told you this, but they've wanted to sell the land since several years ago. I told them I'd buy them out first before I sold the land."

The news bulldozed Bo's defenses about the ranch into rubble. The conflicted feelings rolled like an angry storm. "How can you be so calm about this? I expect you to be angry and yelling down the house." He thought about his cousins who used to live on the ranch and shared each holiday as one family. When did things start to fall apart?

"Guess I'm getting too old. Sometimes you can hold on to something too long."

Bo exhaled. Enough with the philosophical claptrap. He'd deal with his cousins. "When are they coming?"

"It'll be next week. Monday morning. It'll be at the hotel because Carlyle has a presentation they want to show us."

"I hope this won't be a circus. Have you called Harvey?" Bo felt that their lawyer needed to be present.

His father nodded. "It's one of the reasons I pushed you

to take over because I knew you had it in you to bring unity back to this family. After your uncle had his stroke and passed away, Clarissa, Todd, and Leon were like hungry animals after the money. It didn't help that there wasn't a will. But it's their legacy, too, so who am I to say anything."

Bo pounded his fist on the desk. "Once we start cutting up the land, it will snowball until we have nothing worth keeping. We're strong as long as we stick together."

His father stood to leave. "Sounds good, but if there's no one interested in running it, then it's all just rhetoric. Look at me." He patted his paunch. "I'm gray, battling high blood pressure, a back that can barely keep me upright, and your mother's yapping in my ear." He chuckled. "I can't do this much longer." His eyes never strayed from Bo's.

His father's words said one thing, but the silent urging permeated his conscience.

Bo slumped in his chair after his father left. As kids they had all been so proud of being Pemberton kids. It had its prestige, earning them a place of high regard with the city.

He figured that going away to college, alone, free from parental authority, free from the family traditions, seeking their own identities was when everyone drifted away. Joe rented Uncle Wayne's house. Uncle Theo's house burned down and never was rebuilt since he didn't have any children. None of the cousins lived in Texas, which didn't help.

How could he blame them when he had no intention of returning home? After graduation, all he could think about was hitting a big city and making lots of money. He used to hate coming home for the holiday dinners, going through the rituals of listening to stories about ranch life.

The memories stifled him. This room stifled him. He

walked out to the closet, grabbed his coat and gloves, and headed out the back door toward the stable.

This rugged land that could prove heartless had so much character. Its openness never denied him, never placed barriers or prejudices in his path. His boots crunched over the frosted dirt as he walked. The visual vastness of the West, still wild in some areas, appealed to his sense of beauty. Yet there was the sound of the coyotes at night, the thundering hooves of the wild horses, the snort of his cattle that tantalized the core person that he was. He knelt, picked up a handful of loose red dirt and waved it under his nose. This land had welcomed back its prodigal son with no reservation.

Once he mounted Onyx and led him out to the open pasture, he dug in for the galloping freedom ahead. The landscape blurred as he hunkered down into the neck of the horse. The cold air blasted his lungs and he gasped to catch his breath. He squinted as his eyes teared. The freedom was what he craved. It was what he loved.

Instinctively he aimed Onyx toward his favorite spot. When he was a little boy, he'd often fantasized about being a sheriff riding to find the outlaws. His bad guys ended up at the clubhouse in the shape of his brothers, who he would lead back to town. And when he entered town, he'd be greeted with roaring applause and cheer. Usually his parents were outraged at him for tying his brothers up.

The weather-beaten wooden structure came into view. He clicked his tongue and tugged the reins to slow the horse, then he dismounted and hitched it to a tree. Behind him a horse snorted. He spun toward the sound.

A familiar dappled gray horse pawed the ground. He tossed his nose up to sniff the air in their direction. Bo frowned,

wondering who took the horse for a ride. He surveyed the **area**, but didn't see anyone.

"Is someone out here?" His voice rang out clearly. He walked up to the clubhouse and pushed open the door. A loud squeak cut through the silence.

"Oh, I didn't know you were here." Amber's voice startled him from behind. A wisp of steam formed as she spoke. "I liked this spot when you showed it to me."

"You rode out here by yourself?" He didn't mean to sound so astounded. But this was the same woman who, only a few weeks ago, dreaded the sight of a horse.

"Yep. I've been riding a little every day. Your mom said it's the best way to feel comfortable around the horse and for the horse to feel comfortable around you. I thought I wouldn't be able to find this spot, though." She chuckled and then stopped abruptly. "I hope you don't mind."

"No, no, not at all. I needed a taste of the open, too, which is why I came here." He motioned. "Let's walk a bit. It'll keep the chill off." He hadn't expected to see her here, but he welcomed her company.

They walked along a rough path. Bo picked up a branch lying on the ground to keep his hands busy. He stripped off the leaves, giving it more attention than necessary. Anything to keep him from acting like a nervous schoolboy around Amber. She always seemed in such control.

"I can see why the American cowboy holds so much charm. It's man against nature. Man conquering the wild," Amber said.

"It's more than that. It's man with nature. Man living in the wild respecting his environment."

"You're putting a spin on it, but according to Hollywood, it's man's taming of land and beast that stimulates our sense of civilization."

Bo shook his head, readying himself to debate Amber. No matter what the subject was, he always seemed to be in a battle with her. Actually, he enjoyed the sparring. If he wasn't mistaken, there was always a twinkle in her eye and he wondered if she instigated much of their debates.

"Come with me."

"Where?"

"I'm riding with the men to take the herd to another area for grazing. It'll take us about three days and then we can ride back to the ranch."

Amber didn't immediately answer. A frown settled on her forehead and she looked off into the distance. "I'm not sure if I can handle it."

"Don't you want to experience the cowboy lifestyle? Watch us stamp across nature? Conquer—what was it you said— the beast?"

Amber pointed at him. "Now that you've laid it out with dripping sarcasm, then, yes, I'll take the challenge."

When was the last time he had taken his housekeeper on a trail? He denied any other reason for doing this than that she was a great listener. "Let's head back. I'm glad to hear you're not a wimp." He caught her gritted teeth grimacing at him. "Oh, by the way, you'll need to get some thicker clothing."

He examined her from head to toe and raised his gaze to her eyes. What the heck was he thinking? Just looking at her face, radiating an innocent freshness that stirred a part of him he had buried and locked, had his pulse pumping. And now he had invited her to ride alongside him, share the campfire, be in his world for days . . . and nights.

He raised his hand to touch her. A few inches from her cheek, he caught his senses and curled his fingers into a tight fist. All this clean air must be muddying his reasoning.

Not this time. Amber refused to let him give into his doubts. She reached up and enclosed his hand with hers, then stroked the back of his hand with her thumb until he relaxed and uncurled his fingers. Using the slightest pressure, she guided his hand to her face and kissed his palm. Her eyes locked on his, the desire bouncing off each other and growing.

She closed the space between them, stepping into his arms. Bo encircled her body, holding the back of her head as she gently rested it on his chest. His throat ached for air as he intermittently held his breath and then exhaled in loud gasps. He closed his eyes and inhaled the fruity scent of her freshly shampooed hair.

"Please kiss me." The words were slightly above a whisper. "Kiss me. Hold me tight."

Her pleas nipped away at his weakened defenses. He moved his head and looked into her upturned face. Her lips drew him and slowly he kissed her. Gently rubbed his lips against hers until the coldness dissipated. Her softened lips opened, urging him with actions instead of words. Her sweet breath teased him and he slowly tested her with his tongue.

Her mouth drew him in like a bee to nectar. Their tongues darted and twirled in their own dance to a natural beat, sensual in origin, laced with passion. The heady mix proved more intoxicating than any drink he ever had. He kept kissing her, leaving her lips to touch her face with equal attention. Soft whispery kisses on her cheek, eyelids, forehead. Anywhere that showed her emotions with a wrinkle, twitch, any movement, he touched with his lips.

Onyx snorted.

The sound distracted him enough to bring order back to

his senses, his emotions. "Think it's time to go back." He stepped away, deliberately dropping his arms to his side. The cold air quickly resumed its place, pushing away the comforting warmth their bodies had just shared.

Amber remained with her eyes closed. She touched her face, cupping both sides of her cheeks. "You're a powerful man, Bo Pemberton. I can't seem to keep my wits about me when I'm with you." Her eyes opened, but she did not look in his direction. Instead she walked away from him over to her horse. After she mounted, she looked down at him. "I think I shouldn't go with you on your cattle-grazing expedition after all. I don't like being out of control. You just broke up with Cassidy. You couldn't possibly be ready for anything else."

Bo saw the tears that brightened her eyes. Hurting her was never in his thoughts. "Cassidy and I were over a long time ago. I didn't plan any of this, Amber." Words meant to reassure rushed out in a jumbled heap. Suddenly it was important for her to understand.

She blinked away the tears. Her lips drew into a straight line. Bo noticed the tightening of her emotions and didn't protest. She needed her space, just as much as he needed his. He guessed.

Getting the house key was so easy. Eddie silently thanked Sylvia for being so clueless. He had gotten used to her hovering presence and suffered it because he could glean so much information about Amber.

In his darkened bedroom, he booted up the computer. The latest achievement uplifted his spirits as he wondered how he would get in touch with Amber. He clicked on the Internet engine and logged on with a few addresses he'd taken. Then he selected WRITE AN E-MAIL. Each letter he typed was slow and deliberate as he spelled out Amber's e-mail address.

Sylvia, the trusting soul, left not only the keys handy, but also left her address book on her desk. He found both the e-mail address and a number scribbled near her name. The area code looked like Texas. He'd check that out later.

He typed the note, stating that he missed her and looked forward to her return. Then, as a P.S., he wrote that he hoped she hadn't changed anything about herself—not her long black hair, not the amount of makeup she wore, or the usual color of her lipstick. After he ended the note and positioned the cursor over the SEND button, he paused.

"Amber, I forgive you for your sudden departure. I'll wait here for you to get back. Please don't disappoint me," he said aloud. He added the smiley face and sent off the message.

He could never check the previous e-mails to see if she had responded to his three messages. And you never knew if the authorities were monitoring the line. Nope, he'd much rather send out his messages every couple days under new e-mail addresses.

"Honey, are you coming to bed?"

Eddie snapped off the computer with annoyance. In a few seconds, Sylvia would come into the room and drape herself over him.

"It's cold in this room, how can you stand it?"

"It's fine for me." He didn't keep mirrors in the apartment, but could see the reflection of himself and Sylvia in the computer monitor. "You go on, I'll be there."

If she only knew how sick she made him, she'd leave him alone.

"Well, I'll just go call Amber. Gosh, I miss her. Chatting with you isn't exactly easy, Eddie. Kind of like our love life."

"I told you I want us to focus on each other. I want our relationship to be with the purist intention." He slammed his fist on the table. "Stop badgering me."

Sylvia had backed up. He realized he'd kept a tight rein on his anger when she was around him. But the very thought of lying with her sent him into a fit.

"Good night," she said, much subdued. "Turn out the lights when you come to bed."

He nodded, hoping she hadn't changed her mind to contact Amber. He would listen from his office because he knew he couldn't hide his enthusiasm when he heard Amber's voice.

Sitting in his high-backed leather chair, Eddie turned off the lights, lit a cigarette, and waited. He finished his cigarette after a few long drags. His fingers drummed on the desk, marking his impatience. Once the red light on the phone came on, it was time to put on the headphones and push the RECORD button.

Amber's voice reminded him of a soft breeze that gently brushed his soul. She had the power to awaken feelings he had long buried, ever since Judith Marks a year ago. He never thought he'd be able to enjoy the sense of anticipation and eventual culmination. Once that occurred, it was time to find another perfect mate. He grinned and lit another cigarette.

The light popped on and he almost dropped his cigarette as he hurried to adjust the earphones and stab at the RECORD button.

"Hello?"

"Hey, Ambie, it's me."

"Uh-oh, what's the matter?"

"Nothing much." Sylvia sighed heavily into the phone. Eddie frowned at the intrusive noise.

"Don't play games with me. I've known you long enough

to recognize when you're in need *and* you called me by that silly nickname. So, what's up?"

"Do you have time to talk?"

"Yeah, everyone went out for a family dinner. I'm enjoying the peaceful moment. These Pemberton men are a handful."

"I don't want to hear about men."

"Who broke your heart? The same guy you've been telling me about?"

"Yes, Eddie. Sometimes I think he cares about me and then other days he's so cold that I . . . I don't know." Sylvia sighed again. "Maybe I'm just tired."

"Don't sell yourself short. You seemed to generally like him."

"That's what I thought. But we don't go anywhere, not to the movies, not to dinner. It's almost as if he doesn't want to be in my company. Then I get confused because in that same day, he may be very attentive."

"Maybe he has issues. Do you know anything about him?"

"He says he's the only child, but when I looked in his drawer, I found a stack of pictures. He had cut out the face of the children standing next to him."

"He sounds like a piece of work. You always manage to attract the loonies. On a brighter note, how's the sex life? Let's hope that makes up for the madness."

"You'd think, but he's practicing celibacy."

"You're lying. He must be a real keeper if he's got you tamed in the sex department."

"I didn't say I liked it. I was wondering, though, if I could still bring him to Texas. I want you to meet him and give me your opinion."

"Sure."

"Enough about me. How is it going at your end?"

"Slow, but I'm getting to know him."

"Mmm. Getting to know him. Details. Details."

"I don't think he trusts me, as yet."

"Why should he? You're lying to him."

"He doesn't know that."

"Otherwise, would he warrant a second look?"

"Most definitely."

Eddie pushed the STOP button. He couldn't really consider it betrayal because Amber hadn't opened her heart to him. That would be a matter of weeks. Then she wouldn't have to sound like a tramp talking about other men.

Turning off the light, he exited the room and headed upstairs. Now, Sylvia, on the other hand, held no promise, no predisposition to change or be better. She wasn't capable of it. He had no desire to continue contaminating his space with her.

He opened the bedroom door and hid the shudder that rattled through his body. "Sylvia, did I overhear you talking to your friend?"

"Yes, Amber says hi. Would you like to go to Texas with me? We can tour Dallas while we visit her."

He walked around to the bed and sat on the edge. The movement caused her to roll a little into his leg and he resisted the urge to pull away from her warm flesh. Nothing about her, from head to toe, appealed to him. The sickly sweet bout of nausea assailed him and he bit down to keep his composure.

"Sounds good. Where is she exactly?"

"Breezewood. She's at a ranch."

He stared at her lips forming the words he so wanted to hear. For the first time that evening, he smiled. As the excitement simmered and then bubbled up with a gleeful surge, he could almost dismiss what he felt compelled to do, even if it would be in his apartment, in his bedroom.

Maybe, if the mood hit him, he'd send a note to her family about where to find her body.

Chapter Eight

Cobb salad.

Amber pressed down the pages of the recipe book. The picture of an abundantly garnished salad decorated the page. Today would be salad, soup, and bread. She didn't feel confident enough to make the soup from scratch. The family would have to make do with soup from a can and biscuits from the freezer.

But the salad looked doable. Two heads of lettuce, tomatoes, cheese, meat, eggs. Oh, dear, the eggs. She hurried to the stove to hear the distinctive sizzling of bad news. The offensive odor made her nose crinkle. All the water had boiled away and the eggs had exploded.

"Darn it." Amber grabbed the pot and dropped it in the sink. She turned on the faucet and filled it, not quite sure what to do next.

One thing she couldn't screw up was the soup. She opened the can and poured the contents into a saucepan. All she had to do was heat it for a few minutes. She turned the stove top setting to HIGH.

The biscuits would take twelve minutes. Enough time for her to finish up with everything. She placed the dough on the pan and slid it into the oven.

Now for the salad.

She prepared each ingredient, layering the salad as the recipe suggested. All she needed was the meat. She opened the refrigerator to find the meat. Nothing. "Darn it, darn it." No meat. How was she going to fix a cobb salad with no meat?

There was an opened package of bologna. Maybe she could cut up a few pieces of bologna for the salad. Meat was meat. "It just won't look like the picture, that's all," she muttered.

Sputtering splashes on the burner interrupted her from salad preparation. The burners smoked as the soup boiled over, creating an acrid odor. Amber screamed, ran to the stove, and slid the pot off the burner.

The stove looked like someone barfed split-pea soup. Grabbing a sponge, she soaked it in warm water and wiped up the spill. Cleaning it up didn't prevent the smell of burned soup, though.

"Freak me!"

"Okay. I've been propositioned in my lifetime, but you give it a dominatrix approach." Bo stood off to the side, amusement all over his face.

"Where did you come from?" Amber scowled at Bo.

"I had to make some calls. Then I got hit with the smell of bad eggs." His gaze strayed over to the scorched pot. "Thinking that something must be wrong, I come into the kitchen to see that bubbling stew spewing over like lava." Now his gaze moved to the stove top. "If I'm not mistaken, that small curl of smoke is not promising."

"Oh, my gosh, move out of my way." She shoved him in

the gut and swung open the oven door. The butter-flavored biscuits had turned black and a few had wisps of smoke coming from their tops. Amber groaned. It was not fair. Her perfectly planned meal wasn't fit for man or beast.

She pointed the oven mitt at Bo. "Don't even think about saying anything smart. I don't know why you're here at lunchtime anyway. On Wednesdays you're holding your meetings and then you go into town to meet with the cattle-feed owner or the auctioneer." Her anger needed an outlet and his smug smile provided the necessary ignition.

"Whoa. Maybe that's your forte."

"What?"

"Being a personal assistant. Seems to me you keep better tabs on me than I do of myself." He grinned. "From the looks of things, being a cook is a might tad difficult." He plucked the oven mitt out of her hand and moved all the pots into the sink.

Amber was willing to concede defeat, but only for a few seconds. She leaned against the counter, watching him remove the pan with the burned hockey pucks that were once biscuits. "Since you're in the mood to be helpful, let me remind you that you owe me."

"For what?" Bo's grin slowly disappeared.

"Remember when you invited all the men to lunch here at the house?"

He nodded.

Amber enjoyed seeing the worry creep into his face. "You said you would make it up by doing me a favor. That favor is now—today."

"I have a meeting."

"You're not a man of your word?" She stressed each word to emphasize her sarcasm. "I would have thought you would be up for the challenge; the chance to rectify your wrongdoing."

He held up his hand. "Enough. I get your point." He opened up the cupboards and pulled out a saucepan and frying pan. "Instead of standing there smiling from ear to ear, grab the shrimp scampi from the freezer and the linguine noodles."

Amber sighed with relief. "Oh, and you can't take the credit for it."

Bo tossed the package of shrimp from hand to hand. "I don't think that's honorable, do you? You're asking me to con my parents into thinking that you, the darling housekeeper, made my shrimp and linguine surprise. Why would I want to do that?"

Amber debated on what argument to use. She had several suggestions about being honorable and caring. The wicked glint in his eyes warned her that he was waiting like a preying cat to pounce on whatever she said.

"Why would you do it?" she echoed his sentiments. "Well, let me see." Taking his hand, she placed it on her chest, over her heart. "I need your expertise in an area I'm not familiar with." She moved slightly forward and let go of his hand. It fell heavily against her chest.

Bo pulled back his hand. "I don't really know all this house stuff."

"You could have fooled me. I read that cowboys have to know how to cook, rustle cattle, and camp in the wild. They also are honorable men who save damsels in distress."

He grinned. "Really. And . . . um . . . are you the damsel?" He moved a thick curl of her hair from her shoulder to her back. "The cowboy would also steal a kiss from the fainthearted female."

Amber tried to discern whether a challenge had been issued. Bo still wore a mischievous smirk. Never one to back away from a risk, she grabbed him by his collar and tiptoed, before pulling his head down to hers.

Their lips touched. A warm rush of desire swept through her body, radiating from her lower half and spilling through to her limbs. Under the avid attention of his probing tongue, her body heated with a surprised, intense passion.

Who was stealing from whom?

"Lunch is served."

Amber slowly opened her eyes. She struggled to keep from sighing against Bo's chest. When he took a few steps back, the widening space between them set the tone that the impulsive act was over and dismissed.

Amber didn't claim to be an expert photographer. The large 35 mm camera hung from her shoulder. She'd gotten it from a flea-market sale the previous summer. Besides, she didn't care much for nifty sleek models that were aimed for tourists rather than serious photographers.

As she walked toward the stables, she thought about what shots would help in the creation of her story. What could uncover the true nature of the emotionally distant man? The brooder.

The sunlight wasn't great, with a thick cloud covering that had hung around since the morning. It made the temperature remain in the fifties, slightly nippy, but bearable with her winter coat.

She stopped a few feet from the large building and took a picture of the building and the few workers busy at feeding the horses.

"Would you like to go riding?"

She hadn't noticed Bo's approach. "Not today."

"Don't tell me the horse has conquered you. You didn't strike me as the cautious type." He studied her.

"That would be your inaccurate perception."

"True. But you have to admit that walking up to my door for a job that wasn't posted is pretty damned ballsy."

Amber didn't bother to respond. Instead she admired an interesting cloud formation with the flat landscape supporting it. She picked up her camera to focus on the horizon. It didn't have a place in her story at the present time, but it didn't mean there wasn't a place for it.

She snapped the picture and lowered the camera. "What did it feel like to return home?"

Bo frowned and shrugged. "Probably the same way you'll feel when you return home."

She ignored his piercing gaze. "That depends. By the time I return home, I could be going back a hero or hanging my head." *Don't be afraid. Ask.* "How would you describe your experience?"

"You ask a lot of questions. Obviously you know something about me."

"Yes, the same as any television-watching citizen. Since I'm working for you, I think I should know a little about my employer."

"Correction, you work for my mother. As for returning home, well, that's temporary."

Amber nodded and walked ahead. She entered the stable, wrinkling her nose from the mixture of pungent odors. "Why all the horses?" She walked between the stalls, counting the horses of various sizes and colors. Some chewed quietly, following her movements with their large eyes, others snorted, nodding their heads. She looked over her shoulder to see Bo stroking one of the horses and talking softly to it. "I can't imagine that you keep a horse for each member of the family. Isn't that very expensive?"

"You are like a glass of cold water."

Amber didn't say anything because she couldn't discern whether she had been insulted or complimented.

"You're like a wake-up horn," he continued.

Again Amber wondered. "I guess as long as you don't say that I'm like horse poop, I'll file those comments away." She rolled her eyes and turned her head. "Let's get back to why you have so many horses."

"I started a program that will begin in the spring for at-risk children. We only take a handful of kids, but hopefully it can expand to more. They would come here for a week in the spring, two weeks in the summer, and a week in the fall to learn various skills. But, most of all, it's a chance away from their environment, connecting with people and kids their age that are all positive."

"Where are you getting the kids?" Amber asked, awe coloring her voice.

"We're going to get names from area schools and pastors. I have a set of counselors ready to roll out the program. There are lots of things for them do around the ranch. At the end of the program, we'll have a big outdoor barbecue cook-out and give out ribbons for various achievements."

They had reached the end of the stables. Amber couldn't help being impressed with what she'd heard. Kids having the freedom to enjoy a few days without the threat of gangs or violence outdid the average gift. The ranch and its open environment would appeal to kids' sense of adventure and love of the outdoors.

"I hope it works," she offered. This disclosure dear to Bo's heart threw her off balance. Maybe she shouldn't believe so quickly. If she really thought about it, this setup several months away provided the perfect persona. Yet she couldn't deny its noble qualities.

Her cell phone rang. It was Martha. "I'm ready when you are."

"Okay." Amber snapped shut the phone. "I'll catch up with you later. Heading out with your mother to the farmer's market."

"Uh-oh, that means you should be back in about three hours, and that's if the seafood wasn't delivered to the market."

Amber returned to the house to find Martha dressed in sweats and tennis shoes.

"Come on, honey. We're going to be in the middle of the crowd because we're leaving later than planned."

"Sorry. I was outside hearing about the mini camps for the kids."

"Huh? Don't know what you're talking about. But anyway we can discuss it in the car."

Amber didn't have time to throw a follow-up question. She had to run to catch up with Martha.

Four and half hours later, Amber turned into the driveway. Her feet throbbed. She finally understood Martha's athletic gear. Tonight her feet would be pampered.

"I'll clean the fish and add the seasonings. It'll be perfect for tomorrow." Martha looked over at her.

"I wanted to put up the curtains in the two back rooms. I'll work on that." Although Martha didn't expect her to work beyond six o'clock on weekdays and four o'clock on the weekends, she didn't have any plans for the remainder of the evening. If the time was right, she could conduct a part of her interview with Bo.

The car bounced over the dirt road, tossing its occupants. A woman stepped out of a parked compact car and waved something at them; Amber squinted to figure out what she waved. A few feet away, she discovered it was a brightly colored pocketbook that matched her outfit.

"I wonder who this is?" Martha opened her window and leaned out. "May I help you?"

Amber inspected the woman from head to toe. The small blue car didn't have any flat tires. She thought about her own experience of being stranded to feel some measure of compassion. Instead, her suspicious nature was on alert. She watched the brunette paste a bright red smile on her somewhat attractive face before approaching the car.

"Hello. I'm Tia Buckton from Cincinnati Express. I've a couple questions for you."

"I only have one thing to say to you: leave my property."

The woman ignored Martha, looking beyond her to Amber. "Who are you? The maid?" Amber didn't like her tone or the accurate perception. "How does it feel to work for a man who has committed a few shady dealings?"

"Amber, don't answer. Call Joe on the CB and have him get down here, now."

Amber did as she was told and set down the radio. "Please step back so I can drive."

"In a minute. Did you know that Bodine was at a meeting with the other owners where they discussed the new partnership that was funded by the pension monies?"

"He didn't enter into any agreement," Amber shouted.

The brunette looked surprised. "Was that a direct quote from him?" She tossed sheets of paper through the window at them. "Read. He didn't leave the male-bonding trip until four days later. If he wasn't dealing with the big boys, why didn't he leave earlier?"

The anger rose in Amber's chest. She didn't like this woman's probing questions. A few weeks ago they could have probably shared a conversation at a bar, discussing Bo Pemberton as the devil, but even though Amber didn't have all the facts, her instinct had made her slow down her judgment. She shifted her foot off the brake and poised it over the accelerator. "Back away from the car."

Just then a black SUV barreled toward them, coming to a screeching halt within inches of the car. Bo emerged from the driver's side, while Joe jumped out of the passenger side. "Amber, take my SUV and get Mom out of here," Bo said, then stormed over to the reporter, who was visibly shaken. She retreated a few steps.

"I'm within my rights." Her voice shook.

Bo glared at the woman. One of the reasons for coming home was to get away from the prying eyes and gossip of the media. But every once in a while, one bold one would come crawling up his driveway to upset his family. He didn't have to look at his mother to see that she didn't do well under the media's barrage.

"Lady, you're trespassing."

Just then the police siren sounded. He breathed a sigh of relief that they had responded so quickly. Only when the police cars came into view did he relax.

"Okay, lady, let's see some ID."

The reporter pulled her arm from the cop. "One sec. Ma'am, think about it, okay, don't work for a crook. I'll be staying in the motel down the street if you want to talk."

Bo turned to look at Amber. She had one of the pages in her hand and looked up from it as the reporter shouted her accusation. If his lawyers hadn't warned him against any kind of confrontation, he would have had a public debate for his mother's sake, for Amber's sake.

"Pressing any charges, Mr. Pemberton?" asked one of the cops.

Bo took his focus from Amber and looked at the reporter. She sure had guts and her righteous anger was plain on her face. But he wasn't in the mood to drag this out any longer. "Just get her out of here, please."

The cop nodded and waited for the reporter to get back in her car. She turned a defiant stare toward him. "I'm not through with you yet."

He offered her a mock salute and got into his mother's car. Amber had already left with his mother. He didn't know what he would say when their paths crossed again.

Bo finished his salad. The mood in the house was somber. His mother had retired to her house. Only he and his father ate at the table.

"Heard about the excitement." His father opened the topic that was on their minds.

"Figure it'll get worse as the trial gets closer." He was told it wouldn't be earlier than June.

"You know the family is behind you."

Bo reached over and squeezed his father's hand. "I know, Dad. It feels good to have the family's support."

"When do you have to talk to the lawyers again?"

"I have to go in a week to fill out some more paperwork and meet with the investigators."

"You sound exhausted. What are you doing with yourself to keep grounded? I noticed that you're up before dawn and then back late in the evening. Don't burn yourself out."

"I've got some ideas that will be awesome if everything goes according to plan." Bo shared the basic plans about the camp with his father, taking note of the older man's suggestions.

"I hope this means that you'll be here, even if it's only for a little while."

Bo heard the hope behind his father's request. "Dad, this is your dream, yours and Mom's. I'm still finding out what I want."

"I understand. Your mom and I hooked up early enough that after my military stint I was ready to come home and start my family. It wasn't even about running the farm."

"Really? I always thought it was your lifelong intent."

His father chuckled. "If your grandfather was alive, he'd give you the down and dirty of our arguments. He always took your mother's side when we had our disagreements. Then I said I was moving out—I'd take her back to New York and go on my way."

Bo dropped his fork. "You were going to leave Mom?" He couldn't picture anything breaking up his parents' marriage. They appeared to be so in sync with each other. Plus he had never entertained the thought that his father would do anything less than perfect. "Let me get a beer," Bo said. He shoved aside his salad plate and walked out of the room to get a bottle.

"Bring one for me, too."

"You can't drink, Dad."

"Is it going to kill me? Already got one foot in the grave. Just bring me the darn beer if you want to hear the story."

Bo grinned. His curiosity made the decision. He grabbed two bottles of beer and headed back to the dining room.

After long drags, his father wiped his mouth with the back of his hand, then burped. "Your mother was a feisty gal from the heart of the city. Meanwhile, I was a country boy lacking all the savvy to get her attention."

"How did you do it?"

"She came to a bar with her girlfriends. They sneaked in because she was underage. I spotted her across the room and invited her over."

"Cradle robber!"

"She was only three months underage."

"So you're only a little bit of a deviant. Wait till I see Mom."

"She walked over in this red dress that was clearly too big for her. Later she told me it was her sister's dress. Anyway, she came over and plopped down beside me. I didn't buy her a drink because I suspected that she shouldn't have been there. Instead, I offered to arm wrestle her. If I won, then she'd have to go out with me."

"That was unfair."

"That's what I thought when I made the offer. But I didn't know that I was dealing with a little minx. She stomped on my toe and slammed my hand back. Then she declared that I had to go out with her and not the other way around."

Bo thought about his short string of relationships and his one near-miss to the altar. No one had grabbed his attention with such *umph,* yet he wasn't at the point of despair about ever finding a partner.

A flash of color at the corner of his eye caught his attention. He turned to see Amber walking past the dining area, her arms laden with fabric. Maybe in another time or place, he could think of arm wrestling Amber.

"Don't think so hard, son." His father stood, leaning on his cane. "I'm going to head for bed in a few minutes. You were always my brooder. Zack is like a spark plug, full of too much damned energy. Josh is like a quiet storm, full of subdued power. But you are a worrier, troubled, somewhat of a cynic. It's got its place, but I want to see you lift that black cloud."

"Sounds like I'm a burden. I don't mean to do that."

His father limped over to him and hugged him around his shoulders. They stood motionless for a few seconds. "Life is beautiful, the good, the bad, the ugly. It's a gift."

"I know, Dad." Bo could barely speak, his emotion choked him.

His father released him and walked out of the room. "Life and all its baggage is not a punishment," he added over his shoulder.

Bo drained his bottle. Tears had welled, his feelings too close to the surface for him to bear.

Amber's soft humming swept down to him. He didn't want to think about what he was going to do or say. Taking the steps two at a time, he bounded onto the second floor with a definite pep. He strode down the hallway, his footsteps pounding in sharp contrast to the soft hum coming from the partially opened door of the guest room.

He stopped at the door, his hand only inches away from pushing it wide open. From his vantage point, he could see her busily pulling a curtain from the pile. Her hair was fastened in a ponytail, but hardly neat, yet so heavenly sexy. She climbed onto a chair under the curtain rod and reached to fasten the hooks onto the rod.

"May I help?" he offered.

She turned, startled. Her face flushed, her eyes sparkled. She looked so alive. He couldn't help wondering why he hadn't noticed the full impact of her presence.

"Sure," she replied. She remained rooted to the spot with the curtain clutched to her chest.

Bo walked over and offered his hand. "You come on down, I'll get it."

"Oh, are we playing knight in shining armor?" She took his hand and offered a bold wink.

"Yes, so let a man do it."

"Ahh." Amber sighed. "What would I do without you?" She batted her eyelashes and giggled.

Bo drew Amber into his arms, the curtains wound around her like a lacy cocoon. He kissed her. No self-doubts, no second thoughts. A slight flick over her lips to taste her flavored lip gloss. Under the parting of her lips, he smelled the fruity scent of peaches, her favorite snack. Although he thought it ungodly to keep his eyes open during a kiss, he felt compelled to see her. The thick black eyelashes framed her closed lids. He pulled away just for a moment to enjoy her serene expression.

Her eyes fluttered and he swept her up with another searing kiss. It was not time for Sleeping Beauty to awake. No thoughts mattered about the future ten minutes from now. Only the present with Amber in his arms, sharing the sweetest kiss in his life, was his reality.

Chapter Nine

"Are you ready?" Bo sat astride Onyx across from Amber.

Amber nodded. Her stomach churned. She gripped the reins tightly in her gloved hands.

Bo chuckled. "It's only an overnight trip. We're meeting the herd at the edge of the property. I changed the plans. We'll join the men farther along the trail closer to home."

Other than a petting zoo, Amber couldn't remember when she'd spent time in the company of cows, much less shorthorns or longhorns. The first item for the day was to get used to the snorts and head tossing of her horse.

Be one with the horse. The words had to have some power, or else she'd lose what little confidence she had and slip off the side to firm ground.

"I normally don't take a packhorse on my rides, but for convenience's sake, I am." He led a sturdier horse between the other two horses. It had a small amount of bundles secured to its back.

"What do we have?"

"Food, a tent, sleeping bags. You do remember that we have to camp."

"Yes, I remember, and I must've lost my mind to have agreed."

"Once you said to me that you wanted to learn and experience new things. I think you can add this to your accomplishments list." He stroked her horse's flank, calming the animal. "That is, if you don't back down."

"I'm not a quitter, Mr. Pemberton." She answered his grin with one of hers.

Half an hour later, they headed toward their destination—Harlock Falls. Amber fought to relax and not concentrate on every bump and bounce in the saddle. Even if she had worn two pairs of shorts under her jeans, she imagined that it wouldn't be enough padding for her rear.

"How many cattle is it?"

"We're on the small side with only two hundred–fifty head. The cattle takes a lot of grazing land, among other things."

Amber focused on keeping her horse walking in a straight path. "All this cowboy stuff seems pretty taxing to me. You've got to be up early in the morning before the sun has a chance to peep over the horizon. Then you do paperwork and perform the day-to-day details locked in your office. Then, as far as when you sleep, I have no idea."

"You certainly know how to take the glamour out of the profession."

"And you do this by yourself?"

He shrugged, clearly embarrassed by her candor.

She rode alongside him, her thoughts whirring at high speed. "Who did all of this when you weren't here?"

"My father did." Bo nodded at her obvious confusion. "Bad back and all. He relied heavily on Joe, who has a financial interest in the property. But in his heart he wanted to pass the legacy on to the family. Unfortunately, none of his sons had that burning desire to stand ankle deep in cow poop and ride a horse for more hours than our feet actually touch the ground."

"A little exaggerated, but I get your point. It seems to me that your father picked up on your talents early in life. Over your brothers, he took you in hand and showed you the ropes."

He grinned. "Yeah, and they're all broken up over it." Onyx snorted, clearly enjoying the joke as well.

Amber answered with a smile.

Bo pulled Onyx to a halt. "Need a little break?"

Amber raised her rear end out of the saddle. She grimaced. "Yeah, but I'm afraid if I rest that I may not get back in the saddle." She moaned. "How far have we traveled?"

Brad scanned the horizon. "Maybe three to four miles." He bit his lip in a poor effort to keep from smiling. "We have another three to go."

Amber had dismounted, weighing the decision to get off and head for a big boulder because nature called or bite back the discomfort and stay in the saddle for another couple hours. Her stomach growled. The perfect excuse.

"Let's take a quick break," she stated.

They made quick meals of turkey sandwiches, barbecue potato chips, and lemonade. Already the temperature had dropped as the afternoon sun started its descent. Amber pulled out her gloves and zipped up her coat. Her teeth chattered. Why did she ever think she could sleep outdoors?

Bo gathered up the wrappings and Amber folded the blanket. Neither had said much. Amber was too preoccupied with the numbness in her rear to chat. As she tried to stand from the kneeling position, she couldn't contain her discomfort any longer. "Owww." She stumbled and finally righted herself.

Bo hurried over from the packhorse, arriving in time to give her a much needed supporting boost by the elbow. Never mind that her legs went to rubber because his chest brushed against her back, or his breath gently ruffled her hair. "Steady now, partner," he teased. "Looks like I may have to lift you onto your saddle."

"Not on your life, mister." She couldn't bear for him to lift her. And then there was the other problem. She wasn't sure she'd release him once he had deposited her onto her horse. She pushed him away, gritted her teeth, and walked over to her horse.

Bo's roaring laughter startled her. "You look a sight. Why are you walking like you've got issues between your legs?"

How could a man who looked so good be such a pain in the behind? She waved away his irritating question and concentrated on her immediate mission—mounting her horse that suddenly seemed a mile high.

Bo mounted Onyx with envious ease and perched in his saddle with an imperial air. Amber tried to imitate his posture, but shooting pains in her lower back stopped her. Defeat had its sting. It hurt to admit that she couldn't go any farther. Obviously she didn't have the stamina to be a cowboy.

Bo dismounted and secured Onyx. Without a word, he walked over to her horse and raised his hands to rest on her waist. "You're a trooper, but I can't watch you suffer." Before she could protest, albeit weakly, he raised her off the saddle while she disentangled her feet from the stirrups. Under her fingers, she felt the steely cords of his muscles shifting as he gently set her down.

"Thank you." She gulped. "Guess I get an F."

"I'm going to unpack the other horse and pitch the tent. It's safe to say that we're here for the night."

"Go ahead, make me feel really bad. How far do you usually travel to meet the herd?"

"Actually, I don't meet them. When I was younger, I would go on the cattle ride with them. It was fun being around the men, learning things that would never be in a textbook. I learned how to survive on the land."

"So this was mainly for my benefit?" She asked the question, although it was more of a statement. "It's appreciated. Can I at least help with something?"

"Sure, there are some ingredients for a quick meal."

"Am I doing the food because I'm a woman?" She squinted at him, partly because the afternoon sun blinded her and partly because she was ready to cut him off at the knees if he had any chauvinistic tendencies.

Bo didn't say anything. Instead he lifted the hefty burlap wrapped by thick twine and dropped it down by her feet. Then he took out the can of baked beans and cooked pork chops and made himself comfortable in a cleared area.

Amber couldn't read Bo's expression. Was she being ignored? "What about the tent?" She pointed to the pile at her feet.

"I've got the food, you can do the tent."

Amber frowned, biting her lip. The son-of-a-gun had set her up. "I can't."

He cupped his hand near his ear. "Huh? What's that? You can't?" His voice grew steadily louder.

Amber bit back a swear word that would have made her mother gasp. "I don't know how to pitch a tent."

Bo worked the manual can opener around the baked beans. When he was finished, he set it down and leaned over on his thigh. "Would you like me to set up the tent?"

She nodded. "And I'll get the food," she rushed on, knowing that he couldn't wait to throw it back to her.

It didn't matter. Bo did grin at her, throwing a bold wink her way. "The meat only needs to be reheated. I brought a small dab of mustard for the baked beans. Gives it a nice kick."

"I don't like mustard." She wasn't lying, but if she was going to be in charge of food, it would be to her satisfaction.

Bo unfolded the tent and made quick work out of setting up the frame. Amber knew if she had kept that task, there would be no tent erected. Anyway, all she had to do was heat up the food and serve his lordship. She could manage that.

With the pots filled, plates and plastic ware resting on a rock, dinner appeared to be a few minutes away. There was one more problem, though.

"Uh . . . Bo, I'll need a fire." She blamed her mother for not signing her up in Girl Scouts. Then she could rub together two sticks and "poof," her fire would appear.

The tent was set and Bo stood proudly next to his masterpiece with one hand on the tent and the other on his hip. "Anything for you. Because after all, my time is your time since I've finished with my task."

"Did your brothers ever try to drown you? I mean, I can't imagine you ever winning a popularity contest with that giant-sized ego."

Bo tipped his hat toward her and went into the tent. Amber stopped her speech as she saw him tying the door closed.

"What are you doing?" she asked, too alarmed that she was left outside.

"I'm trying to enjoy a moment's peace without you nagging at me."

Amber looked around. The plains that had looked so fertile and rich now scared her with the creeping afternoon shadow. "You are going to make a fire, right? Plus, it's getting cold."

"It usually does in winter." He left the tent and busied himself with getting the materials for the fire. Meanwhile, she stirred the pot of cold baked beans, wondering for the millionth time why she had agreed to do this. There was no doubt left in her mind that she was not cut out for this, and that she was being the biggest burden.

Within a few minutes, a healthy blaze roared. Bo went to tend to the horses while she unwrapped the meat. She noticed that he'd packed a large fork. She stabbed the thick meat, wondering if Bo would have gone to all this trouble if he was traveling with the men. She squatted before the fire and held the meat on the fork over the fire.

It wasn't quite dusk, but a vivid scarlet and golden hue covered the horizon as a backdrop to the sun. She admired the open air, finally relaxing in her new surroundings. The fire added a comforting warmth. She leaned back her head and closed her eyes, enjoying the heat along her neck.

"For heaven's sake, woman, what are you doing?"

Amber snapped to attention, slightly shaken up at Bo's shout near her head. "Ow." She dropped the fork, which had retained the heat, but not before seeing the pork chop in full blaze at the end of the prongs. "Bo, help me, the pork chop is in the fire."

"I'm about to throttle you." He stood looking into the fire, scratching his head. "There should be another piece. I'm going to heat it."

"I had both pieces on the fork. It fit," she added.

He threw up his hands. "I quit. You win."

"Win what?"

"Whatever it is, you win. I'm going home."

Amber didn't like losing. And she didn't like having Bo think she wasn't capable of the simplest task. "No, you're not going anywhere." She walked over to the horse and pulled out her cell phone from the saddlebag.

"You packed your cell phone?"

"Never know when there's an emergency. Since we're not that far from the house, we should still get reception, right?" She looked at the display window, praying that it'd show a strong signal. Satisfied, she punched in the number for directory assistance.

When Bo started to question her, she held up her hand. She requested the number to the nearest pizza delivery shop close to the Pemberton ranch. Once she got the phone number, she placed the order for a large pepperoni, sausage, and ham pizza.

"Good thinking, we'll have pizza when we get home."

"We're not going home." She dialed the ranch and spoke to Martha. "Take the phone. You mom needs directions." She crossed her arms as Bo gave his mother directions to their camp.

Bo snapped the cell phone shut. "My mother is actually going to bring the pizza out here?"

"Yes."

"Both of you have lost your minds. Why are we staying here?"

"Because you've no faith in me. Your mother didn't even ask any questions. She understood."

"From one nut to another."

She waved off his remark and retired to the tent. A thick comforter and blankets lined the ground. She plopped down on the soothing cushioned floor and popped off her boots. Screaming of self-indulgence, she lay on her back and wallowed in the softness against her tired muscles.

"And what do you mean I have no faith in you?" Bo's sudden intrusion startled her soft moan of satisfaction. He was partly in the tent with his lower half poking out.

Amber propped herself onto her elbows. "I can see it in your eyes. You think I'm a total flake, and when I make a mistake, it's great amusement, or in this case, major irritation. I don't know why I'm all thumbs whenever you're around, but I am capable of successes." She'd made her speech in what she hoped was a grand manner full of confidence. Little did he know how close she was to throwing her hands up at her new career choice.

"All I seem to do around you is apologize," he muttered. "I'm just a little hungry and when I saw that juicy pork chop on fire, I short-circuited." He crawled into the tent. "Here, I'm going to hang the lantern up here."

Amber scooted over, keenly aware of the tight surroundings, with Bo's large frame overpowering it and her senses. They sat next to each other, her arm brushing heavily against his. His body heat sent her emotions reeling in a delightful dance. She could have floated as she entertained the thought of kissing him.

She looked up into his face, searching for some acknowledgment that he was equally affected. The smokiness of his eyes staring back at her with smoldering desire set her body tingling. If she dared speak now, she would utter sheer gibberish.

A car horn honked nearby. The mood broke. She crawled to the exit, grateful for an excuse to breathe under the open sky. Another minute next to Bo and she would have draped herself around him and probably begged him to kiss her. She groaned at the thought. Decidedly pleasurable.

"Amber? Here's your pizza. Where is my grumpy son? I know he must be giving you hell."

Amber felt some need to defend Bo. "I'm sure he's hungry."

Martha surveyed the area. "The temperatures are supposed to drop tonight. Are you sure you want to do this? You rode a horse, pitched a tent, started a fire. There's not much more to a cattle drive, you know."

"Did you ever go out with Will on a cattle drive?"

"Yes, I did several times, but that was because we didn't have enough help at the time. Once the boys made their appearance, I chose to stay home with them. When they were old enough, they went with their father on the trip. Jake was the only one who didn't like it. On one trip, I had to meet them fifty miles away to pick him up. That boy complained about his back, his butt, his legs. All I could tell him was to soak himself in the tub in some really warm water. I don't even know if he still rides." She chuckled over the memories.

Amber looked back at the tent. Bo had emerged and was retying a few of the anchoring ropes around the tent. He looked up in their direction and waved. "Hi, Mom. You're playing pizza delivery. Must be pretty boring at home."

Amber ignored the sarcasm, especially when she saw Martha grin. "You're darn right it's boring. Heck, if you had space in the tent, I'd spend the night with you, as your chaperone." She threw her head back and laughed.

Heat shot up Amber's neck to her face. She kept her gaze fastened at her feet. Only Martha's hilarity pierced the embarrassing silence.

"You're quite welcomed to stay, Mom. And I can return home where I can actually do something productive."

Amber glared at him.

"The pizza is getting cold. Martha, thank you so much for

bringing this out here. Your generosity is certainly refreshing at this time."

"Okay, but if you need me to come get you, I'm a phone call away. Bo, be a gentleman, even if it kills you," Martha scolded.

Amber remained where she was until Martha had driven away. "You certainly know how to destroy a mood."

He grunted at her, then relieved her of the pizza box. "Like you said, it's getting cold."

Pizza and soda made up dinner. Amber discovered a baggy of chocolate chip cookies Martha had provided as a wonderful dessert treat. They lounged comfortably against a couple boulders, enjoying the comforting heat from the fire.

Evening had now fully descended. Without the lights from a city or buildings, the area was pitched into an eerie darkness. Only the full blaze of the fire provided an intense brightness in their immediate area. Amber paid notice of every animal call, rustling, and distant echoes of unfamiliar sounds. She could do this. The experience would add a great flavor to her article.

"Do you plan to keep silent all night?"

Bo shook his head and stood. "What I am planning to do is to get some sleep. We have to be up early and be on our way." He unrolled a sleeping bag and laid it on the ground.

Amber looked back at the tent a few feet away. There was absolutely no way she was sleeping in it by herself. She looked at the spot Bo was industriously making into a makeshift bed. Sleeping outdoors where bugs could crawl over her face didn't appeal to her either. She bit her lip, trying to decide what to do. "Bo?" She waited until he looked up. "I think it would be best if we stayed in the tent."

"And I think it would be best if I slept right here."

Now he wanted to play games. It didn't matter. She planned

to get her way tonight. She'd rather deal with Bo's ornery nature than a scorpion or some other creepy crawly making tracks over her face. Without providing him with a good defense, she walked over to his bedding and scooped it up.

"Hey, wait a minute. Put it down."

"Sure, come and get it." She walked over to her tent and dropped it on the floor. Then she rearranged it to match his set up.

The flaps to the tent whipped back. He stood silhouetted by the light from the fire. "I am not sleeping in here."

"And I'm not sleeping out there. Since I obviously have to remind you, your mother said you should be a gentleman even if it kills you." She patted his bedding.

He stormed out.

Amber smiled to herself. "Oh, by the way, I'm changing into my pajamas, so give me a few minutes before coming back in."

Bo turned to shoot back a caustic reply. The words fizzled away at the sight of Amber's silhouette as she changed in the tent. He lowered his head and walked away. "Damned woman!" He walked over to the horses, who snorted at his arrival. "You'll have to deal with me until she's done." He looked up at the tent, glad to see that she was buttoning her shirt. Yet it didn't erase the memory of the sexy profile of her entire body.

He brushed the horse's coat in short strokes. How could he possibly sleep in the same tent? One thing was for sure, he wouldn't get any sleep, being aware of her just a few inches away. He'd have to be dead not to be aroused by this temptation.

"Bo, I'm finished."

He cringed at how she sang those words. He may not know everything about Amber Delaney, but he did recognize when she felt she'd scored a point. Fine. He would go in, get into his sleeping bag, and close his eyes.

Before entering, he took a deep breath. As soon as he stepped in, he sniffed the air. Vanilla. He glanced down to see her rubbing her hands together. Good gracious. How was he going to sleep when she smelled so sweet?

"I brought a few cleansing wipes. Figured you'd like to clean off some of that dust." She smiled. "I've used tons."

He took the bag. She did look fresh and clean. Now that she'd mentioned the dust, he felt it caked on his body, his face, neck, and hands. Her skin positively glowed. He glanced down at his hands and could see the dirt in the creases of his hand and along his fingernails.

"Use as many as you need. I have a few more in my pocket-book."

He thanked her and proceeded to wipe his face and down his neck.

"Here, let me help you. Take off your shirt. I'll try to be quick, since it's freezing."

He complied. He loved seeing her blush. Her eyes glittered as her gaze wandered over his chest. He discovered that not only did he enjoy her admiration of his body, but he didn't want it to end.

She took a cloth and gently wiped a small area around his neck. "I won't break," he said. She giggled and then wiped again. This time, she wiped across his chest, with one hand on his shoulder to steady herself. His skin reacted to her touch like an electric shock. He closed his eyes to break the spell. She was too close to his face. Her fingers pressed into his shoulder as she continued to clean him with such gentleness that it stirred a very male response he'd managed to put a lid on for a long time.

"Am I hurting you?"

He shook his head, clearing his throat at the same time. He didn't trust his voice to speak now.

"I'm almost done. Let me get your back. Lie on your stomach—that way you won't be as cold."

She could have told him to hit his head on a rock and he would have done it. The woman had the power to make him like putty in her hands. His usual defense was to hold on to any pretense of anger to keep focused and not fall to her feet like a blithering idiot.

"When are you leaving us, Amber?" He rested his head on his arms while she wiped his back.

"I don't really know. Soon." She continued to wipe his shoulders. "I'm all done."

"Thank you. That almost doubled as a massage." He grinned, putting on a thick sleeping shirt.

"Well, I'm sure you needed it after the ride." Amber slid under the blankets and pulled them up to her chin, but not before he saw her mouth tremble.

"Cold."

She nodded. He unzipped his sleeping bag and pulled her bedding over. Very gently, he slipped his arm under her head and encircled her body. "I'll try to be the perfect gentleman," he whispered into her hair.

Amber turned her face toward his; the tips of their noses touched. "Not too perfect, I hope." She kissed him, soft and sweet, like her vanilla scent.

He groaned. Then pulled her toward him. He lowered his mouth on hers, hungry, desperate, craving more from her. Their lips ignited sparks that threatened to make him combust. How long had he ached to come alive, to care, to feel. This free spirit had tumbled her way into his life and he wanted to hang on for dear life, lest it was all a dream.

She raised up and straddled him. Slowly she unbuttoned

her shirt. He wanted to stop her, to tell her it wasn't proper. Employee and employer, and all that stuff. He really did want to protest and be noble. And his mouth had actually opened.

Then she took off her shirt and his chivalric words fizzled. It wasn't about her body and, Lord knows, it was a beautiful sight. From the first day of meeting her when she had knocked down the fence post, he had seen a boldness characteristic of a risk taker. He found it refreshing, like a douse of cold water on a sleepy body. In many ways, it shocked him, even scared him, but he found that when she wasn't around, he felt restless.

Sitting on her hips, she stared back at him. "Give me your hand."

She took his hand and placed it on her stomach, dragging it up her body between her breasts. He felt like a high school boy. As his hand traveled through the valley and slid over a breast, he had to concentrate on maintaining control and not flipping her to take their foreplay to another level.

Her taut nipples contrasted to the soft mounds. He gently pulled her toward him, planting a soft kiss on one dark tip. She moaned, arching her body. She offered and he took. He flicked the nipple with his tongue, eliciting another moan. And then he sucked, enjoying the softness, the warmth of her breast. She held his head tightly against it, and if he could devour her, he would.

They pulled apart, both needing some breathing space. The temperature in the tent had to have risen several degrees. It might have been winter outside, but under this waterproof home for the night, they had the burner set on HIGH.

"I want you to know that I don't do this. I don't sleep around, especially with my employers."

Her statements were honest, the message sincere. However,

it had the added effect of introducing a dose of reality to their sensual affair. First, he didn't have any protection. Second, his family had employed her.

"No need to come up with an excuse," she continued. "I can see from your face that a mistake was about to be made here." She rolled off him and quickly put on her top, concentrating on each button.

"It's not that, Amber. I don't think it's a good idea for that to be between us."

She nodded and turned away from him, pulling the blanket over most of her head. "There are occasions when it's okay to throw out the rules."

Bo reached out to lay a reassuring hand on her shoulder. She stiffened at his touch and he removed it with a long sigh.

Chapter Ten

Amber only saw occasional glimpses of Bo late in the evenings when he came in, grunted, and retreated to his study. She kind of expected that reaction, given the way they had parted company a few days before. The remedy for feeling ignored was to keep busy.

With that determination, she tied a scarf around her head to keep the cobwebs from falling into her hair. Gloves in hand and armed with a couple large trash bags, she entered the shed. Martha wanted the Christmas decorations to be brought into the house, including the Kwanzaa set.

An hour later, she'd hauled four large boxes out of the shed. Her scarf was long gone, as it had only made her hotter. She didn't see any more boxes marked *DECORATIONS*, although there were many more boxes of various sizes pushed toward the back, seemingly forgotten.

She saw a tall, odd-shaped box partially hidden behind an oversize one. The shape was strange in comparison to the others, but what had caught her eye was Bo's name scrawled across the side with the words HIGH SCHOOL AND COLLEGE.

Immediately, she rearranged the boxes to create a path. Then she tugged and shifted the tall box until she had it in the clear path to be pulled to near the shed's door. It didn't take long, but it was a dusty endeavor. After a sneezing fit, she pulled up a step stool and began her discovery phase.

She flipped through a couple years of yearbooks, giggling at the sight of Bo with his Afro and fat bow tie. She read a few of the autographs for revelations about any infatuations. He definitely had his share of groupies, but she didn't see any particular one who stood out with a declaration of undying devotion.

In the section featuring the high school organizations, he was president of the student government association, a member of the chess club, and vice president of the young business leaders. "Couldn't have predicted otherwise," she muttered.

"Really," a familiar voice taunted.

Even if she wanted to appear calm at Bo's unexpected presence, her pulse raced with excitement. "Taking a breather?"

He ran a hand over his hair and sighed. "Yeah. I'm in the middle of negotiating the price we pay for the cattle feed. I think we're getting shafted, but the supplier won't budge."

Amber looked up at him, squinting against the midday sun high in the sky. His face looked drawn with a slight puffiness under the eyes. She wanted to stand near him and gently kiss away the stress. Simply touching him wouldn't even suffice.

"Why don't you take a load off and plough through this box with me?"

He looked at his watch.

"See you're in the mood for digging up my memories." He pulled over a box and sat. "I can spend a few minutes."

"Good." Amber thanked him with a huge grin. With renewed vigor, she dived into the box and pulled out a shoe box. She sensed that this wasn't a matter of him holding on to his favorite pair of shoes.

"Aaah, I'm not sure you should be seeing this." He reached for the box, but she pulled it away from him.

"Now you know you've made me curious as all get out." Before he could protest, she flicked off the top. The box was filled with letters, postcards, and small notepaper. A soft floral scent wafted up to her nose. "A woman," she stated matter-of-factly.

"I can't believe my mother kept these letters." A small smile played on his lips. "Here, let me take it."

"No way." Amber giggled. "Finders keepers." She wrapped her arms around the box.

Bo looked at the box and then at Amber.

"While you stand there debating whether you can take this box from me, I'm going to delve right in." Keeping a close eye on Bo, she pulled out a letter. Elaborately she waved the letter under her nose. "Was she your first? I heard you usually fall in love with your first and it ends up being your first heartbreak."

"Is this like girl talk? I don't plan to spend another minute discussing that part of my life with you."

"Discuss with me or I go to your mother." She flicked the letter in his face and gave him the biggest grin she could muster.

"Mere threats don't move me. Wait!" He raised a staying hand against her arm. "Why don't we compromise? You tell me a few juicy details and I'll tell you mine."

Amber mulled over the proposition. With a careless

shrug, she nodded her agreement. There wasn't much to tell. "I'll ask my question first. Did being rich give you an advantage with the girls?"

Bo exhaled. "Heck, woman, you know how to sneak in a punch. We never thought we were rich. My father and uncles struggled to keep this ranch going. Even now, there's not that much profit, but it's become our way of life."

"When I go into town, the people talk about your family in this reverent tone. You may act like this ranch and all this property mean nothing, but you know you're a rich man."

"And that makes me a bad guy?"

"It gives you opportunities and privileges that regular folk don't enjoy. It's only natural for me to think that some women would sell their soul to be with you."

"What rich guy turned your heart to stone?"

"Look, I'm not saying that all rich guys are bad or that money makes you evil. But if you're honest with yourself, you'll admit that I have a point."

"No, I will not play along with your idiotic theories. You don't think there're bad poor guys, bad middle-income guys? Give me a break, Amber. You carry around that big chip on your shoulder like a trophy. You're ready to tip over from the weight."

"Coming from the man who ran home to hide and picked up where he left off with the family business."

"I think our conversation is over." Bo stood and took the box from her hands. "You're a strange one. I constantly wonder why you bother to work for a family you hold in such scornful contempt." He took a few steps and then turned to face her, opened his mouth to address her, then shook his head and turned away.

Amber's face burned. Embarrassment and annoyance with herself made her want to run and hide. The moment had been laced with flirtation, but somehow took a turn for the worse. Since she seemed to be in a mood to be brutally honest, she had to admit that she had put her foot knee-high in the muck.

Once her task of cleaning out the shed was completed, Amber faced having to reenter the house. She didn't know if Bo was at home.

She walked into the house with the intent to head straight for the shower. Her muscles ached and she wanted to wash the dirt, both real and self-imposed, from her body.

"Oh, I didn't know anyone was here." Bo stood at the counter, staring out the window. He had to have seen her approach. Yet he didn't turn in her direction when she came into the kitchen.

Amber paused a few seconds to observe, to judge the level of his anger. Only the constant tic of his jaw proved that he hadn't turned to stone.

She cleared her throat. "I guess an apology is in order."

His jaw continued working.

"I'm taking my frustration out on you. Some things in my past made me leery. I'm truly sorry for offending you."

He turned his head slowly. Amber braced herself as he cast a frigid glare upon her. "You'll have to do better than that. I'm tired of having to defend myself to you. What do you mean 'some things in my past'?" He crossed his arms and leaned against the counter for her to begin.

A lie could suffice. But she felt genuine remorse for her loose tongue and didn't want to detract from her apology. "When I was younger and my parents separated, my mother's brother gave us a helping hand. He was quite wealthy with a huge house, a young wife, and no children.

"While my mother traveled to find work, I was at the mercy of his stiff rules and his wife's fickle choices. We stayed with him for six long months. When I needed clothes, he took me to the secondhand shop and loudly announced that he needed to get clothes for a relative who had landed on his doorstep. At each dinner meal, he'd say a prayer. The prayer always referred to our penniless state and how he was saving us from being a burden on the state welfare rolls.

"My mother swallowed her pride and focused on earning enough money to get us out of there. I wouldn't tell her what he'd say, but I didn't have to hide it because I could hear him berate her whenever she returned home. Things really heated up when his wife said she wanted my mother to leave.

"Do you know what that does to a child to hear that message about being a burden every day? You start to believe it. Believe that it's a crime to be born without wealth. Although I'm older now, I have to consciously battle against the prejudice. At times, it has such a hold on me, I feel as if I'm choking." A tremor shook her words, but she bit back any feelings to break down and cry. She couldn't admit that her uncle was the owner of the newspaper she worked for. After all these years, she had turned to the same man who'd made her feel like dirt and asked for a job.

Her uncle hadn't lashed out the way he had so many years ago. Instead he'd given her the job and salary without a second thought, as if she wasn't even worth further consideration. That's when she vowed that she would be his best reporter. At this moment, she realized that as much as she hated the power his wealth gave him, she always sought his approval.

The lump in her throat threatened to choke her. She blinked rapidly to fend off the tears. Her blurred gaze caught Bo taking giant steps over to her. She felt herself being crushed in the safety and warmth of his powerful arms. All she wanted to do was surrender against his hard chest and stay there until her world righted again.

"I appreciate your honesty," he said softly.

His hand stroked her hair. Although it would be a tad bit awkward if his father or mother came in, she kept her head against his chest, listening to the heavy beat of his heart.

Bo stepped back and tilted up her chin. Staring deeply into her eyes, he said with a touch of gentleness, "I'm not ready to let you go. Would you come with me to a dance tonight?"

Amber wiped her face. "I don't think so. It wouldn't be appropriate."

"You sound like someone out of a historical novel. My mother and father will be there, if you're in need of chaperones. The dance is the annual holiday celebration thrown by the mayor. It's more a political necessity than a social event."

"Then you don't need me."

"I do need you. And I want you there." He sighed. "You really do a number on my brain."

She snorted and pushed him away. She'd keep it to herself, but he did a number to her brain, as well. Going to a dance and standing at his side for the evening would place her in a difficult position.

"You're thinking too much. It's yes or no."

Amber admired his direct approach, but it didn't make her decision any easier. "You're my boss. I just don't feel comfortable. Plus, we've already crossed the lines and it makes both of us very uncomfortable."

"Okay. You run along and go play with more curtains upstairs."

Amber didn't bother to respond. She walked away and headed for the shower. Now she was not only dirty from working in the shed, but also overheated from standing so close to a man who had her emotions in knots.

An hour later, she heard the family gather in the foyer. *Let them enjoy themselves.* She, in the meantime, would hem the curtains, like a proper housekeeper.

"Amber?"

Amber stopped drawing the needle. "In here." The door pushed open wider.

Martha stepped into the room. "So you're really not going with us."

"I don't think it's my place."

"When I told Bo to invite you, it wasn't meant to be as the hired help."

Amber hid her surprise. She thought Bo had been caught up in the moment of her confession and invited her to attend with him. She bit back the smile at her vanity.

"Please say you'll change your mind?" Martha begged.

Amber looked at Martha's Western boots and prairie skirt complete with ruffles and fringed top. "I'm not sure I have anything in my closet for the occasion."

Martha grinned. "It's a square-dancing theme. You could wear jeans and a shirt. I've got a hat to loan."

Amber shook her head. Martha's excitement always drew her in. "I'm sure I would have a wonderful time, but I don't want to keep you."

"Fair enough. I'll have Bo drop us off and then come back and get you." She waved her hand. "Nope, I don't want to hear anything else but a yes."

"Yes." Amber set aside the curtains. The night would have proven to be extremely lonely with only the curtains to keep her company. Although she wasn't the social-butterfly type, it mattered that she would be spending a few hours with Bo.

* * *

"Why are you playing the wallflower, young lady?" Will offered Amber a glass of punch. "I'm the only one allowed to stand on the sidelines." He switched his cane to the other hand and pointed. "Out there is where you need to be. You look absolutely stunning in Western gear." He motioned to another man also standing on the sidelines. "Tim Walkerman, I'd like you to meet Amber Delaney. It's her first time line dancing." They shook hands and exchanged the regular pleasantries.

The band started a new song on cue. The lively toe-tapping beat worked its way into her head. One glance at the synchronized dancing moves between the men and women had her mesmerized as their feet danced intricate choreography. The room would have to be darkened by several degrees before she would attempt the dance.

"Want to give it a try?"

"Oh, no, thanks." Amber didn't want to make a spectacle of herself; maybe if she saw another woman who looked liked it was her first time, she would feel more comfortable.

"How about a glass of punch, then?" Tim asked.

Amber nodded. She remained off to the side while Tim battled his way across the room to the bar. It would take him a few minutes before he returned with her drink. She continued to scan the room, knowing in her heart that she was only looking for one familiar face. She spotted him on the dance floor smiling with an exuberant young woman in a shockingly red-fringed outfit. Her skirt swished sexily around her legs as she flicked her foot in a high stepping march.

Briefly, partners were exchanged. She noticed that whenever Bo had the woman who perfectly matched his height in his arms, they chatted. And, really, did the woman have to giggle so much? It was starting to become annoying.

"There you are. I thought you'd run off," Tim said, startling her. He had her glass of punch as promised and she thanked him.

"You can't leave here without trying out one dance step. It's my duty as hospitality chair."

Amber offered a perfunctory smile and inched her way to the left so she could still keep an eye on Bo over Tim's shoulder.

"Are you a relative of the Pembertons?" he asked.

"No." Amber offered a quick smile and averted her eyes.

"Oh, a friend?"

Obviously he was going to be persistent. She looked at him, debating on what appropriate reply could satisfy him, yet still maintain her privacy.

"Staying at the ranch? You know, some of us call it our very own castle. People love the Pembertons. They are a generous lot."

Amber felt her eyebrow shoot up and she worked to keep the irritation off her face. The man had no idea how sickening he sounded, fawning over the family. It always came back to money.

The song ended and another followed without a break. However, she noticed that Bo escorted the woman off the floor, his hand lingering along her waist. They continued their walk through the crowd and exited the room. She tiptoed to try to see if they, or at least Bo, would return soon.

"Looking for someone?" Tim turned toward the doorway.

"I think Martha is calling for me." Amber offered an apologetic shrug. "Excuse me, Tim. Well, it was nice meeting you." Quickly, she walked away before he recovered. She hoped Martha would stay right there talking to Will until she made her way over to her.

* * *

Bo stood alone in the lobby, enjoying the cool night air that managed to blow in whenever the oversized entrance doors opened and closed. He had spent the better part of the night keeping up with the dance steps and keeping an eye on Amber across the room. She'd been at Tim Walkerman's side, smiling up into the imbecile's face. He gritted his teeth, frustrated with himself for that reaction. After all, why should he care with whom Amber chose to be friendly?

He shoved his fists into his pockets and headed for the door. He wanted more than a few whiffs of fresh air. The confines of the dance hall and even the lobby bore down on him. He pushed open the doors and braced himself for the crisp, wintry night air.

Without his coat, the chilled air had a bite. He wrapped his arms around himself and rubbed his arms vigorously. Costumed folk came and went from the dance hall. The men tipped their hats or gave him a short wave as they went about their business. A few of the single women cast flirtatious smiles and even a brazen wink or two at him.

He leaned his shoulder against the balcony post, staring up at the sky. The stars twinkled alongside a full moon that threw an ethereal glow along the landscape. Even though urban sprawl had taken over the major Texas cities, he still loved the rugged terrain of his birthplace. In his bones, in his blood, he was a Texan. He supposed that it took leaving and sitting in the corporate world to figure out that this is where he should be.

He shifted his position, leaning over the balcony. Maybe he was indulging in childhood fantasies about the romantic life of a cowboy. Practicality had to reign because he had to think about his pension, retirement, his future as a businessman.

"Oh, I didn't know you were here."

He jumped, but didn't turn. Amber walked over and took a position next to him.

"Needed some air," he said.

"I can understand. It's a bit stuffy in there with all that dancing. I see you can hold your own in that department."

He smiled appreciatively at her compliment.

"You and that lady make quite a couple. Almost looked like professionals to me."

"Frannie is a dear friend of mine." He waited for Amber to say something, but when she didn't, he continued. "I like dancing with her."

"Well, it's getting cold out here. I'm going to head back inside."

Bo blocked her path. He didn't like the edge in her tone as if she was mad at him. But there was no reason for her to be angry. "Stay a while. Please." He looked into her big brown eyes, willing her not to take flight.

She tossed her chin over her shoulder, although her eyes pinned him. "Won't Frannie mind?"

"Probably." He shrugged. "But only because she's trying to make a point to her husband that he should take dance lessons."

"Oh."

He loved the way her mouth made that perfect O. "Did that bite a bit?" He grinned. "Seeing me with another woman?"

Amber scowled. "That would mean I cared about you." She walked over to the balcony and hiked her hip onto the rail while her legs dangled. "Not happening, Mr. Ego."

He admired her legs where the hem of the skirt rested. He'd never seen her work out, but her body was firm and toned. Conscious of his open admiration, she placed her hands on the bare portion of her thighs. "It's not every day that I get to see a woman blush," he said.

"I'm not blushing."

Either she was blushing or suffering from a hot flash. He noticed her attempt to fan herself with her hand. He pulled a handkerchief out of his pocket and handed it to her. "Mind you, it's not unattractive, but I know you'd kill me if I didn't let you fix that eye makeup that makes you have features similar to a raccoon."

She snatched the handkerchief, hissing between her teeth when he laughed. He enjoyed teasing her. Actually, he liked her company. The thought sobered him. It stood on top of the tumultuous emotions she managed to inspire within him. "Will you be here for Christmas?" She didn't answer immediately. "I noticed that you didn't go home for Thanksgiving. I wasn't sure if you had plans for the holidays, because you could stay with me . . . my family, that is." His words tumbled out, leaving him winded.

He waited for a few seconds. "What's waiting for you at home?" After he asked the question, he regretted it. Her shoulders had visibly slumped and she now looked down at her hands. "I didn't mean to intrude." Although he could offer words of reassurance that he respected her privacy, in reality he wanted to know everything.

"I haven't really thought about it. But even if I stay, I won't hang around the house for Christmas."

"Why not? The day after, we begin celebrating Kwanzaa. Mom is not going to be happy if you're not there. Nope." He raised his hand to stem her objections. "I know what you're thinking, but there will be no compromise. You have to stick around for Kwanzaa." Besides, he had his own selfish reasons to see that she stuck around.

"I haven't decided, as yet."

"There you two are. I was wondering where you'd gone." Martha cleared her throat and stepped in between them. "It's a beautiful night, isn't it? Bo, you should be in there getting to know the city council."

Bo looked at Amber over the top of his mother's head. She didn't look his way, but he saw the small smile tug at her lips. She was aware that he stared at her.

"Why?" Most of them looked at him as if he had committed a crime.

His mother touched his arm, waiting for him to look at her. Who he saw sent all his rebellious thoughts out of his head. She had always been a strong figure in his life, willing to play warrior when necessary or the shy, retiring housewife to get what she wanted. Under the soft moonlight, in the midst of a fund-raising dance, he saw his mother without his prejudicial baggage. She had aged, gracefully by fashion magazines' standards, with a few deep creases along her forehead and around her mouth. The once-black hair now was stark white and was restrained in a bun most of the time.

She glanced over her shoulder in both directions. Bo leaned closer as she hunched her shoulders. "I've heard from a reliable source that there are several on the council who don't believe in preserving what belongs to us. They've bought into the idea that we must copy the big cities' philosophy to expand and cover every acre with a concrete monstrosity." Her voice was no longer an angry whisper. At the moment, her passion overtook any caution she held in reserve. "This is why you need to focus on meeting them and getting our position across."

"Why would they listen to me?"

"Some will believe you," Amber offered. She didn't look up at him, but it warmed his heart nevertheless to hear the sincerity in her words.

"And some won't," he replied. He wanted to ask her whether she believed him. After spending some time together and sharing a few passion-filled kisses, the importance of her belief in him mattered.

"Please do it for me," his mother gently urged. He nodded. He always seemed to do whatever his mother told him.

His mother took his hand and Amber's. "On another note, guess who will be coming to celebrate the first night of Kwanzaa with us?"

"Um . . . let me guess?" Bo pretended to give the matter some thought. "Amber?"

His mother elbowed him, eliciting a grunt from him. "Amber will be there anyway. No, it's Tim Walkerman." She placed her arm around Amber's waist and squeezed her. "I think he's got the hots for you, dear."

Bo could actually feel the pupils in his eyes contract, along with the muscles in his face and entire body. "Why did you invite him?"

His mother didn't take her attention from Amber, who remained looking out toward the golf course. "Because it's a wonderful cultural celebration we should share with everyone. Besides, Amber is alone entirely too much."

"That's thoughtful of you, Martha, but actually I've decided to go home."

Bo's scowl deepened. Did she suddenly decide this because of his mother's ill-timed matchmaking stint? "You know, Tim gets on my nerves. He pretends he is so worldly, but comes off sounding like an idiot."

Martha clucked her tongue. "You know better than that," she scolded him. "Now, Amber, I'm surprised to hear that you won't be here. But I understand. You know you're welcome here if you change your mind."

Amber finally looked at Bo. How could she tell him how

difficult it was to be around his family? The mission that she had stood steadfastly behind had wavered with the doubts that swirled in her mind.

"I'm leaving and I'm not coming back."

"What!" Martha and Bo echoed their surprise.

Amber nodded. She hadn't planned to quit the job, but now that she declared it, there was no turning back.

Bo stepped in front of his mother. "When is your last day?" He grabbed Amber's hands tightly.

"Two weeks. I'll give two weeks' notice."

"Did we upset you?"

"Why are you looking at me when you say that, Mom?" Bo glared at his mother and then at Amber.

Amber raised her hand to fend of the objections she was sure would come from him. "It's not that at all. I've left some unfinished business and it's time for me to rectify it."

"A man?"

"Bo!"

Amber didn't have time to deny Bo's accusation, as he had strode off with his shoulders rigid and his face tight and angry.

"I'm sorry, Martha. I've got to go." Amber turned back to look out into the blackness that seemed to go on forever. She couldn't possibly admit that she had fallen in love with her son.

Chapter Eleven

Amber opened the door to her house and stepped over the threshold. She was home. When she'd made the decision to return, she'd expected Bo to stop her or even make an attempt to keep her at the ranch. Instead, after his initial flare-up, he'd retreated into his busy schedule. As it got closer to her departure, it didn't seem that he even slept at the house.

Her fantasy life was over. She had spent too many weeks pretending that she had no responsibilities. Her boss knew she'd be returning to work tomorrow. At the moment, the return to the familiar appealed to her.

The phone rang. She ran across the living room to answer. It had to be Sylvia. She hadn't heard from her in a while. "Hello," she sang, expecting to hear Sylvia's cheery response.

"Hello?"

Amber didn't recognize the male voice. "Can I help you?"

The caller stuttered. "Is this Amber Delaney?"

Great. She had just arrived and already a telemarketer

wanted to be a pain. "She's not here. Would you like to leave a message?"

"No. No message."

Amber hung up the phone, shaking her head at the poor telemarketer who couldn't use her call in the quota for successes.

It was time for her to be practical and face reality. She pulled her suitcase up the stairs. Her mind was already busy with the long list of tasks she had to do in the upcoming days. The top one on the list was to head into work with a close-to-perfect draft of her story. Considering that she had only toyed with a few openings and had a sketchy outline of how she wanted the story to unfold, most of her night would be spent writing. Tomorrow she would be prepared to sit in front of her boss and take his criticism. She also expected a fair amount of respect and praise for taking the initiative to do so much research.

Amber sat in her boss's office, waiting for him to get off the phone. From her end of the conversation, she was comfortable saying that he was his usual humorless self. Some poor person in marketing had been unable to close the deal to get a major advertising account and now had the misfortune to face the boss's wrath. He slammed down the phone. She jumped.

"Decided to act like you have a job, Miss Delaney?"

She placed her folder on the desk between them. "It might need cleaning up in a few areas, but I think it's ready to go."

"Oh, do you, now? So in addition to your vacation, you've learned a thing or two about running a successful newsmagazine, Miss Delaney?"

No one could massacre a name like Barkman. He dragged the vowels that didn't need to be dragged and shortened syllables as if saying them properly offended him.

He picked up the folder and opened it. She knew better than to interrupt him or to attempt to leave his office. Now she was under his microscope. Then she saw him reach for the infamous red pen. In a few seconds, she expected her work to become an illegible mass of red scribble. He emitted an occasional grunt and an annoying ticking sound as he read and turned each page.

"How was your trip to Texas?"

"Okay," she replied, thrown off by the casual opening.

"How did you get so much insight?"

"I played his housekeeper."

His eyes bored into her. "Really. You walked up to the door and they decided to hire you as their housekeeper."

"It wasn't planned. Actually Martha—his mother—hired me."

"Then you must have seen or heard quite a few private moments?"

Amber shrugged. "Nothing earth-shattering, just the regular family life."

"Don't you think the reader would've liked to see some of that 'family life'? I mean, explain it to me: I am sitting at the breakfast table facing the same woman for twenty years with kids badgering me for money. I have a job I can't stand waiting for me every day. All I want to do is read my newspaper and get a sense that justice is served to the greedy, the crooked, the obscene. I want to see my newspaper not be afraid to tell it like it is because, damn it, my life sucks." He slammed down the folder and slid it back to her.

Amber caught the folder, but didn't open it. Her ears burned from the rebuke and she wanted to crawl out of the office. Yet she remained with her back stiff and her shoulders pushed squarely back. She'd learned a thing or two on her trip. Most of all, she'd learned that she had sold herself short for too long. It gave others the advantage to walk all over her.

"Have nothing to say, as usual? Your story reads like something out of those sappy housewife magazines. I don't care about his ranch and who lived in it and how long it was in the family. I don't care about the family dinners. You had strong opinions about this man and his type who grew up with a silver spoon in his mouth. This man who played around in the corporate world until it collapsed and then went back to his high-and-mighty rich family and didn't suffer any consequences. Instead, you write it like a lovesick bubblehead who has fallen under the spell of these people."

"That's enough," she said in a soft voice. Not only did her ears burn, but her entire body shook with a seething anger that needed a release valve before she exploded. She pushed back her chair and picked up her folder. "You will apologize to me. I'll have my story printed, whether by you or someone else. As of today, I'm turning in my resignation." She walked out of his office through the gauntlet of curious eyes and whispering tongues. In the glass offices, nothing was private. Since Barkman chose to yell, the floor not only saw her humiliation, but heard the drama unfold.

She entered the elevator and pressed the button for the top floor. In the quick ride up, she practiced a few breathing techniques to calm herself. An automated voice announced her arrival on the floor. She readjusted her suit, smoothed a hand over her hair, took a deep breath, and stepped out on the executive level.

Despite wearing the best suit in her closet, she still felt woefully underdressed. The executive assistants behind their mahogany desks could have been clones. They followed the unwritten dress code for the executive floor with their navy-blue or black skirt suits, impeccable makeup, and professional haircuts without any contemporary dye jobs.

Amber headed for the CEO's office. "Hi, Shania, I need to see him."

Shania raised a manicured finger. She pressed a buzzer and announced Amber. Apparently a series of questions were being asked about her. Amber waited patiently as Shania replied with one-word answers. "You may go in." She pressed another button and the massive doors swung open for her entrance.

As a teenager, whenever she visited her uncle, it reminded her of Oz. How many times had she come before him to ask for a favor? Each time she imagined that she was now the lion, scarecrow, or one of the other characters. Now, after turning thirty years old, she still came to him.

"Have a seat." He didn't look up, but kept writing on papers and moving them from one pile to another on his desk.

"I'm sorry to bother you, Uncle."

"I know. You'd rather eat dirt than have to walk into my office. It must be really bad."

"I put in my resignation today."

He put down the pen. "Decided you don't want to be a reporter? What will it be this time?"

Amber heard the sarcasm loud and clear, but the bait no longer controlled her. "I'm not shying away from my dream to be a reporter. When I made the switch from real estate, it wasn't about the money because I had that and more as one of the most successful real-estate agents in the region. I wanted a sense of value that I could contribute to the lives of many." She saw his lips tighten. "That may be too altruistic for your value system, Uncle, but that's something my parents taught me. Maybe when I came to you, I was looking for a shortcut to success. That made me dependent on you again. It also guaranteed that I would get no respect when you had me start as a mail-room clerk." Again his lips twitched. "But I did it and moved up to covering the obituaries, waiting for my window of opportunity, meanwhile suffering the abuse of your chauvinist-in-charge. I don't expect you to understand what some of your employees endure at the hands of your management team. After all, you sit in your ivory tower looking out at the tops of other buildings, concerned about stocks and bonds and what country club has your dinner reservation."

"Careful."

Amber flicked off his warning. She had come up there to have her say and no one was going to stop her. "When I was a child, I was scared of you, and at the same time in awe. You were so powerful and I saw how people worked to get into your good graces. I wanted to be one of your chosen." She shook her head, staring out the window past his head, looking back on those tumultuous times. "Instead, you acted as if I was a ten-ton boulder placed on your shoulders for eternity. Your wife, I can't even call her my aunt, was even more cruel than you." Those memories brought tears and she bit her lip to keep them from falling. She stood. "Anyway, I'm not here to rehash the past, but I want you to know that I will be a reporter and a good one. I have heart and I poured it into my story. It's not sensational, it's not controversial, it's human."

"Let me read the article."

She handed him the folder and watched his face; only the occasional twitches of his lip showed signs of life. He snapped the folder shut. "Sit down." She didn't move. "Please."

She plopped down in her seat. It wasn't that she was waiting for him to be polite. She was queasy at having to listen to another critical tirade about her work.

"One of the few worthy lessons that I can offer you is to have integrity. Your article is good, but not great. As a reporter coming out of the starting gates, you've got to be great to get on the radar. You've shown great insight, but there is too much of you and not enough of Bo Pemberton, the man. I come away from your article feeling as if I just got a snow job from Pemberton's publicist. I don't see any objectivity, the good with the bad, the beautiful with the ugly, the truth with the myths."

Amber heard and understood what he meant. She smiled, feeling suddenly recharged.

"I want you to return."

"What?"

"I want you to get inside his head and his heart. I don't want to know what Amber thinks is there, I want to know what Bo has kept hidden away from the world."

"But I quit."

"Then you're rehired."

"No, I mean that I quit that job."

"Well, I hope you're getting all this quitting out of your system. Because my family didn't raise any quitters. In my own mixed-up way, I thought I was teaching you how to be a survivor. I didn't want you to be dependent on anyone, not even family. I think in my old age, I've softened, but that's a secret."

Amber rolled her eyes. Her uncle's skin was probably the only thing that had softened. Behind the heavily lined face, the iron will was reflected in his dark brown eyes. Only a fool would underestimate the power behind the man.

"You're not a quitter, Amber. I'm sending you back for another reason. You, my dear, are a hopeless romantic. In this article you bare your heart and love for this man. I've followed the Pemberton case—this man is no fool. I suspect that when you make him open up, he will see the beautiful woman that you are."

Amber squirmed in her chair, embarrassed by her uncle's candor, the fact that he immediately picked up on her feelings, and his insistence that she return. "Uncle, I just can't show up on their doorstep."

"You did it once before and somehow managed to get in. You're crafty, I've no doubt that you'll find a way." He picked up his pen and turned his attention back to his papers.

She was being dismissed, but it didn't matter. She headed for the door.

"I'll take care of the other matter."

She frowned, confused by his comment. He didn't elaborate. She shrugged and walked out the door. In her off-the-rack suit, she strutted down the aisle feeling like a million bucks.

On Christmas Eve night, Amber lay in her bed, contemplating her life. Her father did invite her to spend Christmas with his family, but the idea didn't appeal to her. Meanwhile she couldn't convince her mother to return home for Christmas. And Sylvia had either run off with another one of her infatuations or something terrible had happened to her. Amber's gut feeling was the latter, but she held on to the slim thread of hope that her friend was having the time of her life and would come back with the spiciest stories.

As it was the weekend, she had no reason to go out—not for work or shopping. Instead of joining the chaos at the malls, she stretched out on her couch and stared mindlessly at the traditional Christmas movie marathon. She sipped on white wine and nibbled on cheese, wondering what Bo was doing.

She imagined that the ranch house was decorated with stylish Christmas ornaments. The smell of eggnog would permeate the air because Martha had discovered a new, simple recipe. Will would make his small appearances, spreading his cheer and pearls of wisdom. She drained her wineglass.

Then there would be Zack and Josh to add to the lively family scene. She had witnessed several family dinners to know that it would be much of the same for Christmas, probably turned up a notch. The familial bond, energy, people who could love each other unconditionally had her yearning for a lifestyle that mirrored that.

She poured herself another glass, already feeling the effects of her last two glasses. She didn't plan to drink the entire bottle, but it did soften the bitterness and self-pity that now consumed her as the characters in the movie wished each other tearful greetings of Merry Christmas. The emotional scene triggered how lonely she was, which touched off a series of memories of Bo and their misadventures. Then there was the memory that had permanently etched a place in her mind. She could never forget the searing kisses, tender touch, the roller-coaster ride of falling in love and the bitterness of not being able to do anything about it.

She set down the wineglass with a sharp tap. Enough. She wiped away the few tears. Taking a deep breath to bolster her courage, she reached for the phone. While she waited for someone to pick up, she cleared her throat so she could sound normal and not the emotional wreck that loomed right around the corner.

The phone rang into voice mail. Amber hung up, not quite prepared to leave a message, just in case desperation oozed from her voice. She'd have to wish Martha a Merry Christmas another time.

Another four hours and it would be Christmas. She threw off the blanket and sat up, running a hand through her hair. A yawn overcame her and she stretched. She could go to sleep now or watch a few more tearjerker movies. How pathetic her life had become.

Hopefully Sylvia had managed to leave her an e-mail message telling her about her fabulous getaway with some West Indian hunk. She booted up the computer and logged on to her Internet service. Several unread e-mails popped up, but as she scrolled down, none appeared to be from Sylvia. Maybe her friend had used someone else's e-mail address. If nothing else, she might as well get comfortable and read them.

One by one, she deleted them, finally coming to one with the subject heading *Are you home yet?* This sounded like Sylvia. She clicked on the e-mail and settled comfortably in her chair to read about her best friend's latest escapade.

Amber,

> *Surprise! I just got your e-mail address and hope I will have better luck reaching you this way. I sent you a birthday card, did you get it? I wanted us to be together, but I guess you got scared. I don't mean to scare you. I only want to say that I have admired you from the first day we met. I can't get you out of my mind. I know, it must sound sappy. Anyway, please let me know that you got this, okay?*

Your secret admirer ☺

Amber stared at the smiling face. It seemed ghoulish, given its messenger. She hit the DELETE button, but canceled that directive, realizing that it would be evidence that this creep was not in her imagination.

She scrolled down the rest of her e-mails to hunt for more evidence. Her outrage grew intense that he had been able to get her e-mail address. And the mention that they'd met. When? Where?

She poised the cursor over another unread e-mail. This time the subject header read *Why don't you answer me?* She opened the e-mail and read.

Amber,

> *It's difficult going about my life without you. At least respond to me. If you tell me to leave you alone, then I will. But you can't ignore me. I go to our spot and hope to see you there, but you haven't come back. If you want to play hide-and-seek, then go ahead. I will find you no matter how long it takes.*

Yours.

Amber gulped. Her hands shook as she created a folder and filed the e-mails. Sitting in the extra bedroom-turned-office, with only the desk light on over the computer, she felt unnerved. Before she went any further, she had to make a few adjustments. She turned on the overhead light in the bedroom and then ran downstairs to make sure her door was locked. Even then, her vulnerability overpowered her. She wanted to hide from this unknown bogeyman who was very real and very scary.

"I can do this," she said aloud. Back at the computer, she

braced herself to continue. She had to be the investigator for her own case. She had to learn what had triggered this person to latch on to her.

There were only two messages left to read. One e-mail had a subject header that read *Three steps to finding Mr. Right.* Amber snorted at the contrived topic. A better title would have been *How to make Mr. Right know he's your Mr. Right.* She definitely didn't need to read such drivel to punctuate the bittersweet memories of her time with Bo. She deleted the unread message.

Next.

Looks like Mr. Psycho strikes again.

I always knew I was a lucky man. I tell people that and they laugh at me. But what else would it be? I should have come to visit you the moment I knew where you lived, but I'd hoped to gently bring you along the way. I understand if you're uncomfortable with that, for now. As luck would have it, I found out that you've been away. As a favor, I've kept an eye on the house. You have such a beautiful house with your evergreen in front.

I know I'm babbling like an adolescent boy, but I can't help it. You have wonderful taste. I like the gold and beige color downstairs. Yes, I did get to come into your home. Don't worry, I didn't break in. But I can see you're a neat freak, like me. I do wish you would reply to me, then you'll see that we have so much in common.

Amber pushed away from the computer. Her breathing grew ragged. Tears welled in her eyes, blinding her as she stumbled out of the room. She looked around, not sure where to go, what to do. She picked up the phone to call Syliva's cell.

"Please pick up," she begged. Her emotions could no longer be contained. She wept, feeling the rising wave of hysteria mounting.

"Hello?"

"Who is this?" Amber frowned at the unfamiliar voice. "Where's Sylvia?"

"There's no Sylvia," the young male voice answered.

"How old are you?"

Amber heard the giggles from several people who all talked at the same time. Obviously they were egging on the person who had answered the phone. She took the phone from her ear to make sure she had indeed dialed Sylvia's number. It was correct. "How did you get this phone?" she asked, using an authoritative tone.

"Don't answer her, just hang up."

"It's ours now."

"Sylvia will have to get her own phone."

"Hell, I paid for it, it's mine now."

Amber listened to each child throw out their cocky retorts in the background. Since it was so obvious that Sylvia and her phone were separated, she wanted to know the details of how they got the phone. "Listen, I'm not trying to cause any problems."

"Look, lady, you're killing my mood."

The line went dead. Amber stared at the display panel blinking the amount of minutes she'd used.

It was time to go to the police again.

Chapter Twelve

Going to the police on Christmas Day had its drawbacks. The staff was lean and those on duty clearly didn't want to be there. Unfortunately, criminals didn't rest on certain holidays and the station had a small contingent of drunken individuals about to be booked.

Amber had never been inside a station, and once she had walked through the doors, hoped never to return. As far as decor went, the vast room sported a dismal gray wall—or maybe it was white that had turned gray. The ceiling panels had brown stains and some panels were missing, exposing overhead wiring and air ducts.

No one seemed to know the concept of indoor voice. Cops yelled to each other from their desks. The desk sergeant barked at whomever was standing in front of him. The arresting policeman even had a permanent teeth-bared expression to go along with his orders.

Amber shuddered and headed for the information desk. "I had called earlier and I am here to see Mr. Banner." She

couldn't remember his rank and didn't want to offend anyone by making a guess.

"He's gone for the day."

"But he told me to come in."

"I'm sorry, but he left about an hour ago."

What a jerk. He'd left after she'd called. "Then I need to
see someone else."

"I'll notify Officer Pritchard."

"Fine." Amber crossed her arms and waited. She didn't
want to sit in the institutional-style chairs. As a matter of
fact, she didn't want to stay in that depressing place any
longer than she needed to.

"Hi, I'm Officer Pritchard. May I help you?"

Amber looked up to see a middle-aged woman in a casual
suit smiling at her. Drawn to her friendliness, Amber smiled
and followed her down a hallway. Maybe things weren't so bad.

The officer led her into a small conference room. After
she turned down the offer for coffee, Amber told the officer
her story. She even mentioned her unease at Sylvia's disappearance. The officer asked few questions, but wrote copi-
ous notes on her writing pad. When Amber stopped talking,
the officer looked up.

"Sounds like you definitely have a stalker. Problem is that
you don't know who it is, but he's finding out personal details about you. I don't think it's one of your friends because
then he wouldn't have made a big deal about mentioning the
inside of the house."

Amber snapped her finger. "Maybe it's a friend of one of
my friends. I had a small party at my house about six months
ago. There were people there I didn't personally know." She
puzzled over the thought. "I really don't know a lot of people. One thing I do know is that I'm scared to death of this
person popping up on my doorstep."

"Is there someone you could stay with as we investigate the e-mail addresses? I also want to send someone around to the house. I can have one of the patrol cars drive by a couple times a day for a few weeks. Maybe that will scare the person away."

"I ran away once. I feel like I'm giving up my life for this person."

The officer nodded her understanding. "Just for a little while. It's better to be safe."

"I have my uncle." She said the words with little enthusiasm. Although she had a momentous visit yesterday, it didn't mean she wanted to run over and have dinner with him and his wife.

"Let me get on this. Take my advice: drastically change your routine and stay somewhere for a couple of weeks. It won't be hard to track down the origin of these e-mail addresses. What may be difficult is that they could be anywhere in the world. I have a few more questions."

Amber propped her chin in her hand. She patiently answered the officer's questions. Quite easily this had to be the worst Christmas she had experienced.

Eddie didn't go back to his apartment. He had shed it like a snake of its skin. It had been no easy task to get rid of Sylvia's body and then wipe down the entire apartment. The stupid woman had even managed to send off an e-mail to Amber from his real e-mail address about three ways to find Mr. Right. He almost had a heart attack when he read the e-mail, which talked about how she had met him, where he lived, and her stupid infantile dreams of a life with him.

It had been a stupid, careless move on his part to strike up a friendship with her. He'd felt reckless and a little desperate to maintain contact with Amber. Anyway, he'd driven all the way to Philadelphia to drop off the body at a landfill. He planted a pole and tied her panty hose to it, so that the police could locate her upon his directions. The twit's family should be grateful that he phoned in the tip, on Christmas Day, nevertheless.

Sitting in his hotel, he planned his next move. He made a list of all the items he would need. Flying didn't appeal to him, and with the security checks in place, he wouldn't be able to carry onboard some of his choicest tools for the job. Time was dear, but he didn't want to be impatient and not get it right.

He drank his beer and ate pizza while watching a Christmas movie starring Whitney Houston and Denzel Washington. Amber could play the good girl and he would be her angel. The difference was that he played for keeps.

Christmas morning blended into the afternoon, which blended into the evening. After returning from the station, Amber filled up her bathtub and submerged her body until the temperature made her reach for her robe. So much had happened in the last two days, she didn't know which direction to take. What path could or would lead to success or happiness?

She called Sylvia's family again to see if they'd learned of anything. This time Sylvia's father answered the phone to tell her that the police were investigating a tip. She hung up feeling the dread slither its way through her. Right there at the dining room table over her half-eaten grilled salmon and broccoli, she lowered her face in her hands and wept. She didn't need the police to tell her what she already knew. Sylvia was gone. Forever.

The phone rang and she stared at it. Maybe she was wrong. She picked it up on the fourth ring, praying for good news. "Yes." She wiped her face, waiting.

"Amber? It's Mom."

Her shoulders slumped. "Hi, Mom."

"Merry Christmas, sweetheart. How is it going?"

"I've got a stalker. My friend may be dead. I'm spending Christmas alone. How do you think I'm doing, Mom?" Her anger over the helplessness of her situation created a tight cord in the pit of her stomach. Her mother's perky voice irritated her.

"A stalker, honey? Aren't you being overly dramatic about one of your boyfriends?"

"I don't have any boyfriends, Mom. I'm not stupid—I know that I'm being watched and my life could be in danger."

"Calm down. You really ought to come out here. Everyone is so relaxed. I think the weather makes a difference. In the northeast, people are too uptight."

That did it. The powder keg had ignited. "Mom, here's a reality check. I have a job. I'm an adult and acting like one. Unlike you, I am not running away just because my marriage fell apart and I don't want to deal with life. I've got an uncle who likes to play the omnipotent one, a mother who decided to become a groupie of every author who had enlightened her soul, and a father who occasionally remembers he has a daughter from a previous relationship. Sorry if I feel like my life sucks right now. But life sucks right now!" She screamed the words and sobbed into the phone. She wouldn't be surprised if her mother had hung up. She always hated her daughter's tantrums.

"I think this is not a good time for our conversation. Think about coming to California, Amber."

Amber's anger had spewed with the force of a volcanic

eruption. Now her shoulders heaved from the exertion and only dry sobs choked her throat. She pressed the button to hang up the phone.

The doorbell rang. Startled, she leapt to her feet. Who would be ringing her door at eight o'clock? What if it was the stalker? She started to dial 911 and stopped herself. Paranoia was taking over her common sense. She set down the phone. At least she should check the door. Using the peephole, she looked at her caller.

"Yes," she called through the closed door.

"I have a delivery for Amber Delaney."

"Just leave it at the door."

"Ma'am, I'll need Miss Delaney's signature."

"I'm not opening my door."

"I was given specific instructions to make sure she received it and not to leave it."

"Who is it from?"

"Martha Pemberton."

Amber snapped back the locks and opened the door. "What is it?"

"Dunno."

She signed the paper on the clipboard and took the thin envelope from him. "Thank you." She stepped back into the house and locked the door.

Turning over the envelope in her hand, she forced herself to wait until she was in her bed before opening her surprise. She ran upstairs and slid under the covers, a small smile on her lips. She knew that whatever it was, Martha's thoughtfulness would come through.

She slid her finger under the flap and popped it open, then pulled out the contents and gasped. "Oh, my. Oh, my." In her hands was a one-way ticket from Baltimore/Washington International Airport to Dallas/Fort Worth Airport. A small handwritten note on cream paper was stuck in the ticket folder.

Amber, please forgive my arrogance, but I took it upon myself to send you this small token for purely selfish reasons. I sensed that you may be in turmoil about many things. I want you to know that the Pemberton ranch is a safe haven and you are welcome here anytime. The ticket is for December 26 because it is the first day of Kwanzaa. I feel that it is a perfect way to rediscover the joys of life. Your friend, Martha.

Amber read the note a couple times to make sure she hadn't imagined Martha's generosity. If she was to go, she had to take the nine o'clock flight. She wanted to go desperately, to see Martha and to see Bo. There was no mention of him and she wondered if he knew of his mother's action. She could picture him glowering his disapproval. Maybe after she had left, he had put her out of his mind, grateful to go about his life without her probing questions and strong opinions.

She slid down between the covers and set the ticket on the pillow beside her. She would sleep on it; she set her alarm for six. Then she reached out to turn off the bedside lamp. Her eyes lit on a book that had fallen off her table. She leaned over and picked up the book. It didn't look like any she'd bought lately. Sylvia had probably left it behind when she came to look at the house.

She turned it over to read the title. It was a motivational book about discovering the inner self. She flipped through the pages, curious about the book's premise. Seeing writing in the front of the book, she opened the book wider to read the tiny words. She knew Sylvia's handwriting and it wasn't hers.

She pitched the book toward the doorway. It was from him. How long had it been there? She didn't bother to read the note, but saw her name and the words *secret admirer*. Before he had talked about her living room, but to see that book in her bedroom, she felt violated.

There had to be a solution to this terror. Right now, she knew she had to leave. She pulled out the suitcases she had only just put away. Her father, uncle, even her mother would be possible safe havens.

She opened the drawers and took out her clothes. She needed distance from the man who stalked her. What she didn't have was a haven from herself and her emotions. Staying with any of her family would provide shelter, but not a home, not the warmth and bonding she so desired. That, she found so tragic.

Guiltily she reached for the ticket and held it to her chest. Maybe Martha could provide the healing touch.

Her uncle's message boomed in her mind. Yes, and then there was the mission.

Chapter Thirteen

Amber drove up to the ranch. Nothing had changed. Heck, she'd only been gone for a few days. She examined the grounds, the graveled driveway, the cars parked in front of the house. For the most part, nothing had changed, except that they had company.

After she parked the car and walked up to the door, she suddenly had a case of cold feet. Was this what it felt like for Bo on his return? Did he stand there, waiting, listening for some inner directive to say that it was okay? Once she opened that door and crossed the threshold, nothing would be the same.

The door swung open and Martha pulled her into a warm embrace. "Oh, honey, I'm so glad you came. I kept looking at the clock, estimating what time you would arrive. When I saw you pull up, I got excited because now everyone is here. You'll be glad to know that Tim Walkerman couldn't make it." She softly patted Amber's cheek.

Amber giggled at Martha's exuberance. The insecurities

that had recently nagged at her had fled in the face of Martha's welcome.

"Wait till I tell Will you're here."

A small child ran toward Martha and then veered off into the dining room. A few seconds later, an older version followed, shouting about her CD player.

"Those are my two great nieces. The younger one is Natasha. The one that would like to kill her is Nia. Love them to pieces, but today they are working my nerves. I offered to baby-sit while their parents did some shopping." She pulled Amber into the foyer. "Don't just stand there, head up to your room and then join me. Fill me in on what you've been up to."

Amber watched Martha return to the kitchen. Natasha appeared out of the dining room with Nia still in hot pursuit. The outside of the house may have stayed the same, but inside, she sensed the difference. The family was reuniting for the annual Kwanzaa celebration at Martha's request.

As she climbed the stairs to her room, she hoped that the other family members would be equally welcoming of her. It would be her first experience in the company of a large extended family. She thought about her father and his other family. No, she refused to think about them and entertain the small ounce of guilt for not calling her father.

At the top of the stairs, she looked over at Bo's room. It had killed her not to ask Martha where he was. What she'd really have liked to know was how he took her sudden departure. Did he suffer from loss of appetite, bouts of insomnia, and constant daydreaming about what could have been?

Before she lost her nerve, she walked up to the room and tapped lightly. No sound came from the room. She rested her hand on the doorknob and, with a small turn, opened the door and entered.

The room was immaculate. No stray clothes or discarded shoes littered the floor. Had he slept there? She moved across the room, enjoying the lingering scent of his signature cologne. It brought back the memory of him discovering her in his bathroom. That day seemed a long time ago. She touched the comforter, lightly trailing her hand up to his pillow.

She traced the striped pattern on the pillowcase, wondering if she would ever be able to tell him she loved him. More than that had to be revealed first. Taking a deep breath, she turned and walked out of the room, closing the door gently behind her.

She could stay only for a few days. Years later when she had her own family, she'd look back at this with fondness, but also as a mistake of a fledgling reporter blurring the lines between reality and fantasy.

The young girls' high-pitched squeals of delight startled her. She headed for the stairs to see what had caused their screams and excited chatter. Bo stood midway on the stairs, looking up at her, while the girls pulled at his arms for his attention.

How could one man make her insides flip-flop with warm contentment? The space between them was too great. Yet she restrained herself, something she wished she'd done on several occasions in his company.

Bo had been repairing the roof on the barn when he spied the strange yellow car. His cousins had already arrived, dropped off their girls, and jumped into one of the cars to head for the outlet mall. He walked to the opening, shielding his eyes to see who would get out of the car. He expected to see his cousins' arrivals throughout the day; his mother had issued her summons that this year, she expected everyone to attend the Kwanzaa celebration. She had to surrender to the fact that not everyone could afford to take the seven days off from work for the entire celebration. They all had to promise they would be there for the final day.

While his home was being transformed into the command center, he'd picked up his toolbox and headed to the barn. There was always something that needed to be fixed, hammered, or ripped apart. Once he was done there, he would take Onyx and go riding. Anything to keep his mind from wandering to the same person. He wanted his muscles worked and tired so he could fall into an exhausted sleep and not have to dally over memories of Amber. What she looked like, the sound of her voice, or the way she giggled.

As he turned to go back to his duty, the person emerged from the car. The sun may have been in his eyes, but he recognized the familiar figure. He wanted to run across the field, yelling her name and waving madly. She had come back.

He did run, but then slowed down as he got closer to the back of the house. She had come back. His mind repeated the fact. Why? When she'd announced that she was leaving, there was finality to the words. His mother didn't notice the tension between them, but he understood that she left because of him.

He walked into the kitchen and stayed hidden. He only picked up the last few words from his mother as she came toward him in the kitchen. Opening the refrigerator, he pretended he was getting a drink.

"Get cleaned up, Amber is back."

He poured cold water into a glass. "Why is that an occasion for me to celebrate?"

"Don't pretend with me. Anyway, I brought her back."

He almost choked on the water and set the glass down on

the counter. "What are you doing? Leave her be, Mom." And to think that his life could have returned to normal if it wasn't for his mother's meddling. Instead he had his mother to thank for this new upheaval. "I hope this isn't one of your match-making schemes."

Martha turned off the faucet and wiped her hands on the dish towel. "May I remind you that Amber was the one who came to our doorstep? And maybe I should go to the trouble of being a matchmaker so that you don't bring home any more of that trash you called a fiancée. Now, really!" She pushed him out of her way to get to the skillet from an over-head cupboard.

"Here, let me help you." His mother had never talked about Cassidy to him, but the unusually emotional outburst from her spoke volumes.

"I can manage," she replied in her trademark softness. "Get cleaned up."

"Yes, ma'am." No need to tell him twice.

He headed for the stairs.

"Uncle Bo!"

His nieces screamed his name and launched their bodies onto him. He picked up one in each arm and headed for the stairs.

"You smell sweaty, Uncle Bo," Natasha declared.

"Good. Then I'm going to hug you really, really tight." He laughed as they squirmed to get out of his grasp. He set them down, laughing as loudly as they were. Then he looked up to see Amber standing at the top of the stairs.

Neither one said anything. The girls' chatter had faded. Since they could no longer get his attention, they left. He tore his eyes away from Amber's; his heart raced, his mind screamed for him to do something, anything. If he could just get to his room to recuperate and get himself in control. He wanted to be emotionally detached, distant, safe behind his wall. That wall had started its fall as he got to know her. He hadn't gotten used to feeling exposed to his own emotions.

She hadn't moved while he came slowly up the stairs. "You're back."

She nodded.

He read a little relief in her eyes. Maybe she was equally nervous about their first encounter.

"I'm only here for a couple days. Mainly for Kwanzaa. I've never celebrated Kwanzaa."

What did he expect her to say? Kwanzaa was a legitimate reason. It didn't lessen his disappointment, however. "Make yourself comfortable. I have to get cleaned up. Lots to do."

"Oh, I didn't mean to keep you." She apologized and stepped aside.

He nodded, not taking any chances to look in her direction as he walked past. He was no fool. Amber had the most bewitching eyes, with the power to suck him in and reduce him to a blithering idiot.

All he had to do was maintain control for a few days. Then his world could right itself.

Amber sat at the dinner table, enjoying the company, but equally uncomfortable at having Bo seated directly across from her. She had met so many cousins, she couldn't immediately remember their names. She was grateful that her presence didn't hinder the flow of their animated conversations.

"Amber, more macaroni and cheese?"

Amber hadn't eaten much, but she didn't want to offend. Bo offered the dish to her. Her hands brushed his in the exchange and she almost dropped it in the process. So much hung between them, but she could see that his cold, offsetting attitude was back in place.

"Amber, what brought you to Texas?" Clarissa asked. She was the youngest cousin.

The question didn't unsettle Amber. Even when she first arrived, she had her excuse in place. But it was a bit different when the entire table quieted to listen. And even more so when she looked across the table and saw Bo staring. "I'm what they would call a free spirit. I'm planning to go to California and hook up with friends."

"Yet you went back north?" Bo joined in.

"Visited a friend."

"And when you leave again in a couple days, where are you heading this time?"

"Leaving?" Martha was clearly dismayed.

Amber glared at Bo, who still wore a stoic face. "Yes, it is time for me to move on. As they say, life goes on."

"I envy you," Clarissa said. "You go where you want to go, do what you want to do. No man, no kids, no corporate job to tie you down."

"Exactly."

Bo broke eye contact with her and returned to eating his meal. She didn't need to look at Martha to know that she was still looking at her. She twirled her fork around the food. There was no way Martha could have thought she would settle down in Texas as the happy housekeeper. After their numerous conversations, the older woman had to realize that, if nothing else was true, she had dreams and ambition.

Martha tapped her water glass with her dinner knife. "Quiet down, please." She waited until everyone, including the children, gave her their attention. "I'm so glad all of you could attend our traditional Kwanzaa celebration. We've got Todd and his family coming in on New Year's Eve, which will make it complete. Since you all are staying in different hotels, we will be lighting the candles at seven o'clock each night. Let's go to the living room. It's time to begin."

Martha walked next to Amber into the living room. Bo was somewhere behind her, but she dared not turn around. She didn't want to see the blank look.

The living room had been transformed. Most of the furniture had been rearranged to leave the wall with the large bay-window space decorated with a display of African art and decorations. The framed pictures of landscapes the family had visited had been replaced by various tribal cloths. On the floor lay a large mat in the new design and colors of the South African flag.

Standing in the small group, Amber began to feel the bonds of kinship. It went beyond Martha's valiant efforts to make her feel welcomed and a part of the extended family. Among these African artifacts and decorations, she embraced the connection to her culture. Something important and vital was about to occur and she opened herself to the seen and unseen benefits of celebrating the first fruits.

"Let the children come forward. It is important that they observe the customs because one day they will conduct their celebrations for their families."

Natasha and Nia were only too glad for the attention and jostled each other for their place. Another little one Amber had just met stepped to the front, but when he turned and observed all the adults looking at him, he reconsidered.

Amber didn't know whether she would incorporate any of this in her article. Just in case, she noted every detail about the custom.

A long narrow table made from dark wood and polished to a high gleam now stood in the open area. A bright, colorful, African printed cloth covered the table. The vivid yellow accented the darkness of the wood.

Martha looked in Amber's direction. "This mat in front of the altar is called the *mkeka* and all the other symbols for Kwanzaa are placed on it. The candleholder or *kinara* holds the *mishumaa saba*." Martha pointed to the candles.

"And they have to be red, green, and black for Africa, right?" Amber asked. "Let me see if I can remember what I learned in a documentary. Black is for the people. Red for the blood. Green for growth."

Martha nodded. "The colors represent the strength of our past and the hope we have for tomorrow. In the center is the black candle, on the left are three red candles, and on the right are three green candles. For the seven principles. Every day I will light a candle, starting with the black one."

"What's the corn and the plants for?"

"The plants are *mazao* and are set on the mat, along with the ears of corn. The corn represents our own children and those in our community. Remember the proverb 'It takes a village' because we must be community parents of our youth. The black cup is the unity cup to pour water on the crops, which is *tambiko*—our libation to the ancestors. Every year one of the children does the libation. I'll print out the *Tamshi La Tutaonana* for you to read along as our salute to another year and another Kwanzaa celebration on the sixth day when we have the Kwanzaa feast. The feast is a big celebration with lots of food and music. We have to get you an African outfit for that evening."

"I know where you can get a dress without paying through the nose for it," Clarissa informed.

"Doesn't seem necessary, given the fact that she has to be on her way."

Amber wanted to turn around and punch Bo right in the

nose. "He's absolutely right. I can't wait to get on my journey." Martha had reiterated that each participant should come to the event in the right frame of mind. But what did it mean when she was hopelessly preoccupied with thoughts about Bo?

She stepped back and turned to seek out Bo. He stood off to the side, leaning against the wall. Her sudden actions caught him off guard. She saw a quick smile on his lips before it disappeared, almost as if he'd forgotten to be cold and distant. She stepped toward him until her face was a hand's length away.

"Truce." She issued the challenge, and didn't wait for his reply before returning to her spot. Now she was ready to begin.

"*Habari gani?*"

"*Umoja!*"

"Welcome, Amber, to celebrating your first Kwanzaa with my family, and, as you will learn during the next few days, we are all one family. We, as African-Americans, have an obligation to uphold the best of who we are. I want us to reflect on our culture, family, and community, and our connection with our environment. Hence we celebrate Kwanzaa, as created by Dr. Maulana Karenga.

"Natasha, this year I want you to tell us about the seven principles."

"Yes, Aunty." The eight-year-old proudly stepped in front of the group. She wore a traditional African dress with a matching head wrap. Her serious demeanor continued the mood for the event. She looked over at her aunty, and once she received Martha's nod, took a step forward. "The first principle, *Umoja*, is unity represented by the black candle in the center. The red candles are *Ku-Kuj-Kujichagulia* for self-determination, *Ujamaa* for cooperative economics, and

Kuumba for creativity." Her finger pointed at each candle from the farthest left toward the center. Natasha exhaled noisily.

Everyone laughed, except Martha. She raised her hand to silence the adults. "Good child, now for the other three principles."

Natasha nodded. "The last three principles represented by the three green candles are *Ujima* for collective work and responsibility, *Nia* for purpose, and *Imani* for faith."

"Thank you, sweetheart."

Natasha positively floated back to stand in her place.

Even Amber felt a strong sense of pride at the little girl's accomplishment. At that moment, she wondered what it would be like to teach her own son or daughter about this African-American tradition that could be said to have spread to other nations.

Martha took the head spot again. "As we celebrate the principle of *Umoja*, I would like Leon to share a story about unity."

Leon, Clarissa's brother, told a poignant story about unity among his father and uncles. When Amber closed her eyes to listen to the words and underlying meaning, the message spoke to her, stirring her feelings about her mother and father. Once they were a family, but the cracks dividing them ran deep.

"Bo, please do the honors with the unity cup."

Bo made his way to the front. Instead of walking around the edge of the group, which was easier, he walked up the middle. In so doing, he had to pass her. She felt his hands drop on her shoulders and she reflexively jumped at the touch.

"Excuse me," he said.

Her shoulders warmed under his brief touch. She wanted to lean back against his expansive chest and simply breathe. Before he let her go, she felt him squeeze her shoulders. Not until he faced the group could she study his face. That's when she knew he'd agreed to her truce.

He poured water into the cup and carried it over to his father. Will took the cup and drank. Then Bo took it to his mother, who also drank. The cup was handed from one person to the next. Amber watched the family seal their bond and celebrate their lineage. Finally only she and Bo were left to drink from the cup.

He offered her the cup first. "I'm not family. Maybe I should go last." She didn't mean to sound rude, but only meant to observe in the tradition.

"If it makes you feel better, my mother has adopted you." He took her hand and placed it on the cup. When she had taken her sip, he followed. He blew out the center candle and the entire group dispersed.

Only Bo remained.

Three days. It was her time line before leaving the ranch for good. With only days and hours left, she had to take risks and jump on opportunities. "Heading to bed?"

"No," he said.

"Want to sit on the back porch?"

"Sure. I'll turn on the heater. I'd suggest giving it a few minutes to warm up."

"In the meantime, I'll make us a couple cups of coffee."

They sat on the porch, sipping coffee. The only light in the distance was the one over the barn door. Otherwise, the dark curtain of night had descended like the scene in a final act, yet it was all an illusion because she could hear the animals and insects that used the night for cover as they foraged for food.

With her camping experience under her belt, she had no particular desire for a repeat performance. Of course, she couldn't forget how it had ended in Bo's arms. There had been no satisfying ending and the rejection still took residence in the pit of emotions.

"Where do we go from here?" he asked.

"Nowhere." The last thing she wanted him to think was that she expected something from him. She was a modern woman, independent, maybe not terribly financially secure, but she refused to go to pieces over any man—at least, not in his presence.

He sipped his coffee and then held the cup in his hand. "You can walk away with no regrets, no thought to possibilities, no second chances."

"What am I walking away from—a momentary diversion as you get your life together?"

"It was never a diversion. You know me better than that."

"Actually, no, I don't know you. I get glimpses." She took his cup out of his hand and held it between hers. "And what I saw, I liked. But most of the time, you're pensive, reasoning over every issue in your life."

He turned her hand over in his and raised it to his lips. He kissed it and gently laid her hand on her lap. "Guess I'm a perfectionist."

"And I'm not perfect."

Chapter Fourteen

"Rise and shine!"

Amber awoke, startled by the shout over her head. The curtains were pulled back and she swore she heard the windows being opened. Shielding her eyes, she squinted at the blurred figure in front of her.

"Come with me."

"Bo? What the heck are you doing?" She kicked at his butt, which he had firmly planted at the foot of her bed. "Get out. What time is it?" Her head swam from the sleep she still craved.

"It's six-thirty and I don't want to miss my tea time."

"I don't want any freaking tea at this time."

"You're so adorable." He pulled the comforter off her body.

She screamed and pulled down her nightdress, which had managed to wind its way around her hips. "Why are you doing this to me?" she wailed.

"I'm revealing a side of me. Isn't that what you want?"

The question, his tone, her desire banged at her conscience. As the reporter, this was what she wanted. As a woman in love, this was what she wanted. All she had to do was keep the two separate. "Fine. Let me get dressed."

"Okay." He crossed his arms and waited.

Amber pulled up the shoulder of her nightdress and pushed back her hair, which she was sure resembled a hedgehog. "I guess we're not going, then."

"Party pooper." He grinned and headed for the door. "Don't forget to bring a swimsuit."

"Don't have one. I didn't know when I was coming to Texas in the winter that it was a necessity."

"We'll get you one at the club."

Amber waited until he closed the door before springing out of bed. "The club?" Whatever Bo had in mind, she was game.

Bo looked at his watch twenty minutes later. He should have woken her up at five. What was difficult about putting on a couple pieces of clothing? Instead, he heard her many trips to the bathroom, with containers being opened and snapped shut. Maybe he hadn't made it clear that he was about to miss his tea time.

"I'm ready."

Gawking wasn't polite, but, man, she looked good. Her black jeans molded to the length of her legs. The turtleneck had the same effect with her upper body, making him feel like a leery pervert as his gaze lit on her chest. Like a schoolboy, he finally looked up at her face. He'd expected to see her fully made up after listening to her in the bathroom. Instead her face had a natural glow with a touch of lip gloss. He had said it many times to himself, but this time she deserved to hear the compliment. "You are beautiful."

She blushed. "Thank you."

Neither spoke in the car, but it was a comfortable silence. He appreciated her ease at enjoying a moment without feeling the need to fill it with talk.

He headed north toward the country club. This was only one day, but he wanted to impress on Amber that he enjoyed a normal life, that he could be social, that he may be worth sticking around for a little while in Texas.

He pulled onto the property and displayed his ID for entry.

"You weren't kidding when you said country club."

It was an impressive sight with the southwestern architecture of several buildings. Off to the right were custom-built homes that bordered the golf course.

"Who can afford to live here?"

"They don't sell those houses. They are rented and come with a maid and butler service."

"Have you ever rented it?"

He laughed. "Once. It took my brothers and some friends to be able to foot the bill for a long weekend."

He parked in front of the main building. A uniformed attendant came over, took the keys from Bo, and drove off with the car.

"It's all part of the membership," he offered when she stared at the car pulling away.

"Good morning, Mr. Pemberton."

"Good morning."

"They know you," Amber whispered after the third person addressed him by name.

"It's all part of the membership."

Bo headed for the golf information desk. He got his information and headed for the course.

"What am I going to do while you play?"

"You're playing with me. We will be with another couple."

Not until he heard her voice behind him did he realize she'd stopped. "I don't know how to play."

"Not a problem. Hit the ball and aim for the hole."

"I would've never come if I knew I had to play. And I'm playing in front of other people. They are going to hate us . . . me. I can't do this. I'm not doing it, Bo."

Bo ignored her as he got his golf cart. "Hop in."

"No."

"Hop in or I will come over there and toss you in. You weigh just under a ton, but I'll manage."

Amber gasped and climbed in. She landed a punch on his arm. That was all he needed. He hit the gas, throwing her back against the seat. "Buckle up. It's tee time." He flashed her a grin, which she greeted by poking out her tongue.

He'd decided to play only nine holes. After watching Amber chase more than a few balls from the wooded area or the sand traps, he thanked his lucky stars for that decision. The elderly couple they played with didn't fare any better. The man who looked to be seventy constantly missed the ball and would stand there, looking for the ball to drop. His wife would then pick up the ball after a couple swings, pocket it, and walk ahead. "I do whatever I can to make him happy," she said when Amber and Bo first noticed the variation on the game.

Three hours later they headed back to the golf shop.

"You were really beginning to get the hang of it."

"Don't lie. My hands hurt. My back hurts. I'm hungry and I'm never playing golf again," Amber said.

"Okay, you want me to be real with you: You sucked the

big one. Goose egg on the ninth hole. Even Tiger would have begged you to clobber him on the head to stop the pain."

"I'm going to clobber *you* if you don't shut up. You don't have to be cruel."

"You told me not to lie. I was treating you like one of the boys."

"Fine. I'm ready to go swimming."

He took her into the store that featured a variety of swimsuits. He wondered if he'd made a mistake when she fingered nearly every suit or held it against her body and modeled it in front of the mirror. Why couldn't she just walk up to the rack, pick one, and head for the cashier?

He spied a chair near the beach towels. At least someone in the store had him in mind. He sank into the chair and tried not to look at his watch.

"I'm ready."

"I'm hungry," he said.

"We're going swimming and then we can eat."

"Yes, ma'am."

He entered the pool, which had a few occupants. Why didn't it surprise him that he'd beaten her to the pool? He swam a lap to while away the time. A splash near his head startled him. A body dove to the bottom of the pool and then aimed for the surface.

"Making a grand entrance, I see," he teased.

She grinned. "This feels awesome. By the way, are you buying me lunch?"

"Only if it's a date."

"What if it's because you have to buy me lunch?"

She'd issued a challenge. He knew better than to think she would do that without a reason. He hesitated.

"Scared?"

He sized up the competition. "What's in it for me when I win?"

"We finish what got started at the campsite."

"Okay, let's go." He swam over to the edge of the pool.

Amber leisurely swam over to take her place next to him. "You're so easy."

"Yeah, whatever. You'd better get ready."

"Since we're doing the width of the pool, I say we swim it four times."

That gave him pause, but the reward was too sweet to pass up. "Fine."

"On the count of three. One. Two. Three."

Bo used his legs to give him a powerful thrust out to the middle of the pool. In a few seconds, he touched the edge of the pool and headed back to the original spot. Swimming wasn't his sport in high school, but he knew he had the legs and arms that acted like propellers giving him the needed speed.

By the third lap, his breath grew a little labored. It was also the first time he noticed Amber's easy glide. She was changing up her strokes each time she touched the side like they did in the Olympics. He worked his legs harder. Her waist was now at the level of his head and was slowly moving past him. He raised his head out of the water to see her touch the wall and head back for the final leg. He took a deep breath, swallowing water in the process. In a furious last-ditch effort, he flung his arms over his head in a frenzied windmill fashion and fluttered his legs. His lungs burned from the exertion. He had nothing left in his reserves. By the time he'd touch the wall, Amber was sitting on the edge with only her legs dangling in the water.

"I was regional champ for three years."

Bo gasped for breath, holding his head against the tiled edging. "Not fair."

"I'd like a chicken club sandwich, pasta salad, and a bowl of sherbet." She pulled her legs out of the pool and stood. "And don't keep me waiting."

Completely winded, all he could do was wave her comments away. She knew his hot button and had surely detonated it. Once he thought he wouldn't pass out, he hauled himself out of the pool.

Lunch was pleasant. At least she didn't keep throwing his defeat in his face. He silently thanked her for the small show of mercy.

"What now?"

He shrugged. "They've got tennis. Squash. Horseback riding."

"No. No. And hell, no."

"Massage?"

"Hmm. That sounds fabulous."

He signed the bill. "Let's go."

"Ladies and gentlemen," the public address system announced. "On behalf of North Hill Country Club, we'd like to congratulate Miss Amber Delaney in her magnificent defeat of Mr. Bo Pemberton in a swimming event. Your lunch is on us, Miss Delaney."

The patrons in the restaurant clapped and tapped their water glasses to acknowledge Amber, who stood on a chair, waving. Bo recognized some of the faces and couldn't believe the gleeful cheers in their acts of betrayal. "How did you manage that?" he asked as he propelled her out of the restaurant.

"It's part of the membership."

Chapter Fifteen

Amber stood by the rental piece of junk. The steam curled from the hood, rising along with her temper. Maybe it was supposed to be her luck to be saddled with a broken-down heap during her stint in Texas.

Bundled in her down jacket, she stood on the side of the highway, debating on which direction to head. A couple of pickup trucks rumbled past her with strange characters behind the wheel. Some threw her leery smiles. Maybe hitch-hiking wasn't such a good idea. She promptly stuck her hand back in her jacket.

A familiar beige SUV drove past. Its brake lights flashed on as the tires squealed. The heavy vehicle rocked to a sudden stop. Luckily, no other cars followed. Amber stepped onto the road to verify her guess that it was Zack.

"Hey, lady. Where you trying to head? Looks like you're not going to get too far."

Amber laughed. "You're telling me." Despite her present

inconvenience and crappy mood, she breathed a sigh of relief. "Thanks for stopping."

"Where were you heading?"

"Library. I'd borrowed a few books, which are about two days overdue."

"Well, I'll not only take you to the library, but I'll also treat you to lunch. Sound good to you?"

"Sure."

Amber rode in silence, enjoying Zack's easygoing personality. Every so often she would steal a few glances at him while pretending to look at the view. He didn't really resemble Bo or Josh. Instead he favored his mother, but had distinctive features she couldn't find in the other family members, like his dimpled chin or his ears that stuck out just slightly. The one thing he did have in common with his brothers was the smile that had the power to win arguments, melt reservations, and pique a woman's interest. Whenever he grinned, she couldn't help but think of Bo.

"Where're we going?" Amber turned in the seat to look back at the town as they drove out.

"I don't know how you can stand that microscopic town. We're heading to Dallas. You don't mind, do you?"

"I guess not," she joked.

"Good. I only came home to sign papers that Dad had for me. But staying overnight was out of the question. I have my bachelor pad, but that's off-limits to most." He grinned. "Have to keep some places sacred." He stroked his steering wheel. "As long as I have my ride, I'm mobile. Don't need any Suzy Homemakers to come to my house and move in."

"I can't wait for the day someone has you panting for her attention." The chuckle died in her throat. *Can't wait*. This wasn't home. This wasn't reality.

"No way. Anyway, I'll have to stay for the entire Kwanzaa celebration. That's a command performance."

"That's what I'm gathering."

"It's a tradition. Mom has celebrated Kwanzaa as long as I can remember. Even though we're no longer teenagers, the entire family, including the cousins, has to come home, or at the very least for the last day of Kwanzaa. Only death or sickness is an excuse."

"I know nothing about it. I mean that I've heard of it, but my mother was too much of a free spirit to be tied down to any one tradition. I usually went over to my friends' houses to celebrate with their families."

"That must have had some advantages. From what I can see, you're a free spirit, too—independent, visionary."

"Flattery will get you everywhere, Mr. Pemberton."

"You're everything my brother said you were. I'll enjoy your company at lunch."

Amber blushed at the thought that Bo had discussed her with his brother. She was dying to know what he'd said.

"I can hear the wheels grinding in your mind. Don't worry, he didn't say anything negative or embarrassing about you. I just wondered how long you plan to play housekeeper."

Amber stiffened. "Excuse me?"

"I saw the books you read. I've paid attention to our previous conversations. Cooking and cleaning isn't your bag unless it's for the money. Mom tends to pay according to her feelings, not based on market value."

"What is with you Pemberton boys? I've never met a more brazen lot. Why I'm a housekeeper is none of your business." She kept her tone soft, but added enough of an edge to let him know he was at the line that shouldn't be crossed.

Obviously he didn't care about the line or was enjoying himself too much to hear what she'd said. "Don't get touchy. I just wondered if Bo was the main reason you were hanging around."

"I guess from high school to the present, girls have been scrambling over each other to talk to Bo. That hasn't happened in my case. I'm too old for that and I'm too focused for a throw-down with the boss." She deserved the highest award for the lies dripping from her tongue as smooth as honey.

He nodded. "That's not what my mother says."

Amber screamed, not knowing what else to do or say. "And you are very much how your brother described."

"You can tell me over a plate of food."

"Now that I have no way of returning to town, are you planning to hold me hostage until you glean every piece of worthwhile information?"

"Got that right. We're going to the Crab Shack as the bribe."

"Mmmm, seafood. Good thinking. We'll see." Her stomach growled on cue for an exaggerated touch.

Lunch arrived after a few minutes. Amber was pleased with her selection of coconut shrimp and apple dipping sauce. With the additional side of crab legs, she could have floated overhead from the sheer delight of eating crabs and shrimp.

Opposite her in the booth, Zack had selected a seafood platter that had a little bit of everything and a hearty helping of hush puppies.

They munched in comfortable silence, commenting about safe topics like the weather and the local news.

Her cell phone rang. She glanced down at the number across the LCD screen before answering. "Hi." Her stomach did flip-flops at the deep timbre in Bo's reply.

"It's Bo."

Amber nodded, trying to split her attention between the two brothers. "Where are you?"

Zack pulled her hair playfully. "It's my brother, isn't it? That husky 'Hello' and giggling gave you away." He threw back his head and laughed. "Man, my brother must have put a number on you."

Amber giggled again and tried to shush Zack by throwing her napkin at his face.

"What's going on? Are you with friends?"

"Ah . . . no. I'm with Zack."

"Zack!"

Zack filled his mouth with hush puppies. "Tell him we're having a romantic lunch and sorry he couldn't be here."

Amber emitted a longer string of giggles. "Be quiet, Zack."

"Sounds like you're busy, so I'm going to hang up."

"Come on, Bo. Are you getting an attitude because your brother and I went to lunch?"

"Was this Zack's idea?"

Zack reached across and took a shrimp from her plate. "I used to steal his girlfriends. They always thought I was so cute and adorable. It got so bad that he'd have to pay me to stay away."

"What's he saying? Put him on the phone."

"Nope. You're being touchy for no good reason. My car broke down and Zack picked me up. I'm now outside of Dallas eating seafood."

"Dallas, huh. That's more than an hour away."

"You're right. Did you want something?"

"You are so frustrating. I wanted to talk to you, but you're obviously busy."

"Sounds like you're lonely. Maybe there's a cow you can go tend."

"Don't make fun of me. Once you're finished playing with my adolescent brother, you've got to come back home."

Amber smiled. She liked the sound of that word and every meaning associated with it. "Yes, I'll be home soon."

Zack stretched out his hand for the phone. She complied.

Although Amber could only hear one side of the conversation, she heard enough to make her perception. Bo was jealous of his little brother's Good Samaritan act and Zack was not letting up in reveling in his brother's discomfort.

Knowing that Bo could be an ornery toad, she'd deal with his ill temper later. Right now, she particularly enjoyed the thought that he could be jealous.

The weather didn't bother to cooperate with Bo's foul mood. The sun shone in a brilliant fashion during a spring-like day. There was no wind howling as a precursor to the family discussion about to begin. Instead, from where he could see at the window, the grass in the field barely rustled. The soft wind brushed the tips of the overgrown grass in one direction, resembling a lush green carpet. Bo looked around the room at his closest relatives. He wanted a clear win, but that didn't seem possible.

"I've brought in an accountant who is currently going over the books. I can tell you right now that there is heavy debt."

"And what does that mean?" His cousin Leon crossed his arms.

"It means I'll need more time to let the accountant do her thing. Then I can share the financials with you and we can make a smart decision about what we should do."

"Smart decision? I made a smart decision when I told you I wanted to sell my portion," Clarissa said. "This is about what is right for me and my family."

"We're all family," Martha added quietly.

"Aunty, I don't mean to disrespect you, but we're struggling to make ends meet. It doesn't make sense that we should be living from paycheck to paycheck when we have a means to make that disappear."

"I understand, Clarissa, but you don't want to be short-sighted either. Bo is back and I'm sure he can get things running in top shape again soon." Bo saw the unspoken worry in his mother's eyes.

"Is this true? Are you back?"

Bo nodded. "Yes, I'm back. I promise you that if you give me three months, we can meet again to decide on what to do."

"I'll give you that chance," Leon offered.

Clarissa nodded.

"This is all well and good," Todd said over the speakerphone, "but I don't believe anything will change. I talked to a lawyer and he said that either you buy me out or we can go to the court and request that the property be sold and then divided."

"What?" Bo shouted. "That will destroy the ranch."

"Stop being so dramatic. The only ones that seem to be getting the best deal is you and your family," Todd replied.

"Watch it, Todd," Josh warned. "Don't forget that your father and uncles didn't leave a will and my father made sure everyone maintained an interest in the property."

"It's the twenty-first century and it doesn't make sense to keep hold of something that no longer has the value. Ranchers everywhere are going bankrupt. Bo, you were the one not so long ago who couldn't stand this smelly rat trap."

The room quieted. The truth slammed Bo in his face. He certainly never hid his desire to go off and claim his own fortune. It made it doubly hard to get on his soapbox about saving the ranch.

Todd wasn't finished. "And it wasn't as though he came back because things were rough on the ranch."

Only the ticking of the wall clock punctuated the air.

Martha stepped forward. "Enough. Let's all just simmer down. We'll get back to all of this. "Good-bye, Todd." She pressed the button ending the call. "Right now, dinner should be ready." Her voice was soft, but surprisingly firm. The room emptied in a matter of seconds.

Bo appreciated the reassuring pat on his back from his father. "I can see it in their eyes that they're listening to you. You're the eldest and everyone looks up to you."

"I don't see it."

After a heated exchange, now they had to eat together. Only his mother could have come up with that game plan.

Dinner was simple. Covered dishes sat on the sideboard. The table setting didn't carry too much flair with basic plates, glassware, and silverware. He understood his mother's plan to appear as if there weren't social distinctions within the family.

The muted conversations at the beginning of the meal didn't last long. Discussions ranged from the reigning football teams to the clearance racks at the nearby shopping outlet. Bo kept up his end of the conversations, but his gaze wandered to the doorway on the lookout for Amber. He'd love to hear her opinion of this family squabble.

Bo agreed, but still wanted her there. "Now that we've had a chance to eat and think about what we have, can we at least agree to give me a few more months?"

Bo noticed that everyone nodded except Leon. He locked eyes with his cousin. "What's the problem?"

"Todd already signed a deal. Don't look at me like that. He's in Chicago with a law-school debt over his head."

"But didn't he think he should have talked to us as a family? It's not only his decision."

"Did you talk to us as you increased the grazing land or the head of cattle? After the last drought, when everyone else was getting out of the business, did you ever consider asking our opinions?"

"My father ran the ranch and we shared the profits."

"You know, Bo, all you have to do is pay me."

Bo shot the chair back as he stood.

"Bo!" His mother called. "Leon, sit down."

"No, Aunt Martha. All of you need to think about your future, what little you may have. Thanks for dinner." Leon threw down his napkin and left.

It took every ounce of Bo's willpower to remain at the table. His head throbbed to the angry beat of the vein in his temple.

"Anyone else?"

No one answered, but he could see the indecision in their eyes. Heck, if he looked into the mirror, he could probably see it in his own eyes.

"Bro, we're here with you." His brother came over and hugged him. "Come on, Clarissa, our parents went through too much to get this land and keep this land for us to fight over it. Regardless of what we decide in three months, let's not destroy what we have," Josh said.

The family got up and hugged each other. Martha offered a prayer over their bowed heads. "Please make sure you come back for our day of meditation. I think we are in dire need for sustenance. I've never asked you to contribute to the Kwanzaa celebration, to bring your stories or share your insights. Some of you did and I appreciate it. This time because we are becoming so fragmented, we need to come on New Year's Day in the correct frame of mind. Come with humility and gratitude. Focus on *Imani*—have faith in our people, our victory, our legacy. Okay?"

Later, Bo went up to his room. Out of habit he looked across the hall at the partially opened door to Amber's room. He'd never entered her room, especially when she wasn't there. Missing her made him want to be close to her, even her things. She and Zack hadn't yet returned.

The room, which was already decorated, had small touches of her. The champagne-colored room with gold accents now had a vase with a colorful bouquet of fresh flowers. There were small-framed pictures of people he didn't know. Only then did he realize that Amber had shared some information about her mother, but no mention of her father, extended family, or friends.

Picking up each frame, he contemplated what the occasion was. Based on the various hairstyles and even hair coloring, he assumed they were not recent. He was glad to note that none of the pictures featured any intimate poses with a male friend.

At the desk in the corner, he saw an open notebook. In the evenings he would spy her writing in the book. She'd be so focused, biting her lip as she wrote, that he could watch unobserved. The full page with dark ink drew his curiosity. He walked over to the desk, scolding himself for what he was about to do. He shifted the book with his finger and squinted to make some sense from the scribble. Randomly he skimmed several pages.

His name leaped off the page at him.

"Son, what are you doing?" His mother's voice chastised from the hallway. "How can you go into her room when she's not here?" She opened the door a bit wider, waiting for his exit.

He picked up the journal and turned to his mother. "I see my name in here."

"And . . . ? It's her personal notes, Bo." She crossed the room and snapped the journal shut before replacing it on the desk. With a firm hold on his arm, she pulled him out of the room. "I've raised you better than that. Even if you choose to forget your manners, I'm not going to let you violate Amber's privacy."

Bo knew when he wouldn't win an argument with his mother. Without resistance, he allowed her to usher him out toward his room while she continued to scold his behavior. Maybe he did deserve the rebuke because he felt no remorse. How could he feel sorry when he distinctly saw a sentence that claimed he was a moderately wealthy man with no concept of what real people think and feel?

After his mother left, shaking her head, he contemplated making another attempt at Amber's bedroom. He turned around. Apparently his mother had considered such a maneuver and paused on the steps to look back at him. With a mocking salute and small smirk, he entered his room and closed the door.

His imagination played with his insecurities. Did Amber

really think about him in such a manner? After a long trying day with his family, he didn't need this. He didn't expect such a betrayal—and that was his conclusion—from her.

Amber turned up the volume and bobbed her head to the bass vibrating off her favorite CD. Her mood was light and bubbly. With the afternoon off, she had Zack drive her to the bakery to say hello to Barb and to pick up a treat. She couldn't help but feel proud of herself. Martha was going to hug her to death for the apple and pecan pies she now brought back to the house. She'd surprise Bo with lemon-bar treats.

Winding up the dirt road toward the house, it hit her that this sudden comfort and ease in which she'd lived for the past few weeks came with a price. In that space of time, she'd begun referring to the ranch as home—her home. Life in Maryland seemed so far away, distant, and foreign. One day all of this would have to end. Pretty soon she would have to fulfill her assignment, fulfill the goal she had set for herself, but now that didn't have the same satisfaction.

Amber entered the house with the pies in one hand and the bag with the lemon bar in another. Heading straight for the kitchen, she looked around for any signs that the family meeting was over. Since there were no parked cars, she assumed it was done. The dishwasher changed cycles, providing a soothing whooshing sound in the empty kitchen. She figured that Martha probably went back to her place.

"You're back."

Amber spun around to see Bo standing in the opening between the kitchen and hall. "Hey, how did it go earlier?" From the stern set of his mouth, there was no cause for celebration.

"Didn't know you would leave."

Amber detected a slight tone of accusation. "Wanted to go to the library and then get pies for dessert. Was that okay?" She pointed to where she set the pies. "Got you a lemon bar." She was offering to get him to smile.

He nodded. "Thanks." Yet she got the distinct impression that she had done something wrong.

"Can we have dessert together later this evening?"

"Sure. But can you tell me something?"

She really wished he would smile. So far his eyes might as well have been burning a hole in the middle of her forehead. The steely glint made her hesitate. She shrugged, immediately deciding that any answer didn't bode well.

"What's this?" He held up his hand. Amber recognized her leather-bound journal. Her focus shifted slowly from the book to his face.

She exhaled. "Oh, boy." Her heart sped up its beat. Her mind scrambled for something to say or do.

His eyes narrowed.

"Where did you get that? Did you go into my room? I don't understand—"

"I went into your room looking for you. After my cousin sucker-punched me with his plans, I needed some relief. I needed you."

If it was supposed to be a statement of desire, it fell flat. Amber waited for the full impact of the impending storm. "But you had no right to go into my room. At least not to go rummaging through my stuff as if I'm a common thief."

"I'll apologize later. Right now I want to know what these notes are about me, my family, my business." He opened the book. "Don't bother to protest. I'll read these parts and you 'fess up.'" He cleared his throat. "'*Bodine Pemberton. He's just a man. A man used to privileges, placed on a pedestal by family and friends. In a matter of months, he no longer has his big-title job. His fiancée gives him the boot. And many think he's as dirty as his colleagues, but managed to get away by the skin of his teeth because he copped a plea.'"*

Amber stared down at her feet. The shame and guilt crippled her into a gagging silence. The floor could have pity on her and swallow her up.

"Is this what you think of me?"

Amber tried to meet his gaze, but couldn't.

"Answer me!"

"No. I just . . . I wrote that before I really knew you."

"Oh, really. Then what about this on the last entry—'*Not everyone leads fairy-tale lives where they can go on living happily ever after. Bo must have a lucky penny under his pillow because the thought of being broke for retirement isn't a possibility with successful home business like the Pemberton Ranch.'*"

Martha walked into the kitchen. "I tried to stay out of this, but I think you're making a big mistake, son. Amber is not your enemy."

"Mom, stay out of this." His jaw clenched and unclenched.

His mother responded with a hand on her hip. "I told you not to go snooping."

"Well, the rewards made it worth my while. Obviously today is the day of betrayals."

Amber appreciated Martha's defense. Heck, she held more than gratitude for the older lady. At the same time, she'd grown to dislike her dual role. "Bo, I'm a reporter."

"What?"

"I figured you were." Martha laid a reassuring hand on her shoulder. "Asked too many questions, but I could tell you thought about everything. I truly believe you would be fair in your portrayal of my son and this family."

Bo rubbed his face vigorously and shook his head. "I'm thrilled that you feel comfortable with her. Since I didn't have a clue, I'm not feeling so generous. After everything . . ." He locked eyes with her.

She understood that he wanted her to remember their special night. The impact of her actions hit, then. She mouthed the word "Sorry" as tears welled, creating a shimmering view of him.

"After everything, Amber, honesty means nothing to you."

"So many times I wanted to tell you."

"But we shared so many . . ." He looked over to his mother. She blushed, but motioned for him to continue. "I was going to say that we shared some special times where we talked about our dreams and our fears. But I suppose that was all part of the plan, right?"

"May I make a suggestion?" Martha stepped in between the two. "How about using Amber to write about the real you. Personally I don't see why you should care what people think. Your father and I raised you to do the right thing and we are very proud of you. Working here, it won't matter."

"That's exactly my point. Again I will be tied to this ranch whether I want to be or not."

Martha visibly backed down.

"I'm sorry, Mom. That came out all wrong."

"Bo, Martha, yes, I did come under false pretenses. But my friendship with you was genuine. My journal just happened to be my naked thoughts and you're taking them out of context. I'm so sorry."

Martha walked over and hugged her. Amber melted against her shoulder, grateful for her forgiving nature. "I trust you to be fair and honest. You're a sweet person, Amber, don't lose sight of your values in pursuit of your dreams." She looked over to her son, who had turned his back on them. "Guess I'll step out now. Bo, think about what I said."

He bowed his head, not bothering to turn around.

"Follow me." He led the march to his office.

Amber licked her lips, prodding herself to say something. The stiff set of his shoulders told her it would be a waste of energy to try to dissuade him.

"Have a seat." She complied, straining to see what he had pulled out of his desk. She saw that it was the checkbook. Without looking up at her, he filled out a check and ripped it out of the book. Only then did he look up at her. With his emotions safely shuttered behind the tight face, he handed her the check. "Here's your check. Here's your journal. I want you packed and out of here by six."

"Bo, I never said this, but I love you."

The words shook Bo. Emotionally, he took a step back, steeling himself to remain unmoved. Unlike his breakup with Cassidy, ending it with Amber tortured him like nothing had ever done. He had to bite down on his tongue to keep from talking, and asking why.

"At least I did earn my keep, even if I wasn't the best housekeeper."

"It'll be something you can fall back on if the job doesn't work out."

"I have a feeling that a change will be coming soon."

Bo pulled open his drawer and took out his familiar pills for the headache brewing just under the surface. "Answer me this, what about the stalker? Was that fiction?"

Amber shook her head slowly. "No, it wasn't. The whole thing seems so faraway now. I'm sure he must have gone on his merry way, though."

He wanted to believe her. Let something she said actually be true. He knew better than to take her words about loving him to heart. If their entire meeting was planned and their supposed employment relationship a farce, why should he be gullible enough to believe in those three words?

Chapter Sixteen

Bo stormed through the house, fighting the urge to pick up the large imported vase in the hall and throw it against something hard. He refused to feel guilty about what he'd done. Amber had played him for a fool. What he didn't like and wasn't used to was the physical pain. And it hurt like hell.

"Bo, what've you just done?" His mother ran behind him.

"Can't you leave me alone?"

"I'll let you get away with talking to me in that tone. But you need to calm down and rethink the situation."

"Rethink what!? Amber is a fake, a phony, a con artist. She has had access to us, to me, to everything around here. What do you think she'll do with all that information? She's ambitious and coldheartedly focused on her goal. There's nothing to rethink."

He stormed toward the front door, ready to rip it off its hinges. Not even his horse could calm him down. His ill temper was on hyper speed and he felt out of control. As his hand lit the doorknob, the bell rang. He swung open the door, glaring at the stranger in front of him.

"Yes."

"Good morning, sir. I have this bouquet of flowers for Amber Delaney."

Bo stared down at the roses. Whoever bought these roses had spent a pretty penny. In a quick tally, he knew it was more than a dozen. The blood-red hue of partially opened buds completely blocked the delivery man's face.

After giving a tip, he took the flowers into the house. The strong scent overtook the room in a matter of seconds.

"Oh, my, how beautiful. These are for Amber?"

Bo glared at his mother. "What are you so happy for?"

"Because after dragging her through the mud, she deserves something like this." She stepped forward to take the little envelope. "I'll take the card up to her room. Thirty roses, wow. 'll be too much for me to take upstairs."

"She can get them on her way out." Bo reached for the card and flicked it open.

"Stop doing that!"

He ignored his mother. "See. This proves my point. Her sweetheart is giving her roses 'Just because. . . .'" He allowed his mother to pluck it out of his hand.

Without a backward glance, he walked out the door and headed for his car. Behind the steering wheel, he'd decide where to go. Right now, he craved an open highway.

Amber heard the exchange downstairs behind the safety of her bedroom door. How had everything changed so suddenly? She rested her head against the door and bit her lip to fight back the tears. As much as it hurt, she couldn't blame Bo for feeling betrayed. She'd been so honest about so many things, sharing memories she'd never shared with anyone else. All these things she could do, except tell him about her job and her assignment.

After the chaos and emotional wreckage, her precious assignment didn't seem important at all. Deep inside, she harbored a hollow feeling that knew no cure.

Heavyhearted, she pulled the suitcase from the closet and opened it on the bed. It seemed like months ago when she had arrived in a dusty, tired state and fell into the job of housekeeper. She'd actually learned to boil an egg. So there was *some* good that came out of this. A muffled sob caught in her throat.

Like a robot, she moved back and forth from the drawer to the suitcase. There were more than clothes being packed. She had mementos she'd picked up in town. There was the little bear he'd bought for her on their cattle-rustling adventure. She closed her eyes and brushed it against her cheek. A soft scent of his cologne still lingered. As she recalled that evening and their passionate experience, her legs went weak and she sat on the bed, staring down at the bear behind a curtain of tears.

She ignored the knock at her door. She didn't think it was Bo from the tentative knocking, but she still didn't want any company.

Another sharp knock made her look up at the door. Yet she didn't answer.

The door slowly opened. "Amber, dear. I'm not going to ask a stupid question like how are you doing, but I did want to check on you."

Amber sniffed and hastily wiped her tears away. "I'm

fine. I'll be done in a few minutes." She scrambled off the bed and went about the business of packing again.

"No, child, I didn't come here to chase you away. On the contrary, I want you to stay."

Amber didn't buy into Martha's plea. She knew the older lady had a good heart, but in this case it wasn't enough. "Your son wants me to go."

"I want you to stay."

"I have a job—maybe friends, a home back in Maryland. Remember, I wasn't a housekeeper."

Martha sat at the foot of the bed and closed the suitcase. "Would you stay until we work out all of this?"

Amber laughed. There was nothing funny about this conversation, but she couldn't help being cynical about Martha's blind optimism. "My article is due."

"You can't leave when both of you are heartbroken."

"Martha, that is very melodramatic."

Martha nodded. "You can't tell me it doesn't hurt right here." She placed a hand between her breastbone. "I had my share of heartbreaks in my life and I swear if they took an X-ray, they'd see the damage."

Amber couldn't agree more. But what did having a heartache have to do with her only option—to leave? "Martha, I have to leave. I wish you all the best."

"Before you go, answer a few questions."

"Sure." Amber didn't stop what she was doing. She'd managed to buy shoes and clothes while exploring Breezewood. Her loot couldn't fit in the small suitcase. It didn't matter, she'd throw the entire lot in the back of the car. She would book her flight once she moved into a hotel near the airport.

Martha didn't try to stop her from packing. Instead she made herself more comfortable on the bed. "Why did you choose to write about Bo?"

Amber thought about her answer, wanting to give the cleaner version as to why she had selected Bodine Pemberton.

"Don't lie to me, Amber."

"My childhood friend, Zoe Cantrell, committed suicide. She worked for the same company with Bo. While I tried to come to terms with my friend taking her life, I started researching Bo and his role in the scandal. Bo presented a contradiction I didn't want to believe. A man with a set future in the family business goes off and lands a high-paying job. Then he discloses the company's practice and single-handedly places the company on the edge of bankruptcy. While everyone else's life is in shambles, he returns home, back to his safe and secure legacy."

"I guess I understand how the public may think that way. I see him as a hero."

"He is."

"So you came with this mind-set. You didn't know we needed a housekeeper. What would have been the game plan?"

"I was going to ask him for an interview. If that didn't work, I was going to camp out in front of his house and bug him until I got what I wanted. I was even willing to put an ad in your local newspaper with a plea about how Bo should face the media and tell his story, make apologies."

"You're pretty creative." Martha stared at her with a shrewd expression crossing her features. "Do you think you had what it took to take on a member of this family?"

"I'm pretty tenacious, but after getting to all of you, you could have certainly given me a run." She paused and grinned at Martha. "But I would still have won."

"You've been here about two months now. It couldn't take that long to write your article."

"Actually it did. I wasn't sure how I wanted to begin. How I wanted to introduce the public to Bo. Then I wrote a couple drafts but my editor rejected them, or, I should say, wanted them rewritten in a more sensational fashion."

"Obviously you were going to do it." The humor had left Martha's face. "Amber?"

Amber pushed the suitcase farther up the bed and took a seat. "It's not only the story that brought me here. There was someone stalking me in Washington, D.C. The police couldn't help me. I couldn't get a restraining order because I didn't know who was doing the stalking. It was getting creepier. I took the opportunity to get away."

One look at Martha and the older woman had bundled her up into her arms, hugging her tightly. "You poor child. I knew you couldn't have written anything nasty about Bo. All this time you were in hiding. You should have told me." Martha stood and headed for the door. "Look here, you're not going anywhere until we figure out a few things. Have you talked to the police lately? You should check to see if they're still investigating. Oh, and your house, who's watching it?"

Amber broke down. "My friend Sylvia who was watching the house has disappeared." She wiped away the tears. "I haven't called to find out the latest. I'm afraid."

Martha hugged her and patted her back. "There, there. You've got too much to deal with for one person." She sighed. "You're here as my guest. Nope, don't try to dissuade me. I never rehired you." She opened the door. "Dry your eyes. Then come on down for something to eat. When Bo returns from his tantrum, we'll talk."

The mention of Bo's name brought the despair to the forefront. "I don't think I can face Bo. Martha, I really think I should stay in a hotel until I can get a flight out."

"That's an expensive way to decide on what to do. Come down in a few. I'll have a snack fixed. And don't worry about Bo. What about Zoe?"

"I think it's time I stop beating myself up. It hurts that I can't take back all the ugly things I said. It's time to stop looking back."

Amber heaved a big sigh after Martha left the room. She felt as if a heavy burden had been lifted off her chest. Now she could breathe easier.

Martha's kindness reminded Amber of her mother. After their last fight, she hadn't heard from her mother, which wasn't surprising because she could hold a grudge for a long time. But Martha's warmth and forgiving nature made her yearn for a chance to make things right.

Amber dialed her mother's number. The phone rang and she hoped it wouldn't go into voice mail. The chances of her mother checking the voice mail were not optimistic. She held her finger over the END button, counting the rings.

"Hello," her mother whispered.

"Mom? Why are you whispering?" She heard the fear in her own voice.

"I'm in a workshop—"

"With Alice?" Amber was excited on her behalf.

"No. It's a new author, but I haven't given up on Ms. Walker. How are you?"

"Things are a little chaotic." She sniffed, wiping her nose with a tissue.

"You make the simplest things hard on yourself. Look at your options and choose what's in your heart. I know I can be a pain, but I took it to another level the other day. I don't know what came over me."

"It's okay." Amber stared at her reflection with the phone wedged between her shoulder and ear. She didn't like sharing her feelings. Didn't ever want to have a one-to-one discussion. The fact that her mother seemed to be going in that direction made her uncomfortable.

"It's not okay. I know I made you feel as if I take you for granted. Maybe I do."

"You're scaring me, talking like this."

"When I had just missed seeing Alice Walker, I went to the hotel room. As I was lying there, I thought about how I had allowed my life to drift for a fleeting dream."

"Being a writer isn't a fleeting dream, Mom. You've been writing poetry and stories for me ever since I was kid. Now that you're so close and have made so many sacrifices, don't run from it. Don't be scared." Amber heard her mother's soft sniffles. "Why don't I come and see you?"

"Here, in California?"

"Yep. It's time for us to catch up face-to-face."

"Thank you, babe."

Amber hung up from her mother and wiped away the tears that had silently rolled down her cheeks. Her mother equaled her only family. Martha's hospitality stirred her desire to belong.

The Pembertons' closeness intrigued her, inviting in a mysterious way, but also scary. Their honesty fed a warmth and security she never knew she ached for until Martha and Bo came into her life.

In this house she had allowed herself to become a character that was part of a family. But the fit didn't always suit her, making her itch and scratch in deep places where she'd learned to keep her emotions secured.

Her mother's apology was the tool she needed to pry open her fears and release them. In this moment, she knew she didn't want to head back to Washington, D.C. Since the door was also closed here, despite Martha's invitation, she was prepared to turn to her mother and go to California.

With half a sob and half a chuckle, she imagined sitting with her mother in one of her many writers' retreats. She wondered who would be her artist of choice to dedicate her life to following around the state. They would make quite a pair. She wasn't sure the logical side of her would willingly go.

She grabbed a tissue and blew her nose. Enough of this. She would call her crazy girlfriend for a good laugh. She dialed Sylvia's parents.

The voice mail came on and she hung up.

Eddie called the florist shop for the third time. People could be so rude. He wanted to be sure, though. "Yes, this is Mr. Brown. I wanted to check on the delivery I requested."

"Yes, sir." The salesperson's frustration practically oozed over the phone line. "Your delivery has been received."

"Good. I mean . . . are you sure? Who signed for it? What time was it received?"

"Sir, the shop is very busy. I told you they were delivered."

His temper flared to a roaring blaze. "Look, either you tell me over this phone or I will come down to that shop. And you don't want me to do that."

"It was delivered at noon. Bo Pemberton signed for it."

He slammed down the phone, although his temper had subsided. Now he could relax. Think. Maybe he could even sleep, get up his energy, and go hunting later. With the television off, he stared up at the dingy ceiling until his eyes grew tired and his lids closed.

Two hours later, his eyes popped open. Eddie yawned and stretched. His mouth felt thick and he could actually taste the bitterness of his breath. He felt like a high school boy on his graduation day.

Everything had to be perfect.

He took a quick shower, brushed his teeth, and groomed himself. A quick check in the mirror didn't reveal any magic transformation. He still had a receding hairline that made his forehead look bigger. His pockmarked skin hadn't changed.

Stroking his chin, he wondered what Sylvia had wanted from him. She was the kind of woman who could attract the savvy lawyers and muscle-bound beach bums. Yet she had noticed him. Wanted to be with him.

He flicked out the bathroom light. This was no time for weakness. Sylvia was gone. It wasn't in the plan, but at least he knew how to act on his feet. Once he had Amber, he would treat her like a queen. In his own way, he would repent for his actions against Sylvia. Maybe he would even send a note to her family to let them know.

Dressed in his camouflage fatigues and hiking boots, with a dash of cologne, he headed out of the motel room. He walked past the motel's office and waved at the clerk. Although he'd checked in for five days, he didn't plan to return.

Repeatedly he went over his strategy, planning for the best- and worst-case scenarios. There was no turning back. He had left Maryland with home and job no longer an issue. All he wanted was a life with Amber. They would settle down somewhere. He'd get a job and support her. He had no desire for children.

Driving through town, he imagined her walking through

the town. Did she go into the little shops with their products in the window to entice shoppers?

From Sylvia he learned that Amber had fallen in love with Breezewood. He couldn't fulfill that dream for her to remain in town. More than likely he would have to spend some time convincing her they belonged together. Patience was in huge supply.

He followed the road leading out of town toward the ranch. At the turn onto the dirt road, he waited for oncoming traffic to clear. A sports car coming from the ranch caught his attention. It wasn't really the car, but the thick cloud of dust kicked into the air as the fast-moving tires skidded.

He didn't expect to see Bo Pemberton. That wasn't in the action plan. The man didn't notice him as he turned onto the road in the opposite direction. With the man of the house out of the picture, he knew that the parents lived on the property. He'd have to figure out if they were in the house.

Eddie drove the car slowly up the path, wanting to make the least noise possible. He parked off to the side of the barn and waited in the car to see if anyone had noticed him from the window.

His palms grew sweaty. His breath came short. Leaning across the passenger seat, he opened the glove compartment. He pulled out his self-help book. Nerves on edge, stomach tight, he needed to get himself focused with a confidence surge. On page fifty, he reread the chapter on "Taking Charge." It always helped to give him momentum to achieve.

Amber looked out the window; she thought she heard a car. Maybe Bo had returned. But she didn't see his car and tried to suppress the disappointment. Well, she couldn't hide in her room all night.

"Amber, come on down and eat. You can't stay up in that room all night long."

Amber smiled and ran down the stairs. "I was coming. Just thought I'd heard a car."

"Didn't hear anything. But if it's Bo, I'll deal with him."

Amber sat at the table in the kitchen with a plate of peanut butter and jelly sandwiches and a glass of milk. "Thank you."

"Figured you want some comfort food. Noticed that you tend to fix that for yourself whenever you've had a bad day." Martha sat down next to her. "I also notice that you eat it after you've spoken to your mother." She raised her eyebrows.

"Yes." Amber grinned. "I spoke to my mother."

"And . . ."

"It went really well. I'm planning to head out to California to see her. Spend some time, maybe make it my new home."

Martha brushed away the imaginary crumbs. "Put you first, Amber. I'm not saying that you shouldn't go see your mother. But it's obvious that you're going through a period of self-renewal. I don't want to see you drown in someone else's dream. Okay?"

Amber squeezed Martha's hand. "You're so good to me."

"I've liked you from the first day you came in here with those ridiculous platform shoes. You've got a warm spirit about you. I enjoy being in your company."

"You're going to make me cry again."

"Not over the sandwich, please."

They both chuckled. Amber drained her cup of milk, turning down a refill.

Martha took her dishes to the sink, despite her protests. "You know what? It's not quite evening, but I think we both are in need of some sustenance. Let's strengthen our inner spirits at the Kwanzaa set."

Amber nodded. She didn't want to admit to Martha that she had her doubts about this tradition that her family never practiced. Some of her friends talked about it, but not too many families had participated. Even as she got older and Sylvia invited her to the Ebony Eye Book Club annual Kwanzaa celebration, she turned it down.

"I'm going to pop over and get Will. Then we can begin."

"Okay. In the meantime, I'll think about today's principle."

"Do you remember what it is?"

"*Ujamaa* for cooperative economics."

"Great. You're learning." Martha walked out the back door. "Be right back."

Amber went into the living room. She sat in the wing-back chair and tried to relax, to get in the proper frame of mind. What she wanted more than anything was to find the right words, the actions to make things right. Despite all her actions, deep down she wanted the rift between Bo and her to disappear.

"We're back."

"I'm in here," she called to Martha and Will.

They appeared arm-in-arm in the doorway. Martha took the lead and relit the unity candle before lighting the red *Ujamaa* candle. She turned to her husband for his part. "On the fourth day of Kwanzaa, we will explore *Ujamaa*, which means cooperative economics." Will stood at his wife's side while leaning on a cane. "Cooperative economics is the principle that recognizes our need to have and patronize our businesses and to pool our financial resources for betterment. My father and uncles may not have known the Swahili term, but they had the foresight to pool their money and provide for this family. Not only did this family benefit, but they were able to feed many children and employ from the community."

Amber listened, keenly aware of the pride with which Will reflected about his father. Could she stand and mention the remarkable things that her parents did? Parents who were childhood sweethearts, toured with a small acting troupe, and then settled down in a lower-middle-class neighborhood to have their child? Without all the colorful details, it sounded harmless, plain.

Alcohol, then adultery, tore the family apart into tiny fragments. No one trusted the other for the mending, even if that was an option. Instead her father left to start anew, staying in touch on holidays and birthdays until it became birthdays only. And then an occasional card that would turn up a week early or a month late.

Talking about cooperative economics brought home the fact that her mother's new single-parent role threw them into deep poverty. There was no pooling of resources, unless she counted the times she shook every penny out of her piggy bank. Yet she never crumbled under the misery and she knew that her mother did the best she could at that time.

Amber looked up to see Martha and Will looking at her. "I'm sorry, were you talking to me?"

"It was your turn to share."

"Oh." Amber didn't want to share, but didn't want to be rude. "I was going over it in my head. I'm going to have a hard time saying it aloud."

Martha took a step forward.

"No, dear, let's give Amber her space. We can end the evening now," Will said.

Martha nodded. As with the end of every evening during Kwanzaa, she held out her hands and they all connected as she bowed her head and led the prayer.

Chapter Seventeen

Bo didn't take his foot off the accelerator until the dreaded blue lights flickered behind him. His eyes shifted to the speedometer. He grimaced. Eighty-five miles per hour. The day kept getting worse and worse.

He pulled over to the shoulder and leaned over to his glove compartment to pull out the registration. Maybe if the cop was a female, he could try one of Zack's moves and offer a sly, sexy smile. When he straightened up and turned to the window, a stone-faced male cop with dark reflective shades stared down on him.

Bo groaned. This was *really* not his day.

An hour later he pulled into Josh's driveway. He hadn't called ahead, but his brother's home was always open to him. Josh's car was parked in front of the garage door. Why have a garage if you wouldn't park the car in it? Obviously he had not made his case convincingly with

Josh about protecting his expensive BMW from the elements.

Bo rang the doorbell a couple times and then used his key to enter. "Yo, Josh. You in here?" He looked into the living room, which opened to the dining room. "Josh?" he shouted up the staircase.

He felt thirsty and headed for the kitchen. Unlike Zack, Josh made sure his house was in tip-top shape, with cupboards and refrigerator packed. Thank goodness he had cold root beer. He grabbed one and popped the lid. The drink needed munchies. After searching the cupboards overhead, he looked in the pantry and found an unopened bag of barbecue chips.

Armed with his treasures, he headed for the sofa in the family room. Chips on one side, chair cushions propping his elbow on the other side, he wiggled his back into the sofa and flicked on the television.

"I thought I heard you come in." Josh stood in the doorway in only his shorts.

Bo looked at his watch. "Aren't you working today?" His brother managed two upscale restaurants in the Dallas downtown area.

"I called in."

"What? You called in? Now, that's a first." Bo gulped his soda. "Okay, tell me her name."

"You don't know her. And why are you here? On a Friday night I'd think you'd be out on the town making goo-goo eyes with Amber."

"Don't mention that name."

"Uh-oh. What happened? Is that why you're over here?"

"Not really. I was just driving around and stopped in. Like you're ever doing anything other than work."

"As a matter of fact—"

"Jake, are you coming back?"

Bo halted the soda can to his mouth. His eyes grew wide. "Guess I walked in at the wrong time. Sorry, bro."

"Okay, then take your feet off my table and get out."

"She'd better be worth kicking me out." He shifted his weight on the sofa, but didn't move.

The door opened. "Hey, what's going on? Ya'll having a party and didn't tell me?" Zack strolled into the family room and plopped down in the chair next to Bo. "What brings you out of cow heaven?" He looked over to Josh. "Anything to eat?"

Josh walked over to the television and pushed the power button off. "Both of you, go cause trouble somewhere else."

"What's his beef? I'm hungry. Did you bring any left-overs from work?" Zack rubbed his stomach for emphasis.

"He's got another pot on simmer upstairs." Bo pointed toward the ceiling.

Confusion crossed Zack's face as he looked at Bo and then the ceiling. Then it clicked and his expression changed to a wide grin. "Josh's getting his groove on? Then don't let me stop you. Go ahead. Bo and I will sit here and catch up about the cows and stuff."

"Josh!" A husky voice drifted downstairs. A dark-skinned woman in her mid to late thirties appeared around the corner. This time the sexy drawl had vanished. "Josh, call me when you're serious about us getting to-gether." She zipped up her coat, glared at all of them, and walked out the door.

The three brothers craned their necks to witness the de-parture. Maybe it was the way her well-padded behind sashayed from side to side. The minute the door closed, Zack and Bo slapped hands together, hoopin' and hollerin.'

Josh pointed at them. "You're lucky I'm only a doctor and

not a cop because I'd go get my service weapon and put you both out of your misery."

"Didn't she look familiar?" Zack looked over to Bo.

"Not to me."

"Shut up, both of you. She's a local TV reporter." Josh glared at them.

Zack walked over and thumped Josh on his back. "Get outta here. Where did you meet such a honey?"

"I went to a basketball game. She happened to be sitting two seats over."

"And you had the nerve to talk to her? Is our Josh growing up, Bo?" Zack headed for the kitchen and promptly opened the refrigerator. He pulled out several aluminum-foil-wrapped dishes and a couple plastic containers, lining them up on the counter.

"Why are you in my house?" Josh had taken a seat on the floor, sharing his disgusted look with Zack and Bo.

"Zack, if you find anything good to eat, let me know." Bo flicked back on the television and channel surfed until he came across reruns of a sitcom.

Fifteen minutes later, he and Zack were eating shrimp Alfredo and garlic bread. Even Josh was eating, having given up on getting answers from either one.

After the final scene of the sitcom faded out, the string of commercials that followed broke the viewing mode among the three.

Bo took the dirty dishes to the sink. He had just spent the last fifteen minutes pretending to be engrossed in the show. Instead his mind was on Amber, wondering what she was doing. Did she get a flight out? If he had done the right thing, then why didn't it feel good? Why did he feel as if he had lost more than a housekeeper?

"You can put the stuff in the dishwasher. I need to turn it

on." Josh returned some of the items Zack had retrieved from the refrigerator. A few items he tossed in the trash after a smell test. "Mom said that you might end up here."

"Mom?" Bo had just put a plate in the dishwasher, glad that this revelation didn't occur moments before or it was liable to have slipped from his hands. "When did she call you?"

"I guess soon after you fired Amber and hopped in your car." Josh hoisted himself onto the counter, leaning against the cupboards. "I had to promise that if you came by, I'd call. Mama's little boy."

Bo dried his hands and leaned against the island. He didn't know where or how to begin. "Do your duty. Tell her I stopped by."

"Aren't you staying the night?"

"No, I think I want to be alone."

Zack walked up on their conversation. "What's going on? Bo, you've always wanted to be alone ever since we were kids. I guess you're too thickheaded to realize that isn't going to happen." Zack took a seat on a bar stool. "Now, can someone fill me in? Josh, any ice cream?"

Josh filled his brother's request, while Bo trailed a path with his finger on the counter.

Bo sighed. "Amber is a reporter. I knew she wasn't a housekeeper. That didn't take long to figure out."

Josh chuckled. "Yeah, Mom said if she wasn't so sweet, she would have fired her after the first pot burned."

"I thought she simply needed a job and this one had landed at her feet," Bo explained.

"When did all this come out?" Zack asked. "I spoke to her a couple of times, but I didn't pick up on anything. Thought she was pretty levelheaded—strong-minded is more like it."

"I came across some of her drafts. Not all were particularly flattering. I confronted her about it. She didn't deny it. Didn't say that she wasn't using us to achieve her own means. She befriended Mom. Used her." He didn't add that she used him nor that their mom had forgiven her.

"Mom said she understood Amber's motivation."

Bo pounded the counter with his fist, making the cooking utensils clatter in their place. "Well, I don't understand it. You don't come into someone's house and settle in while spying on them. She'd even sat in on some of the arguments about the land. This wasn't a problem until I read how she thought I was living a privileged life while the people who worked . . ." His voice faded.

"She hurt you," Josh said. "You trusted her, liked her, and you're angry because you were betrayed."

"Whoa, man." Zack shook his head, making sympathetic noises. "I don't know what to say."

"There's a bright side, though." Josh walked over to put a comforting hand on Bo's shoulder. "You love her. If you didn't, it wouldn't tear you up so much."

Zack nodded. "I agree. I think she loves you, too. It's true," he defended when Bo's eyebrows drew down into a single line. "Amber couldn't possibly have spoken with such passion about the family, the business, and you without having some feeling. And if you'd seen her face, her eyes that made you agree with everything she said or believed, it wouldn't be so hard to realize that she loves you . . . very much."

"I see she's wrapped you around her finger. First Mom and Dad, and now you." Bo glared at Josh. "Did she manage to get her hooks into you, too?"

"Well, I—"

Bo waved his hand aside. "I don't want to hear it. I didn't see you protesting that Cassidy loved me."

"Because she didn't. And you didn't love her."

"I don't love Amber." He even heard the weakness in his declaration. "I can't."

Zack yawned. "I thought you had some major problem. When Mom told me to swing by here, I canceled a date to do so."

"What?" Josh and Bo echoed.

"Yeah, I got called, too. But you're wasting my time with this stuff. Go get your girlfriend, tell her how much you love her, and then kiss the hell out of her. I bet she'll tell you she loves you, too."

"She already did."

Josh slapped Bo on the back of his neck. "That's because you're a fool. Now, since we've both blown our evenings for your sorry butt, get out. Go home and tell Amber you're the brother with the stupid gene."

"She's gone. I told her she had to leave."

"Do you think Mom would have let her go? If I know Mom, by now she, Dad, and Amber have done the cooperative economics principle."

They all nodded.

Eddie stood up from the crouched position near the window. He was cold and hungry. Now that the night had fully descended, covering the landscape in shadows, he'd gained his strength and confidence. During the day he was just a regular joe, somebody blending in with the other robots who went to work. Mindless fools who slaved in their cubicles, typing incessantly and dealing with the moronic public and their problems. He had mastered that disguise, even getting awards for his customer service.

He stretched out his muscles, constantly keeping an eye

out for anyone. Bo's absence worried him when the sun was still up, but now he didn't really care if he did return. As a matter of fact, he looked forward to it. Getting rid of Bo would help Amber to realize he meant business.

He saw the mother and father head out toward the newly added portion of the house. He figured that was their apartment. Didn't matter. He'd still have to take care of them.

Amber walked into his view. Despite the many weeks he'd missed seeing her, he drank in the vision. The nippy air no longer bothered him because he felt a warmth radiate throughout his body. No one could tell him this was not real.

Therapists had claimed that he suffered from fantasies—delusions. For one thing, he didn't believe he suffered, not one bit. Creating fantasies would be a shallow activity, and even perverted. As he watched Amber straighten up the living room and turn off the lights, he breathed deeply. He wanted to remember her soft scent that had attracted him the night of the speed dating when she sat next to him, chatting to her date while he spoke to his.

That night he had eavesdropped on her entire conversation. And when she'd risen to leave, he had brushed her hand with his. No one could tell him she was a fantasy. Her smile toward him was friendly and warm.

With only minutes separating their eventual union, he relished the thought about how happy he would be to see her. She headed for the stairs before he lost sight of her. He didn't think she had set the alarm on the house. If he tripped it, he'd have to abandon the car and then it would be a matter of time before they caught him. He wiped his shaky hands on his coat.

He nervously ran his fingers over the window and pushed slightly. It didn't budge. He headed toward the back of the house and tried the storm door. It opened. Then he turned the knob to the door, which opened with a soft click. Tonight was his lucky night.

Eddie slid into the kitchen and closed the door behind him. He remained still until his eyes adjusted to the darkness, then walked into the kitchen and stopped. Amber could wait. Martha and Will Pemberton were at the top of his list.

He walked through the connecting hallway and came upon their door. Could he be lucky twice? He turned the knob, but this time it was locked. He looked around the door frame to see if there was a key. The lock seemed simple enough. They probably relied on the outer door to provide more of the security. He grinned.

After rummaging through the kitchen drawers, he came back to the door armed with a skewer, a thin knife blade, and a screwdriver. One of these items had to work.

On the second try with the knife, he popped the lock. These all had to be signs telling him that his mission was the right thing for him to do. Tonight was the night that would alter his destiny.

He opened the door with the same hesitation he'd used when entering the main part of the house. It didn't matter because before he could duck, he saw Martha swing an iron skillet that caught him on the side of the head. The impact lifted him off his feet and threw him against the door before he slid into a heap.

"I'm going to call the police," she threatened.

Eddie blinked to clear the sickening dizziness. The old woman rushed him and he barely moved before her foot missed his face within inches. He swore and lunged for her.

Luck continued to be on his side as his hand closed around her ankle. He brought down the slightly plump woman and pulled her to him. She screamed and tussled with him, clocking him in the forehead with her other foot.

"Damn it. Stop it or I'll kill you."

That seemed to make the elderly woman even angrier. "Kill me. The only person who can kill me is God. That's not you!" She did a martial-arts chop to his throat. He bit his tongue before grabbing her throat with both hands.

He could feel the blood welling in his mouth. He swallowed. "Look, old woman, either calm down or I'm going to bust your head wide open on this floor."

Martha struggled, but the momentum died as he kept a fairly tight grip around her throat.

"Where's your old man?" He couldn't imagine anyone sleeping through the ruckus.

"I'm a widow."

Eddie had no choice but to respect Martha's will to keep up the fight. But he was losing patience. She had already given him a lump on his head and a bloody mouth. What would Amber think when she saw him?

He pulled the duct tape from his pocket and taped her hands behind her. Then he cut a piece for her mouth and stuck it to his sleeve. He needed some information first. "Let's go."

They headed toward the bedroom. He had her in front of him, just in case anything came flying out at him. "Turn on the lights."

She complied. Eddie stared at the bed, a bit confused at the sight. "Is he dead?"

"No."

"What's wrong with him?" He picked up the cane.

"No, please don't hit him."

"I'm not going to hit him." He poked the old man's leg. "If he isn't dead, is he close to it?"

"He suffers from insomnia, so I gave him his sleeping medicine."

"Well, thank your lucky stars that there isn't a fire."

"Yeah, just a lousy crook."

That earned her the piece of tape he'd stuck to his sleeve. He forced her down to the floor with her back against the foot of the bed and taped her to one of the legs. Next he tended to Will and simply taped his legs and wrists. He woke, but was so groggy that Eddie didn't waste any time in explaining what was happening to him.

After dealing with Martha and Will, Eddie headed for the bathroom. When he turned on the light, he gasped. Damn that old woman. He washed his face, but it still reflected the old woman's unleashed fury. He ought to make her pay for it, but he'd already spent more time than he'd planned in this part of the house.

He walked through the house and turned off all the lights, just in case someone walked past the room. He headed into the main house and stayed still to listen.

Satisfied, he headed for the stairs. Slowly he took the steps leading to his own Sleeping Beauty. At the top of the stairs, he surveyed the area, noting that all the doors were closed. He picked the one closest to the stairs and turned the knob. It was the master bedroom and, thank goodness, Amber had not taken up residence in it. He walked to the opposite side of the hall and opened the first door. It was obviously a guest room. When he opened the next door, relief washed over him.

The soft scent of roses alerted him that he was in the right room. The covers were thrown back, but Amber wasn't in the room. Then he heard a bottle or something hit a tiled floor. A pencil-thin strip of light emanated from under the door off to the side.

He closed the door and looked around wildly for a place to hide. But he also wanted easy access to her when he was ready. There was no more time for decisions because he heard the knob jiggle. In a mad dash, he ran to the closet and stepped in. There was no time to close the door because he could already see Amber step into the room, clothed in her baby-blue pajama set.

He had to place his hand over his mouth to keep from gasping. His excitement at her close proximity made him breathless. She hummed to herself and he closed his eyes, wanting to concentrate only on the sound. She turned off the bathroom light and the room was pitched into inky blackness.

The moonlight offered some light, but not enough from where he hid to be able to make out her features. Was she a deep sleeper? What if she didn't fall asleep quickly? Plus, how could he be sure that Martha hadn't managed some superhero action to free herself?

Ten minutes later he took the risk and eased out of the closet. He struggled to keep the door from opening any wider than necessary. Not until he was free did he dare breathe. He looked over to the bed. She had her back to him. He wanted to trail his hand over her form. All in good time.

He pulled out the duct tape, hating himself for having to do it. But he knew she would initially resist him until she learned to trust him. "Amber," he whispered. He didn't want to startle her awake. "Amber, wake up."

She stirred and moaned softly. He leaned closer to hear what she said. The tape almost fell from his hand when he heard her moan, "Bo."

"Amber," he called with an angry sharpness.

Her eyes opened. "Bo? What are you . . . who are you?" Then she screamed, clutching the comforter to her chin.

He taped her mouth first and then her hands. At first she

was scared, but that didn't last long as the panic flooded into her eyes. The muffled screams that came from her throat distressed him. He didn't want her to be scared. If she would only calm down, he could explain. "I won't hurt you, baby. I told you I would find you."

The endearment stunned her. She squinted at him, shifting her face away from his hand. He only wanted to smooth the hair from her eyes. He motioned for her to quiet down. Then he reached over and turned on the light.

She looked at him. He could see her trying to figure out who he was. "I brought that sexy outfit you were in the night we met." He dropped the pantsuit onto her lap. "I'll help you get dressed. You looked so beautiful, along with your intelligence. I figured that it was my lucky night when you walked in. Then we touched and you smiled. I knew then that we were meant for each other."

She shook her head, the muffled screams rising. To his dismay, tears fell. This was not supposed to be an unhappy occasion.

He had to think. First he'd get her into the car and then head to Colorado for a national park. He had the camping equipment. They could tough it out for a few months before heading into a town.

He taped her legs and then dragged her into the closet. There was no chair in the room for him to prop under the knob. He checked out the chest of drawers and decided that it would have to do to keep her imprisoned until he was ready.

The sound of a car made him stop. He paused to hear if it was really a car. Then he heard the garage door roll up. A grin crossed his face. He finished sliding the chest of drawers. "Honey, I'll be right back. Looks like Bo just got back." He was surprised by the wail behind the door. Then when he heard her throw her body against the door, it motivated him to finish up his business. "I'll be back."

Bo pulled up to the house, not sure how he was going to go about having his talk with Amber. He couldn't sleep anyway and his mind kept working in overdrive about what she would think. On the passenger seat lay the box of chocolates and bouquet of mixed flowers he'd bought. Small tokens of his feelings that were all mixed up and confusing.

Out of habit, he looked up at the house. His mother's lights were all out. They had worked out a code that if ever her place was dark or if the porch light was out, he should check in on her. Maybe she'd called him. He pulled out his cell phone to make sure there wasn't a message he'd missed. There were no messages.

Amber's light was on, though. So his mother was probably okay. He'd check on her once he got in. Right now he was heading straight upstairs to pull Amber out of bed if he had to.

He walked through the inner door in the garage into the house. As he crossed the doorway, he saw a shadow cross his path before a blinding streak of pain sent him crumpling to his knees. The front of his face throbbed and he saw drops of blood plop on the floor. His vision wavered as if he were underwater.

A second blow on the back of his head shut him down completely.

Amber strained to hear anything. Instead, it was eerily quiet. She took two steps back and rammed the door again. Her shoulder had to be bruised, but she didn't want to stop.

She couldn't stop. All she could think about was Bo. What was this crazy man doing to Bo?

She wanted to sob and rage, but what good would that do? One more time she bumped the door and shifted the chest of drawers enough away from the door for her to squeeze out.

"I came back just in time," Eddie said from the doorway. "Well, now that you're free, come on. Take this bag and fill it with some clothes."

Amber didn't reach for the bag as it landed near her feet. She didn't risk not doing what he said, but he'd have to take off the tape, which she motioned by raising her bound wrists.

He obliged and cut the tape loose, even from her mouth. "Behave and you'll be fine."

Amber walked around the room, gathering her items. She took things that would be of no use, but it slowed her up so she could think. "Did Bo come in?"

"Yes."

His matter-of-fact tone struck her with its coldness. "Is he okay?"

"He might have a concussion and a broken nose. But I'm not a doctor."

"I want to see him before I go." She could tell that made him angry. "I simply want to make sure he's okay and then we can go."

He didn't acknowledge her wish. Instead he picked up her bag, gripped her arm, and headed downstairs.

"So you're the guy who has been sending me all those notes."

"Yes."

"You're the reason I left home."

"Sorry about that. It took me a few weeks to decide to see you. Now all of that is behind us."

Amber didn't say anything. She was too busy filing every feature, intonation, mannerism into her memory. "Where are we going?"

"Can't tell you."

"You said you met me at the speed dating, but I don't remember you."

"I know you're lying. You sat next to me during one of the sessions. We chatted briefly about the weather, but you gave me your view about the whole dating scene. I thought and continue to think you are very intuitive."

"Are you crazy?"

"No!" He pulled her hard against his body. "Don't make me mad, Amber."

She realized instantly that that was definitely the wrong thing to say. "Sorry. How did you track me down?"

"I work with the DMV. Once I got your license tag number, I had everything I needed."

"Have you done this before?"

"I don't want to talk about it."

Amber wondered what that really meant. She pulled away from him slightly to look into the rooms. "Where's Bo?"

"If I show you, do you promise to come along quietly?"

She nodded, afraid about what she had just agreed to.

They walked into the kitchen. Amber looked down on the floor to see Bo lying on his stomach, face turned to the side. His face was partially in a small pool of blood. Without thinking about her captor, she ran over to hold Bo's head. She felt his neck and found his pulse. She closed her eyes to stem the flow of her tears.

"Let's go, now."

She complied, sensing that Bo was an emotional trigger for him. "By the way, what's your name?"

"I've been calling myself Eddie. When we've spent some

more time together, then I'll tell you my real name." He pulled her away from Bo. They walked out the back door and around the house to the car.

Amber couldn't help stopping before the car. The thought of getting into this man's car scared her. What would be the chances for anyone to find her once she got into his car?

"Come on, Amber."

"I don't think I can." Her legs refused to move.

"Maybe this will help." He walked over to the car and pulled out a newspaper and flicked it open. "Read the front page."

In the newspaper, in a single column, was Sylvia's picture. She read the entire article, learning about her friend's disappearance.

"Now get in. They've probably found her by now."

Amber concentrated on not throwing up. As the car pulled away from the ranch, the tears flowed for Sylvia, Martha and Will, and Bo. No matter what Bo thought of her, she had him firmly in her heart. She sent out, with all the power that she could muster, a silent plea for him to come and save her.

Chapter Eighteen

The police swarmed the Pemberton property Saturday morning after receiving a call from Bo. Uniformed police and plainclothes investigators arrived armed and ready to do battle. Martha greeted them at the door, hair in place in a matching pantsuit. If it wasn't for the bruises around her face and the slight tremor in her smile, it could have been any other day.

Bo sat on the arm of the chair where his father sat. Thank goodness his father fared the best because of his sleepy state during the ordeal. Since Bo refused to go to the hospital, his mother had their family doctor come to the house.

"I'm okay, doc." Bo kept the ice pack on the front of his face, waiting for the painkillers to kick in. It felt as if he had been run over by a truck.

"Your nose isn't broken, but you took a massive hit to the face. Lots of swelling and, I'm sure, pain to go along with it. What I am worried about is a chance of a concussion. Do I need to tell you the dangers of suffering a blow to the head?"

Bo shook his head and instantly regretted it. He groaned and fell forward.

The doctor caught him and laid him back against the couch. Bo couldn't say anything, even if his brain functioned enough for him to do so. He only wanted the throbbing to quiet and the fuzziness to disappear. He needed to find Amber.

As he was rolled out of the house on the gurney, he knew he had lost the battle. His mother was directing the doctor to take him to the hospital. He opened his mouth to protest and another groan escaped. Helplessly he could only observe as they lifted him into the back of the ambulance and closed the doors.

His body surrendered to the onslaught of the pain and injury. Like a valve being released, he welcomed the blackness that washed over him.

Bo returned to the house two days later. He dismissed all the protests and warnings about leaving the hospital. How could any of them expect him to stay in the hospital when Amber hadn't been found? He'd wasted two days lying on that bed.

The house still looked like a command center with several police vehicles scattered in front of the house. The media, on the other hand, had taken up positions on the perimeter. Vans with extended antennas added to the invasion.

Some of the stories being reported tried to find a link between Amber's kidnapping and Bo's case against his company. As he entered the house, he could only wonder how many reporters had called the house.

"Welcome back, bro." Josh hugged him and then it was Zack's turn.

"It's good to be home."

His mother appeared in the hall. "I knew the doctors wouldn't be able to hold you for too long. But at least your swelling has gone down. Come on in here. Your father is talking to the chief investigator. There're so many of them, I can't keep them straight."

Bo followed his brothers into the room. A man in a suit talked to his father. A few more cops helped themselves to the sandwiches, coffee, and fresh fruit. Only his mother would think about being hospitable at a time like this.

He poured himself a cup of coffee and walked over to listen in on the investigator's report.

"Bo, this is Special Agent Briggs, he's been keeping us updated on everything."

"It's been two days." The accusation hung in the air.

"Yes, Mr. Pemberton, we got close to him and then somehow he managed to disappear. We think he's still in the area, though."

Bo sipped the coffee to drown his frustration. It didn't work. "What did you find out about this guy?"

"His name is Cory Steel—a two-year employee with the Maryland Department of Motor Vehicles. Kept to himself a lot. Never dated anyone from the department. Once we searched his place, he had a completely different personality from his work life."

"How different?"

"He stayed in a basement apartment. Rented it from a graduate student near the University of Maryland. They found photos of various women, some of whom happened to be his co-workers. Most of the pictures were taken without the subject's permission. He would be what we call a Peeping Tom."

"Is he dangerous?"

"Since we don't have anyone who has filed a complaint against him, he doesn't have any criminal records. But in my opinion I'd say he has the capability to be dangerous. We read some of his journals and he repeatedly mentions Amber Delaney."

Bo slapped down his coffee and grabbed Briggs by his shirt. "What did he say?"

"Sir, calm down." Briggs removed Bo's hands. "We have folks pouring over every word in that journal. But it appears that he came into contact with her at some party and then selected her for his crazy fantasy."

"I'm going to look for her. He'll hurt her or kill her. I just know." Bo looked at all of them. Why weren't they all out there looking for her, instead of standing around discussing the possibilities?

"Mr. Pemberton, I'd strongly advise against it. We know they are still in the area because we've got roadblocks and helicopters covering the surrounding areas. There were some tracks found heading back to your property. And we've got the dogs."

On cue, the dogs bayed, causing quite a racket. Bo hurried over to the window and saw about twenty dogs on their leashes, straining to get on their way. The howling and baying sent chills along his arms as he thought of the historic use of dogs to find his ancestors a long time ago. Yet, in the brightness of the day among his family, in the presence of the police, the dogs provided hope that the day wouldn't end without Amber at his side.

Bo nodded. "Thank you. Just keep us posted, will you?"

"Sure." Briggs shook their hands and walked out of the room.

"Close the door," Bo ordered. "I'm going to find Amber."

"Right there with you." Zack stepped up.

"Me, too." Josh closed the gap between his brothers.

His dad placed a hand on his. "Don't think that you're going to leave me out in the cold. I'll keep tabs on what's going on with the police and call you with any updates."

"Sure, Dad."

Martha studied each of her boys' faces. "Make sure you take some food for the road."

The traumatic events had taken its toll on her. As she stared at Bo, it was as if she searched his soul. He in turn studied her, noticing the dark circles around her eyes. Her face was drawn, her movements slow. Whenever she turned to her right, she gritted her teeth in pain. "Thanks, Mom." He knew that she understood why he was grateful. She didn't offer any resistance to his plan because she believed he would find Amber.

All he knew is that he wanted to get Amber. Once that happened, Cory Steel, or Eddie, may have to pray for his continued existence on this earth. This vicious sociopath had crossed the line by bringing the war to his home against his family and the woman he loved. He wanted vengeance.

"Let's get going. The horses are ready." The three men strode out of the house with purpose. They ignored the police and the media that waited like scavengers for their feeding time.

Bo walked in the lead. He didn't know how long it would take to track down Eddie, but he was prepared to camp out. He walked into the stable. Joe had prepared Onyx. The horse seemed to sense his important role as he pawed the ground and tossed his head in the air.

"Thanks, Joe. Keep an eye on my parents."

"Will do, sir. Good luck."

"Where are we heading to?" Josh asked.

Zack pulled up on his horse. "The police said they found his tracks heading west off the highway. You know that trail is going to eventually give way to brush and his car will get stuck."

"Then let's start over there." Bo stuck his heels into Onyx's flank.

The three brothers galloped away from the ranch, Bo in the lead, head tucked behind the horse's mane. Josh and Zack rode abreast of each other, following their brother.

Half an hour later, with much ground covered, Bo pulled up to check their progress. The horses munched on the soft grass at the base of the trees.

Zack placed the call to their father. Bo paced the area until he was finished. "Anything?"

"They found some clothing—female's—in a bag. They're dusting for prints on the buttons and the dogs have got a scent."

Bo stooped and picked up a twig. "Look at this." He drew a few diagrams on the ground, situating rocks in strategic positions. "This is our border. The river runs through from here to here. He'll know he's being tracked. He can lose the scent right here before disappearing into the forest over here." Forever. The stick dropped from his hand. A sickening thought came to mind as to what Eddie was capable of doing. He wished he could turn off his imagination. It fed his fear and that highlighted the fact that he wasn't in control, despite all this bravado. He needed a little bit of luck.

Josh stood at the edge of the diagram. "We'll find her, Bo. Let's head over there now. The clouds are pretty thick and there was a fifty-fifty chance of rain. That would muck things up."

"Then we'll split up so we don't waste time. Josh, you head to the point where the stream crosses the property. Zack, you head to the other point where it crosses. I'll hit the middle section."

"Are you sure? If we're wrong, then we've wasted a lot of time," Zack pointed out.

"Do you think that I don't know that? It scares the hell out of me that I can't be everywhere all the time. But until they say he's gone from this area, I plan to canvass this place inch by inch." Bo's chest heaved from the panic he struggled to keep at bay. He wiped his face, bit back the tears, and swallowed the bitter anger welling in his throat. "Let's get a move on."

No one spoke. Even the breeze seemed to stop to listen to him explode. Nature echoed its sentiments. Thunder rumbled in a powerful vibration, introducing the monstrous dark clouds. The ominous sky darkened as the clouds unfurled and connected into a thick blanket of premature darkness.

Bo mounted his horse. He needed to be elevated, to feel empowered that he could make a difference. As the sky cloaked the area from the sun, its various shades of gray and muddy blues played against the rugged landscape. Lightning shot forks of its wrath to the earth. Under this natural phenomenon, he struggled with how inconsequential he felt.

"We'll touch base after this storm. Be careful," Josh warned.

Bo touched his brow in a salute and then turned Onyx to his destination. He squinted as the clouds opened up and the rain poured. It unloaded with such ferocity, he strained to see ahead. Hopefully he hadn't passed any clues.

By the time he reached the midpoint of the lake, his shirt stuck to his body. "I could really use a break now!" he screamed up to the sky. The rain stung his eyes. A chill made him shake uncontrollably. His impatience inhibited his thinking. How was he going to outwit a man he didn't even know?

He dismounted in ankle-high water. There was no flash of color among the trees. No visible campsite to alert him that they had been in the area. Meanwhile, the rain kept its furious rhythmic beat.

Onyx snorted, tossing his head. "Sorry, boy. You were dry and warm in your stable and I came along and dragged you way out here." He buried his head in the horse's neck, glad for the muscular strength against his face. "We can't give up, boy." Onyx snorted and turned his head toward his voice. He nudged Bo as his owner, in turn, stroked his snout.

Bo left Onyx and walked a few paces, staring intently at the ground. Just as he was about to turn and do the same thing in the opposite direction, he stepped on something. He moved his feet and bent down to retrieve it.

The object was a red rock. He tossed it in his hand, wondering if it was a clue. He walked away from the water and spied another rock in the low grass. Then it clicked. He and Amber had picked up several of the rocks when they'd camped. Amber had admired the rocks and they had spent most of the hour picking them up.

The excitement paralyzed him momentarily as his thoughts scattered in several directions. He kept following the rocks, picking them up and storing them in his pockets. So intent was he on his task at hand that he didn't notice the change in weather until the rock trail had stopped.

The clouds had finally heard his plea and parted like the curtains to a second act. Even the sun had turned up its heat, which he appreciated since his wet clothes clung to his body like a second skin.

Bo clicked his tongue for Onyx. The horse ambled up to

him. He hoped he could see better once he was perched on his horse. The rocks were still leading a trail, but with more space between each rock. Bo figured Amber got low on rocks and started dropping them several yards apart.

His cell phone rang. "Yes."

"It's me," Zack answered. "Didn't see anything here."

"I found a trail I think Amber left for me." Bo twisted around in his saddle, trying to discern where he was. "As a matter of fact, I think I know where she may be leading him. Get in touch with Josh and meet me at the clubhouse."

"Shouldn't you wait until we get there?"

"Yes, I should, but I'm not going to. I'm heading to the clubhouse and if I see any signs of that man—"

"We're on our way."

Bo pushed his horse and kept riding toward the spot he'd claimed as his favorite. The place he shared with Amber.

Eddie sat hunched at the base of a tree, frantically trying to get his brain to think complete thoughts. It angered him that Amber could look so calm. She hadn't said a word, not even to ask him anything. It was as if a light dimmed when she looked at him. This wasn't how he had imagined their heroic escape.

He had definitely not imagined that he'd be running in circles in this godforsaken land. After they'd abandoned the car, they ran until his chest felt like it would burst. With the police on his heels, he couldn't afford to waste any time, but he had to catch his breath. Tired, hungry, and itching under his sweater, he contemplated his next move.

"I don't think it's a good thing to sit here for too long." Amber unfolded herself to stand.

Eddie didn't budge, mainly because every muscle hurt.

"I'm the one doing the thinking," he retorted. He simply wanted to lie down.

"It's going to rain."

"What are you, the weather girl?" He looked at his watch. The second hand didn't move. "We have to find the road again." This time he struggled to his feet. Obviously she was going to talk him to death after saying nothing for hours. Nothing like a woman to scramble his senses and make him go crazy. "Let's go." He headed back into the trees.

"I wouldn't go that way."

"Why should I listen to you?"

"Because I've been living in this area for the past two months. I may not know every inch, but I do know that if you go in that direction, you're liable to get picked up by night-fall. It's near a federal prison."

Eddie blinked. "Prison?"

"Yeah, but if you go this way, you cross into Oklahoma fairly soon, then Colorado."

He squinted at her, looking for signs that she was lying. He had thought she was perfect—until they came on this trip. She never seemed to warm to him. Her eyes left him cold, and if he wasn't mistaken, she wore her dislike of him in a scornful manner.

"This isn't what I had planned," he explained.

"I know."

He wiped a hand across his nose. "Are you going to leave me when we get out of this?"

Amber raised her bound wrists. "I don't think so."

"I can't take those off you. Not yet. I want to trust you, Amber." Eddie opened his arms to hold her and let her feel the sincerity that came from his body.

She recoiled.

"You hate me," he said.

Amber shook her head. "I still have to get to know you, Eddie. You've got to admit that all this is a little scary."

"I haven't touched you. I haven't hurt you."

"I know and I appreciate that. I like that you haven't forced me, Eddie. This is why I want to make sure we're safe. We need to go this way."

Eddie loved the lilt in her speech. It was her words and small giggle interwoven in her speech that caught his attention. He wanted to believe in what she said. Take a chance. Out there in no-man's-land, he couldn't do it by himself.

"If we don't see the road in half an hour, then we'll go your way." She smiled.

Eddie wiped the sweat out of his eyes. "Okay."

They trudged their way over a few low hills, across the flat pastures that seemed to go on endlessly. Eddie wheezed from the exertion. For some reason Amber was now in the lead and she moved with a speed that had him stumbling. "Slow down."

"We can't." Amber turned her palm upward. Fat drops of rain hit them. Seconds later the sky opened, soaking them in the process.

Eddie swore. With each step into a mud puddle, he swore some more. It didn't help when Amber kept up her pace. Her nimble leaps and sidesteps reminded him of deer flitting around without a care.

"Hey, what's that?" Eddie grabbed Amber by the back of her neck, pulling her off balance. She landed against him. "What's that building?" He looked over his shoulder, whipping around in case anyone came out from the dense trees over to his right or from behind the run-down building to his left.

"Let's hide in the building until the rain stops." Amber pulled at his arm as he shielded his eyes from rain. "Please,

Eddie, let's get dry. Then we can head out for the last leg. Aren't you tired? I know I am." She exhaled.

With his lungs threatening to explode, he warmed to the idea of resting. His legs had turn to rubber as he worked the hills. "You did good, Amber." They stumbled into the building. It was dark, but at least it was dry. "I'm going to close my eyes, but I want you sitting next to me. If I feel you trying to escape, I'm not going to be happy."

Amber nodded quickly. She offered him a big smile and then settled down next to him.

Slowly Eddie's ill temper fizzled away. His confidence that had fallen to the bottom fed on the comforting security that now warmed him. Everything would be all right.

Amber closed her eyes, pretending to be asleep. She hoped Bo had seen the rocks she had dropped for him. Now that she was still near the ranch, she had no plans to leave without a fight. As long as she could get Eddie to bend to her will, she would act as the pliant victim.

He groaned and shifted his shoulders. Amber eased open her eyes, watching him through her eyelashes. She watched his chest rise and fall, evenly. She cleared her throat and sat up slowly. No movement. Only a gentle snore came from him.

Although the clubhouse didn't have electricity, there were enough cracks in the planks of wood that walled the building. Now that the storm was over, the sunlight streamed through the cracks, providing sufficient light for her to examine the surroundings.

She crept slowly forward to an opening and peered out. There weren't any signs of anyone. A squirrel scampered up a tree. A wild rabbit hopped into the clearing, nibbling on grass. She strained to hear anything. Only the sounds of nature greeted her.

She bit back the disappointment. She couldn't have come this far to crumble under her fear. With her head leaning against the wall, she reached for something that could give her strength.

Kuumba. Creativity.

Martha had told her to learn the seven principles of Kwanzaa. At first she'd resisted because she didn't see the need for another celebration, but when she read about Dr. Karenga and the philosophy behind the African-based tradition, she embraced the tradition. Still, each evening when Martha led the recognition of the principles, it hadn't connected on a personal level.

Sitting there, cold and hungry, she had time to think about lots of things. She loved Bo with all her heart and the hope of being able to tell him that again in person gave her determination.

Her strength came from thinking about the principle of creativity and her role as a reporter. She had lost sight of why she changed her career after being a successful real-estate agent: the financial gains did not make up for the emptiness it left within her.

She focused on whether she could write a story about Bo Pemberton. None of her creativity would benefit him or her community.

On New Year's Eve, hidden in a shack, she made her resolution to use her talent with care and consideration. She thanked Martha for waking her up to her heritage.

She laughed. "It always seems when you're in a tight spot that you make promises." She drew her knees up to her chest and rested her head. "Bo, oh, Bo, please come and get me."

"What are you muttering over there?" Eddie sat up, rubbing his eyes. He yawned and stretched. "Good, the rain stopped. It's time for us to get moving."

Amber's head popped up. "I'm still tired."

"We're moving. I don't like it here."

Amber knew in her heart that if she left that building, she may never see Bo again. Eddie was growing desperate and irritable. It was only a matter of time before he would turn ugly toward her.

She remained huddled, still keeping a watchful eye of her narrow view of the outside. Over the rise of a hill, she saw the familiar cowboy hat appear. She gasped. Then the man she had begged to come and save her came over the hill. She couldn't see anyone with him, but it didn't matter. The tears threatened and she was afraid that at this critical moment she would become an emotional wreck.

"What is the matter with you, girl?"

Amber looked up at him and wailed. "I'm so tired. So hungry. Can't we stay here? I'm scared. You're scaring me."

Eddied frowned at her. "Stop it." He walked over and shook her roughly. "You're making too much noise."

"Would you sit here and hold my hand?" Amber kept up her performance until he settled down next to her. She'd angled herself so that Eddie would have his back to Bo's approach. Now she would wait.

Bo heard the wailing. His blood boiled, spurring him into action. There was no time for his brothers or the police. He used the trees as much as he could, running and ducking as if it were a game.

If only it were a game.

Another wail came from the clubhouse. That did it. He

emerged from behind the tree and ran toward the building, aiming for the door.

His breath formed wisps. His feet pounded the hard ground. His hands clenched into fists pumping at his side. He felt like a locomotive charging down the track. With a loud roar, he bulldozed the front door and dive-rolled to a crouch position.

Face to face, he stared back at Eddie. Amber's scream pierced his ear and he glanced over to her to make sure she was alive and well.

A split second later, he launched his body toward Eddie, hurling their bodies hard against the floor. "I'm going to kill you." Bo had one hand around his throat. The other warded off Eddie's blows.

Out of the corner of his eye, he saw Amber scramble to the doorway. She waved her arms. He couldn't really concentrate on her because Eddie was pounding his face with his fist. He relied on his college wrestling skills to toss him over his head.

"Amber, you okay?" Zack entered first and hugged her. Then Josh stumbled in, hugging her.

"Could someone help me, please?" Bo sat on Eddie's back with one hand pinned under his knee.

"Get off me."

Zack bent over and tapped Eddie on the head. "You're lucky we arrived in the nick of time. You were about to be cattle feed in a few seconds."

Josh was on the phone, providing the police with their exact location. He gave Bo a thumbs-up sign.

Once Eddie was secured with rope, Bo turned his attention to Amber. No words were needed. Amber ran into his arms and he swooped her into a bearlike hug. He felt her warm tears on his neck. He didn't want to let her go. They spun around until he grew dizzy, before kissing her.

He dropped kisses all over her face. The softness of her lips drove him wild and he still couldn't believe she was there in front of him. It seemed like a lifetime ago since their disagreement.

Chapter Nineteen

"I feel bad," Amber complained.

"Everyone understands. They know that going back to the house may be hard on you." Bo sat on the edge of the bed in the hotel room. "We're all happy to have you back safely." He jingled his keys. "I'll come back for you later this afternoon for the *Imani* celebration. Mom insisted, thought it would help. But if you'd rather be alone, I can understand that, too."

Amber noticed the visible signs of Bo's unease. After Eddie's capture, they had barely seen each other because the police had whisked them away for the long hours of paperwork. Bo had waited for her at the station. With so much drama hanging between them, her penchant for fleeing kicked in. Instead of getting the heck out of town and turning her back on the entire situation, she invited him in for her great escape.

Alone at last, she didn't want to waste time on what could have or should have been. She sat next to him and placed his hand between hers. "I don't want to be alone, not without you. I couldn't take any more questions or the cameras flashing in my face." She interlocked her fingers with his, feeling the slight reassuring squeeze of his hand. "Peace. I crave a peaceful setting with only you at my side." She pulled his hand to her cheek and brushed it with her lips. "Don't walk away, Bo. Stay?" She had so much to say, but his quiet attitude gave her pause. His face reflected tiredness and a certain sadness. The bruises around his eyes and nose were now only discolored. Her hero, he had saved her, but nothing between them had changed. His accusation, her guilt—it created a nasty mix that wedged its way between them.

She'd recently outwitted an enemy. Although the circumstances lay closer to her emotions and was on the brink of destroying her, she couldn't let go, not without a fight.

"I'll stay," he answered, his voice husky and tight.

Amber nodded. "Okay." Putting on a brave front, she smiled. "That oversize tub is calling my name. All I want to do is sink under a ton of bubbles and lie there until I shrivel." She gave him a small smile. "Maybe then I'll relax enough to fall asleep. Would you believe that I'm afraid to close my eyes?"

"I'll be here." Bo bent over and kissed her forehead. "I'll draw your bath, milady, and order room service for a small army."

Amber giggled. "Ah . . . just watch the expenses. My card does have a limit."

"And I have an account with the hotel."

"Oh, really." She raised her eyebrows. "And how many damsels in distress have you brought to your lovebug hideaway?"

The smile she ached for, the signature feature she treasured, flashed brilliantly. "Did I say I had an account? The family has an account. Any cousins, business associates, special friends can use this hotel. The hotel chain is actually owned by a family member on my mother's side."

"Good answer." She poked him in his belly. "But you know, you don't have to do everything for me, although I appreciate it."

"Don't try to be Miss Independent with me." He left her to head for the bathroom.

Amber heard the water pour into the tub. Her idea of a quick retreat was to stay in one of the better motels outside Breezewood. Bo wasn't having it. Instead he brought her west of the city to a hotel and spa resort. Driving through the massive ornate gates, walking through the pristine and expensively decorated lobby, she knew this would not be the regular hotel experience.

Their two-door suite opened to separate areas with an inner connecting door. Sitting on the king-size bed that sat as high as her hips, she wondered how much a place like this cost. The door leading directly into her bedroom seemed half a mile away. Most of the size was taken over by the massive tub and surrounding area of the bath.

Sliding off the bed, she went to the other room for closer inspection. It contained a sitting room and small dining area. A multimedia entertainment unit took over most of the wall space on one side. The other wall had a small bookshelf with a mixture of the classics and recent best-sellers.

Thick cranberry-colored curtains hung from the sliding doors that led onto a balcony. Although it was daytime, if she didn't have the lights on, the room would have been pitched into blinding darkness. Privacy was definitely a priority. So was being tied down to any schedule or time constraints. The room did not contain a clock.

She remembered Bo saying that the hotel kitchen provided breakfast, lunch, and dinner at whatever time the guest requested. She pulled the thick robe, compliments of the hotel, closed. Her fingers trailed the lush fabric, playing with the embroidered design on the chest. It wasn't until she stood in front of the mirror that she realized the robe had the name *Pemberton* stitched on it in old-English style.

"Wow. Must be nice." She stifled a yawn. If she could be sure that nightmares wouldn't come, she could sleep for hours.

"Do you want me to pour in some of this pink stuff or the blue crystals stuff?" Bo shouted from the bathroom.

"Both. What the heck." After her bath, maybe she could have Bo make use of the fireplace. A romantic thought crept in, with the marble-paneled fireplace as the backdrop. It would be up to Bo. But if he thought he could resist her, he hadn't learned a thing or two since she'd arrived at his doorstep.

She wanted Bo Pemberton for keeps.

Bo popped his head around the bathroom door. "Are you decent?"

She nodded.

"Your bath is ready, ma'am. I've set the radio to the classical station. I think they're playing Beethoven now." He sidestepped her when she approached.

Amber, oozing innocence, touched his arm. "Thank you, Bo, for everything." She drooped her shoulders enough to cause the front of the robe to gape. Subtlety was the key. She knew the robe provided a peekaboo of her cleavage.

Poor Bo. If his eyes were pinballs in a machine, they would be pinging off the walls. Fighting to keep the grin off her face, she tried not to notice him looking at her chest and then catching himself to look away, at her, at the floor.

On tiptoe, she leaned into him and kissed him softly on

the edge of his mouth. As if she couldn't help herself, she kissed him again, this time flicking the corner V of his mouth with her tongue. When she felt the jolt of his head and the slight movement as he turned his head to capture her mouth, she dragged her slightly opened mouth across his cheek to his ear. "I'm sorry," she whispered. "I don't know what came over me." Then she stepped back, tightened her robe, and sashayed into the bathroom.

Behind the closed door, she fanned herself. Seducing Bo had some pleasant side effects. She needed to get into that water to cool down and this was only the first inning.

Amber dipped a toe in the water to test. Just perfect. "Bo, I think I want red meat." She slid into the tub and settled back under the chin-high suds.

"I'll place the order."

"Why don't you have them deliver it to the sitting room?" She examined the area next to the tub, looking for the controls.

"Is that where you want to eat? I thought you'd want it in the bedroom."

"I do, but you won't be there to receive it, so have them just take it straight to the sitting room. We can bring it over."

"Did you need me to go get you something?"

"I sure do." Neither of them had clothes. But if she had anything to do with it, they wouldn't need clothes anytime soon.

He knocked on the door.

"Come in."

He popped his head around the door, staring up at the ceiling. "Sorry, I couldn't hear what you said. Did you need me to do something?" he repeated.

"Yep, two things. First, I need you to turn on the jets. Then I need you to massage my back, please."

"Oh." He didn't move.

"Problem?"

"No. No. The control for the jets is right over here." He pointed to the panel of buttons positioned over the faucet.

Amber waded over to the spot and stood up to push the button. She gave him enough of an eyeful to see him back up in the mirror, but he didn't turn away, didn't take his eyes off her. She slid back into the tub and turned a winning smile toward him.

"There's a bottle with some yellow lotion cleanser that is supposed to be good for the skin. I wanted you to rub it on my back. I did try." She made a halfhearted motion of reaching around to her back and winced. "I can't."

"No problem." Bo rolled up his sleeves, took off his watch, opened the top button of his shirt.

Amber wondered if he was going to take off his socks and shoes, too. He'd pay for making her wait.

From the first wide stroke of his hand across her back, she had to hug her knees to keep from responding in animal-like sounds. He not only rubbed on the lotion, but gently massaged her back. Despite her game of seduction, she genuinely needed his assistance with easing away the kinks in her back and neck.

His hands rose up her back and swept out along her shoulders. He framed her neck in his large hands and brought them down to the front of her chest before sliding away.

"Oh, my gosh," she gasped. The muscles in her stomach, in her thighs, anything below the waist quivered. She had no control. They simply reacted each time to Bo's strokes up her back, around her neck, and down the upper part of her chest.

"What's the matter?"

"I . . . I . . ." She blew out a breath. "Guess it's getting hot in here," she finished weakly.

He stopped.

"What's the matter?" She turned to look at him. He couldn't just stop like that.

"I think you're fine."

"I'm not." She hunched her shoulders. "Still feels tight right here." She craved his touch.

"Probably need to rest."

"I don't want to rest." Okay, now she sounded like a shrill housewife. But the man drove her nuts.

"Then what do you want?" He frowned at her.

Amber stood and stepped out of the tub. The water drained off her body into a small puddle at her feet. Staring into his face, unreadable, mysterious, withdrawn, time slowed. She was acutely aware of the water trickling down over her breasts, her nipples, the additional trail over her belly, disappearing into the hair below. A small trickle cruised down her back and over her butt cheeks.

"I want you, Bo."

He shook his head. "I'm not looking for a woman who only wants me." He stepped away from her. "I need a woman who can love me with the same passion I love her. Are you this woman, Amber?"

She nodded.

He unrolled his sleeves and rebuttoned his shirt. "I don't think so."

Amber pulled the towel off the rack and covered her body. She admitted defeat. "Why?" Despite the shame and humiliation, she couldn't just walk away.

Bo took a seat on the dressing-table counter. "Because you haven't begged me."

Amber blinked. "What?"

He crossed his arms and grinned at her. "Did you really think you could seduce me? If I wanted, I could have had you eating out of my hand when I massaged you. You're such a sucker for my massages."

"Oh, really? You shouldn't declare victory so early."

"But I think we're at the finishing line." He pulled her to him and nuzzled her neck.

She moaned. "You're not playing fair."

"I'm learning from the pro." He nibbled her earlobe and blew gently on her ear. "You know, Amber, I should have told you something the day I lost my head."

"Yes?" If it wasn't for the desire she saw on his face, she would have been afraid of what he was about to say.

He tilted up her chin. "I love you, Amber Delaney." He kissed her before she could respond.

She closed her eyes and surrendered to the moment. With his declaration, he had single-handedly won her heart, body, and soul. As she returned his kiss, she savored the firmness of his tongue, playfully partnering with hers in a sensual dance. They broke apart, gasping and laughing in each other's embrace.

"Think the water is too cold?"

"Doesn't matter." She unbuttoned his shirt, popping the last two buttons that stubbornly wouldn't come undone. "Is this how all the cowboys are built?"

"Of course, in case we have our clothes ripped off by sex-starved city girls."

She planted feathery kisses on his chest, smiling when his muscles contracted in response. His deep brown skin rippled under her touch, his stomach taut as her finger trailed a lingering path to his waist. She rubbed her hips against his for her own pleasure as much as for his.

They kissed, wild and passionate. He unfastened his belt

and she pulled down the zipper, brushing the front of his pants to tease him.

He grabbed her wrist and pulled her arms above her head. When he crushed her against his chest, her nipples grew taut. The soft brush of chest hair titillated the desire burning its own course through her. She saw the determination that he wasn't done yet. And she didn't want the moment to end.

The time that they spent together, the secret kisses, the occasional body contact she had begun to yearn for, it all became a preview of what would be.

In one sweep, he picked her up, took her in the bedroom, and laid her on the bed. While she readjusted herself among the pillows, he finished disrobing and slid on the condom.

"Tell me something."

"Oh, gosh, woman, this is no time to talk."

"Yes, it is. I want to know why it took you so long to tell me you loved me. When I told you my feelings, you stared right through me."

He sat on the edge of the bed to take off his shoes. "I was firing you. You only said it to shake me up."

She stroked his back with her foot. "So now you're calling me a liar."

"Not you, sweetheart."

"I hear sarcasm. Are you still bent out of shape because I didn't tell you about my job as a reporter?"

He stood at the foot of the bed. Naked. Aroused. Without answering her, he climbed onto the bed, nudging her legs apart with his knee. "No more secrets."

She could have promised him the entire world as he lay on top of her. Her legs wrapped around his hips, pulling him toward her. When his body brushed against the sensitive spot between her legs, she raised her hips to welcome him.

He propped himself on his elbow. "I mean it, Amber. We

can't have secrets between us. You have to trust me and I have to be able to trust you."

She nodded. "I never enjoyed living the lie, except when I started falling for you. Then I didn't know how to end it without losing you." She kissed him, long and hard. "I never want to lose you."

Bo tilted up her chin, stroking her bottom lip with his finger. She kissed it. Slowly he slid into her, his eyes never leaving her face. Her body moved with his, same rhythm, same timing. She hooked a leg over his butt, arching to quench her body's thirst. So long had she waited for this very moment. Bo had been good about not taking advantage of her, not wanting to be an employer who would lie down with his employees.

She kept her legs locked around him, her eyes shut tightly. She clung to his neck for fear of drowning in rapture and never coming back to reality. Touching him fed into a deeper need to verify that this wasn't a dream. She cupped his butt cheeks, going with the erotic spasms that shook his frame.

But her body wasn't going to be left behind. It answered with her insides exploding as desire crested and sent over-sized waves crashing and retreating. All she could do was hold on and enjoy the ride.

Chapter Twenty

Returning to Pemberton Ranch with Bo was truly a home-coming. Amber couldn't stop smiling and the two couldn't stop kissing each other. They held hands and moved to each room together.

"Enough already. Bo, let that girl go so we can get started."

Bo obeyed his mother, but not before kissing her. Amber didn't mind the teasing comments from their affectionate display. As a matter of fact, nothing much affected her at this moment.

"Thank you, Martha, and everyone for postponing the last day of Kwanzaa on my behalf."

Will stepped forward. "Think nothing of it. We wanted the entire family here to participate and be a part of the tradition. You are a part of our family, now and forever."

"It had better be forever. If Bo can't handle a woman like Amber, I'm here," Zack piped up.

"Zack, you're too much of a player for me. Plus, I haven't won any beauty pageants, so I'm not 'keeper' material. On the other hand, Josh and I could be an item," Amber flirted.

"You can be so exasperating, woman," Bo growled. "Everything has got to be your way." He pulled a small box out of his pocket. "Amber—"

"No!" the women screamed at him.

"If you're going to do it, you'd better do it right," Clarissa demanded.

"On your knees, boy," Will added.

Amber trembled with emotion. She had come with such high expectations that were selfish and false. After everything they had been through, she was afraid to believe that something as truly wonderful as this moment could happen to her.

Bo took her hand. "Amber, would you marry me?"

She knelt opposite him. "Yes."

The screaming and dancing around occurred overhead, but she only had Bo in her vision. They kissed and then sank into each other, giggling at the commotion around them.

"Welcome to the Pemberton family," he whispered in her ear.

Later that night, after the Kwanzaa feast, the family moved into the living room. Will took the lead by stepping forward. "Kwanzaa may be over, but we have an obligation as a unit. Ask yourself this question every time you feel like you're drifting from your true purpose, whether it's career, personal or spiritual: am I being faithful to the world I inherited? If the ancestors were to return, could I honestly say I've taken up the responsibility of their legacy and added on with my contributions?"

Bo raised his right fist and the family followed. Amber

followed. She had closed the door on Zoe's story. Her friend wasn't lost, but she could do better by honoring Zoe's memory rather than looking in the dark for answers only Zoe could answer.

"Harambee!"

They lowered their fists and repeated the salute six more times.

"This concludes the *Karamu* celebration until next year. Remember your commitment to your people, your community, and your environment."

Dear Readers:

I hope you fell in love with the romantic journey of Amber and Bo in *Making Promises*. The history of the African-American cowboy provided the foundation for Bo's character and the Texas setting for the Pemberton ancestral home. This house that has sheltered the family, past and present, with strong parents at its helm, also provided the appropriate stage for the Kwanzaa celebration.

I enjoyed the research process followed by weaving the information into a heartwarming tale of self-awareness and renewal of spirit. When I started to write this story, it was not my intention to have a series. However, Bo's brothers provided enough fun moments to earn their say. Stay tuned for more from the Pemberton boys.

On another note, mark your calendars. The sequel to *Finders Keepers*, featuring the quaint town of Glen Knolls, will hit bookshelves May 2005, tentatively titled *Circle of Love*. This time, Toni and Derek (Brad's brother) are on the path to love, with the famous bed-and-breakfast in the background and the familiar cast of girlfriends to liven things.

You may contact me via email at michellemonkou@aol.com or write to P.O. Box 2904, Laurel, MD 20709. My website is: http://www.michellemonkou.com.

Peace,
Michelle Monkou

ABOUT THE AUTHOR

Michelle Monkou sold her first contemporary romance to BET in January, 2002. Her advice to aspiring authors is to be disciplined and to respect the craft. She is an avid supporter of writer networks such as Romance Writers of America.

Born in England and raised in Guyana, Michelle attributes her creative source to the nuances of cultural diversity that she experienced. She currently resides with her family in the Washington, DC metropolitan area.

More Arabesque Romances by
Donna Hill

__TEMPTATION	0-7860-0070-8	$4.99US/$5.99CAN
__A PRIVATE AFFAIR	1-58314-158-8	$5.99US/$7.99CAN
__CHARADE	0-7860-0545-9	$4.99US/$6.50CAN
__INTIMATE BETRAYAL	0-7860-0396-0	$4.99US/$6.50CAN
__PIECES OF DREAMS	1-58314-183-9	$5.99US/$7.99CAN
__CHANCES ARE	1-58314-197-9	$5.99US/$7.99CAN
__A SCANDALOUS AFFAIR	1-58314-118-9	$5.99US/$7.99CAN
__SCANDALOUS	1-58314-248-7	$5.99US/$7.99CAN
__THROUGH THE FIRE	1-58314-130-8	$5.99US/$7.99CAN

Available Wherever Books Are Sold!

Check out our website at www.BET.com.

The Arabesque At Your Service Series

Four superb romances with engaging characters and dynamic story lines featuring heroes whose destiny is intertwined with women of equal courage who confront their passionate—and unpredictable—futures.

__TOP-SECRET RENDEZVOUS – _Air Force_
by Linda Hudson-Smith   1-58314-397-1 $6.99US/$9.99CAN
Sparks fly when officer Hailey Douglas meets Air Force Major Zurich Kingdom. Military code forbids fraternization between an officer and an NCO, so the pair find themselves involved in a top-secret rendezvous.

__COURAGE UNDER FIRE – _Army_
by Candice Poarch   1-58314-350-5 $6.99US/$9.99CAN
Nurse Arlene Taft is assigned to care for the seriously injured Colonel Neal Allen. She remembers him as an obnoxious young neighbor at her father's military base, but now he looks nothing like she remembers. Will time give them courage under fire?

__THE GLORY OF LOVE – _Navy_
by Kim Louise   1-58314-411-0 $6.99US/$9.99CAN
When pilot Roxanne Allgood is kidnapped, Navy Seal Col. Haughton Storm sets out on a mission to find the only person who has ever mattered to him—a lost love he hasn't seen in ten years.

__FLYING HIGH – _Marines_
by Gwynne Forster   1-58314-427-7 $6.99US/$9.99CAN
Colonel Nelson Wainwright must recover from his injuries if he is to attain his goal of becoming a four-star general. Audrey Powers, a specialist in sports medicine, enters his world to get him back on track. Will their love find a way to endure his rise to the top?

Now Available in Bookstores!

Visit our website at **www.arabesquebooks.com**.

Arabesque Romances
by *Roberta Gayle*

__**Moonrise** $4.99US/$5.99CAN
    0-7860-0268-9

__**Sunshine and Shadows** $4.99US/$5.99CAN
    0-7860-0136-4

__**Something Old, Something New** $4.99US/$6.50CAN
    1-58314-018-2

__**Mad About You** $5.99US/$7.99CAN
    1-58314-108-1

__**Nothing But the Truth** $5.99US/$7.99CAN
    1-58314-209-6

__**Coming Home** $6.99US/$9.99CAN
    1-58314-282-7

__**The Holiday Wife** $6.99US/$9.99CAN
    1-58314-425-0

Available Wherever Books Are Sold!

Visit our website at **www.BET.com**.